RUN OF RUIN

PRIDE OF PRAXIS DUET
BOOK 1

NIKKI ROBB

PART ONE

THE CHALLENGERS

CHAPTER
ONE

BEX

I MEMORIZED every face on that stage, knowing one of them would soon be dead. Someone had to remember them. Someone needed to remember who they were before they were reduced to another name on a list. For me, it was easy, I remembered everything. Every detail. Every second. Every breath. People called it a gift. My little brother, Jax, called it my superpower. But it wasn't a gift... it was a burden. Because what people don't get is that the bad things stick just as hard as the good. The screams, the blood, the moments you'd give anything to forget, they never fade. So I learned to use it. If I had to carry the memories anyway, I'd carry the ones no one else would. The ones that mattered. The ones that might otherwise be lost.

Every year, in the last few painful minutes before the vote, I studied the faces of the candidates, giving them a private eulogy of my own. It's not supposed to be this way, of course.

Nova Locksley, the polished puppet of Praxis, never fails to remind us that they're not meant to die. But they almost always do. The truth is, no one from Canyon Collective ever survives the Reclamation Run. So, I make sure to memorize their fearful expressions, imprinting their faces in my mind. It's the least I can do for them, after our people have condemned them to a death sentence they never stood a chance of escaping.

My feet sank into the dusty covered ground, wedged between sweaty bodies as we waited for the result of the vote. My brother's good hand clung to mine. I looked down at him, smiling softly. He squinted up at me against the brightness. If he could, he would've raised his free hand to shield his eyes, but he lost the use of it months ago. Shifting my body, I leaned into the sun's path, casting a shadow over him to offer a brief reprieve for his eyes.

"Who did you vote for, Bex?" Jax had asked me this morning, as we sat across from each other at the kitchen table. The table's surface was worn and uneven, the legs wobbling drastically beneath it. We'd lost the lumber trial last year, so new furniture was a luxury the Canyon Collective wasn't allowed. Not that I'd have enough money to pay for it even if we had.

I paused, considering his question. He asked it so casually, as if we weren't sending someone to die to secure our survival. He was too young to fully understand, and his innocence made it all the more painful. I gave him a soft smile, my gaze drifting over his fragile form.

He held the spoon in his right hand, his grip wavering. His fingers trembled slightly, the joints of his hand stiffening with each movement, struggling to maintain their grip on the utensil. The tremors were subtle, but I could see them. The slow, steady progression of the illness that claimed him. It had started with his legs, making it harder for him to walk, to run. And now, it kept stealing more from him every single day.

"I voted for Rexen," I said, lifting the cup to my lips, letting the warmth of the bone broth seep through me. Rexen was the oldest candidate and the only one with any real schooling under his belt, a reminder of the years when the Canyon Collective used to perform better in the education trials. He was the only one who might have a chance in the mental challenges this year.

I lowered the cup slowly, my fingers curling around the rough edges. "He's got a shot at the medical trial," I added quietly.

We had a few herbal remedies, simple, but effective against minor ailments. Still, there was only so much that we could do for Jax. His illness was beyond the reach of our limited resources, and I couldn't ignore the weight of that fact any longer.

For years, I'd used my vote to try and send someone who could win the mental challenges. Someone who could think outside the box. But more often than not, my choice was over-ridden. They'd always pick some muscle-bound contender, hoping they could secure the physical resources. I understood the logic, even if it was flawed. Those Challengers were usually dead before the medical trial ever started. And I needed someone who could help Jax, someone who might stand a chance of saving him. For a brief time, I wondered if I could have done it. If I were one of the elected. Would I be able to secure what Jax needed?

But I'd never be one of the candidates. Not if I could help it.

"I voted for Ezra because I like his name!" Jax giggled, his eyes sparkling with an innocence that made my chest tighten. A wave of guilt rushed through me. Every member of the

Collective could cast their vote for the Challenger, even if they didn't truly understand what it meant, or what it cost. Even Jax, so young, had no real grasp of the consequences. I hadn't done a good job of raising him to understand it either. Maybe I'd tried too hard to shield him, but I wasn't exactly prepared to become a parent at twenty when our mother died giving birth to him. Seven years later, and I still don't know what the hell I'm doing.

"By the will of the Praxis, you are welcome," Nova's screechy voice pulled my attention back to the stage.

"For the will of Praxis, we arrive," the crowd murmured in unison, our voices flat. Nova's eyes scanned us, disappointment flickered in her gaze at our lack of enthusiasm. She stood tall, draped in the signature color palate of Praxis, metallic silvers and golds. Her skin-tight jumpsuit clung to her, the fabric clearly unsuited for the desert heat. I felt sweat begin to bead on my skin just watching her.

I wore a much more lightweight garment, fit to protect my skin from the sun's harsh rays, but cool enough to keep my body temperature from spiking to dangerous levels. Nova was going to pass out in ten minutes if she didn't get out of this sun. I'd be lying if I said that wouldn't be entertaining to see.

Nova smiled warmly at the camera, her face instantly flooding the massive screens towering behind her. Overnight, the barren desert outside our Hub had been transformed into a vibrant, overblown and chromatic spectacle. We hadn't won a technology trial in over two decades, so there was no infrastructure here, no equipment to stage their little show. At least not to their standards. Not like Steelheart, where screens lined every street corner from what I've seen on my outdated screen. Outside of Praxis, they were the next biggest purveyors of entertainment and technology.

Most of our Collective still watched the Reclamation

Run on ancient, half-broken screens, some flickered, colors warped and distorted, with audio that crackled like it was underwater. Praxis a few years ago, despite our pathetic performance in past technology trials, donated a few screens for common spaces. Out of the goodness of their hearts, they claimed. But we all knew better. They just wanted to make sure we could watch our Challenger win or die in vivid, unflinching detail.

"Who do you think is gonna win?" Jax whispered up at me, leaning his tiny body into mine for support. I tried to get him to stay home, this much excitement and walking was bound to prove too much for him, but he insisted and I can't say no to him.

"I don't know, sprout," I replied quietly. But what I wanted to say was 'Nobody ever wins.'

I sensed someone approaching and turned to find the familiar grey eyes of my best friend.

"Ava," I said, a small smile tugging at my lips.

She returned it with one of her own, steady and warm, as her crutches pressed into the sand with each step. The soft crunch of their weight was rhythmic, almost comforting.

When we were kids, she lost her leg to a relentless infection, one that would've taken her life if it hadn't been for the rare luck of having medical personnel in our Collective that year. One of the last years we were granted that kind of grace.

She survived, scarred, altered, but unbroken. Down a leg, yes, but she never let that slow her down. Ava never let the loss affect her. If anything, it seemed to make her fiercer. Stronger.

"Morning," she said, reaching around me to smile at my brother, and rub her knuckles along his scalp. "How's it going today, little dude?"

"Hi Ava!" He beamed brightly at her, swatting her hand away from his dusty blonde hair with a chuckle. "I'm great!

It's election day." Ava tensed beside me and I offered her hand a soft comforting squeeze.

Her older brother was our elected Challenger when we were girls, and the pain of his death still lingered for her. It did for me, too. That was the year I understood what the Reclamation Run really was.

"Sure is, buddy," she replied softly, doing her best to hide the haunted echoes in her eyes.

"You doing okay?" I whispered to her.

She nodded a few times, but I could see the faint sheen of unshed tears in her eyes, and I knew it had nothing to do with the stinging sand that whipped across our skin in the wind. I squeezed her hand gently, my fingers drifting to the inside of her wrist where the small moth tattoo rested. She'd gotten it after her brother died, her way of keeping a part of him with her, a permanent mark of mourning and memory inked into her skin.

Before I could probe further, the discordant and familiar anthem of Nexum began to play. Too loud for anyone to think or speak. As the music died, Nova took her place at center stage, the five faces I've memorized stood in line behind her.

"Please join me in giving our candidates a round of well-deserved applause!" Nova exclaimed, her voice dripping with over-the-top theatrics. The crowd clapped, half-heartedly, but I saw the way her smile tightened, frustration flickering behind it. We weren't giving her the energy she craved. They'd probably just replace our lackluster cheers in editing anyway. I remembered a few years ago, when they dubbed over the video of our election, layering on what sounded like thousands of screaming fans. It felt hollow, wrong, but then again, so did everything Praxis did.

"These five candidates have proven themselves to you, campaigned long and hard for the opportunity to represent the Canyon Collective at this year's Reclamation Run!" Nova gestured to each of the individual's standing on the stage beside her.

'Campaigned' was a generous term, and it didn't even come close to describing what the five people up there actually did to earn one of those 'prestigious' spots. Five people must make up the ballot each year, and those spots can be voted on in a primary election, or filled by candidates volunteering. In some Collectives, they carefully cultivate their candidates, prepping them to compete in the Run for most of their lives, but in Canyon?

Our five candidates are criminals. People our Collective viewed as expendable. Leadership in Canyon has come to use this election as a way to punish them. That might be why we never win any of the trials.

My eyes trailed to Rexen. He was up there because he created a poison that couldn't be identified, smelled, or tasted. By the time you knew you'd ingested it, you were already dead. He was a murderer, but he was also a genius. He had at least a small chance against the brainiacs they typically send from other Collectives.

That's why he had my vote.

Next to him stood Ezra, the one Jax had voted for. He was the youngest on the stage by a mile, maybe a few years older than me. I wasn't even sure what his crime was. His trial had been quick, quiet, over before anyone really had a chance to talk about it.

Not that it stopped the rumors. They spread like wildfire, each one more outlandish than the last. Smuggling contraband. Theft. Murder. Conspiracy against Praxis. Some even claimed he caused the mining collapse that killed a bunch of people a few months back. Whatever it was, it had to be bad enough to land him up there.

He was probably Rexen's biggest competition for the vote. Young. Fit. And there was that air of mystery, the kind that makes people lean closer to their screens. If he got in front of the camera, maybe they'd finally find out who he really was. He was also handsome enough to warrant garnering a fan base. Something I'm sure the producers would be excited about.

"As you all know, the Reclamation Run is the method Praxis uses to provide for the Collectives of Nexum," Nova began, her voice smooth and practiced. "One hundred years ago, the world as we knew it was collapsing, resources were dwindling, people were starving, and it led to a war that changed everything. Praxis emerged from the ruins of a broken society, bringing order to the chaos." She delivered the same tired rhetoric she spouted every year. A story of desperation, war, and the monstrous acts people committed when survival was at stake. It was easy enough to swallow, though, since I've seen first hand what happens when humanity is stripped away. Of course, I wouldn't claim that the people of Canyon aren't suffering, we are, but Praxis offers us just enough hope to stave off the worst of it.

"Now, please stand by for a message from our Archon, Evanora Veritas," Nova exclaimed, turning her back to us to watch the screens behind her.

The image on the screen shifted before focusing on a woman who seemed almost too perfect. Her dark brown hair was slicked back into a neat bun at the nape of her neck, and her eyes were framed by just enough makeup to still be considered subtle. She wore a sharp, golden blazer, its lapels gleaming as if they had never known a stain. I was never good at discerning ages just by looking at someone, because in my experience, the more suffering life has dealt you, the more it shows in the lines of your face. Her unblemished and unwrinkled skin could mean anything in Praxis, but I'd be willing to bet she'd lived a fortunate life.

"Good afternoon, Collectives," she spoke, and her silken voice echoed in the empty desert. "And allow me to welcome you to the first day of the 90th annual Reclamation Run."

Nova broke out into applause, and the crowd meekly followed suit.

"Our Earth has a finite amount of precious resources, resources that our ancestors took for granted. They were used and abused until the world we inherited was unrecognizable. Now, Praxis understands the necessity of rationing, of making deliberate, thoughtful decisions to preserve what we have. For the sake of both our present and our future."

I scanned the crowd, taking in the faces around me. Hungry, desperate people. Last year, we finished dead last in eleven out of twenty-one trials. And in this challenge, last place gets you nothing. No resources. No seeds to grow food, no electricity, no lumber, no water filtration. That was just the beginning. You'd think we'd finally try sending someone with a real shot at winning. But maybe we've just accepted this life of constant scarcity, where survival means learning how to live with less.

I looked down at Jax. His little face was twisted in pain, and I knew his legs were straining under the pressure of holding him up. I never should have let him come, I cursed myself.

"Come up here, sprout, so you can see." I said, leaning down to let him hop onto my back. He did, with a little extra strain that cracked my heart wide open. I settled him onto my back, holding him tightly.

"The Reclamation Run was created as a fair and honest way to divide our resources amongst the Collectives," Archon Veritas continued. "Because of this practice of preservation, Praxis has been able to provide for all the citizens of Nexum."

Fair and honest weren't words I typically associated with Praxis, but I didn't dare say that aloud. No one would if they wanted to keep breathing.

"In celebration of our 90th year, and in show of Praxis' commitment to building a stronger future for everyone, especially those who may otherwise remain unseen, we are amending the rules of this year's run." Murmurs of interest and confusion rippled through the crowd.

"In addition to each Collective's elected Challenger, we're excited to announce a new addition. A lottery to randomly select a second participant to represent your Collective in the Reclamation!" She delivered the words like it was some kind of gift, as if she wasn't just sending another person to their death. "This generosity is to remind you that everyone has the chance to benefit from the goodwill of Praxis, not just the most popular among you."

The crowd's whispered confusion grew heavy and worried.

"May your Collective's Challengers embody the strengths of your people, and may the Reclamation begin."

The video cut off, freezing on Archon Veritas' smiling face. But that smile never quite reached her eyes, and it left a sour feeling in my stomach.

The crowd rippled with tension, shouts of discontent bubbling up like steam ready to burst. Nova's voice crackled through the speakers, sharp and commanding. "Attention!" she called. The crowd dipped into a low murmur, though the anger still simmered beneath the surface.

"I know we're all absolutely thrilled about this exciting new development!" she chirped, her voice too sweet. "So, let me answer a few questions I'm sure you all have. One, yes, every member of the Collective has their name in the drawing. If you can vote, you can Reclaim!"

A collective gasp rippled through the crowd. My grip on Jax tightened instinctively. His name was in that lottery somewhere... if he was chosen...

I shook my head, shoving the thought away before it could root itself too deeply. But the fear now had a prominent place in my chest.

"Two!" Nova shouted, raising her voice over the growing rumble of panic. "There will be no substitutions for any reason whatsoever. The chosen winner is our second Challenger. Simple as that."

The outrage exploded this time. Parents shouting about the fairness of sending young children or the elderly, and kids wailing as the reality began to sink in.

I met Ava's eyes and I could see how terrified she was. She knew exactly what this experience does to a person, and I don't think she'd survive if she had to follow her brother's ghostly footsteps.

For a few chaotic moments, it was a storm of voices and panic. Then Praxis guards in gaudy silver armor began slipping through the crowd, calming or silencing... depending on who you asked.

"So much excitement!" Nova beamed into the camera, her cheerful tone as fake as the smile on her lips. I had no doubt they'd scrub the outrage from the final broadcast. By the time it aired, we'd all look like eager participants in this game of chance.

I wondered if the other Collectives reacted similarly to the news. I guess I'd never know.

Nova pulled out two envelopes. Both held closed by the seal of Praxis. My heart raged against my ribcage as I watched her break the first seal and slide the card out into her hand.

"Canyon Collective!" she cried out into the microphone. "Your fairly elected Challenger is....Ezra Wynstone."

Damnit.

Disappointment curled in the pit of my stomach. I didn't know Ezra, but I did know everyone in Canyon who could read at a higher level, or had basic understanding of science and arithmetic... and he wasn't one of them. We could all but kiss the medical trial goodbye. Ezra stepped forward, a look of quiet resignation on his face. He held his hands clasped behind his back, which only accentuated his broad shoulders. On the bright side, maybe we did have a chance at some of those physical trials this year. It would be nice to get more livestock.

I leaned my chin on Jax's arms which were hanging around my shoulders and sighed deeply. Livestock was well and good, but it wouldn't help him.

Ava leaned into me, a quiet gesture of comfort. She knew exactly who I'd voted for and why, and she knew, just like I did, that this Challenger wasn't the one who was going to save Jax.

"Maybe next year, hon," she offered gently.

"Yeah... maybe next year," I whispered back, the words bitter on my tongue.

But I wasn't sure Jax had another year. With the way his illness was progressing, even six months felt like a stretch. I couldn't imagine a world without him, without his infectious smile, his endless curiosity. Even on his worst days, when the pain had to be unbearable, he was still the sweetest kid I knew. Sharp as a tack, always ready with a joke or a question that made you think.

His frail arms tightened around my shoulders, and I placed my hand over his, feeling the slight tremor in his grip.

I blinked hard against the sting in my eyes, refusing to let the tears fall. Not here. Not now.

Ava gasped softly beside me. When I turned to her, she had one hand covering her mouth, her eyes wide and glistening. Panic jolted through me.

"What?" I asked, heart pounding.

She didn't answer. More sets of eyes were landing on me now, confusion rippling through the crowd. My pulse hammered in my ears.

And then I saw it... my face, projected on the massive screen behind Nova. My confused, dumbfounded expression staring back at me.

"Come on down!" Nova's voice rang out, cheerful and bright, but all I heard was the roaring in my head.

It all snapped into brutal clarity.

It was me.

I was the second Challenger.

"Bex..." Ava's voice cracked, trembling with shock. I barely heard her. Everything around me felt distant, the crowd, the shouts, the gasps, all of it was muffled, like I was hearing it through thick glass. My limbs felt like they weren't mine, shaking uncontrollably as the weight of what just happened slammed into me.

Slowly, with agonizing reluctance, and trembling hands, I slid Jax from my back. He clung tighter, his small arms wrapping desperately around my shoulders with as much strength as his muscles could muster. He didn't fully understand what the Reclamation meant, but he knew I was leaving him.

"Bex, no," he whined, his voice high and panicked. "Don't go."

I knelt down, my heart breaking as I gently cupped his face. "You need to stay with Ava for a little while, okay, Jax?" I tried to sound calm, but my voice was rough, strangled.

He shook his head, tears welling in those wide blue eyes. "I don't want you to go," he cried, voice cracking on the words.

"I know, sprout... I know." My voice dropped to a whisper. I pressed my forehead to his, closing my eyes against the hot sting of tears. "I love you. I love you so much... and I'm going to get you a doctor. Okay? I promise. I'm gonna take care of you."

He nodded through his tears, but his grip on me only tightened as much as his little limbs would allow. He buried his face in my neck, shaking in my arms. I held him, squeezing him like I could imprint the memory of this moment into my skin, his warmth, the sound of his breaths, the way his hair tickled my cheek. I felt my chest crack open as I forced myself to move.

I stood slowly, holding him against me for just a second longer before meeting Ava's gaze. Her eyes were rimmed red, her cheeks blotchy with tears. I could see how much she was trying to hold it together, for Jax, for me.

"I need you to look out for him," I pleaded, my voice barely holding steady.

"I will," she promised through broken sobs. "You know I will."

I squeezed her hand.

"May the stars shine on you, Bex," Ava whispered with a serious sort of reverence.

I nodded, thankful for the support embedded in the words, even if I didn't recognize the phrase. "Thank you."

"Come on, sprout," I whispered, trying to peel him off me. He fought it, clinging to me with all the strength he had left.

"Please don't go," he sobbed. "Please, Bex."

"I have to," I whispered back, my voice breaking. "But I'm going to come back. I swear."

It took everything in me to pass him into Ava's arms. He cried out, thrashing, his little hands reaching for me even as she tried to soothe him. The sound of his sobs cut through me, carving me hollow. I took a shaky step back, then another.

"Come back to us," Ava whispered, clutching Jax tightly against her chest. "And come back in one piece. Don't let them write the end of your story."

I nodded because I couldn't speak. If I opened my mouth, I'd fall apart.

"Time to come on down!" Nova's voice rang out over the speakers again, dripping with false cheer. The impatience in her tone turned my stomach.

I tore my gaze away from my best friend and my brother, my whole world, and forced my feet to move. The crowd parted around me in heavy, reverent silence. No one spoke. No one whispered. It was an eerie, suffocating kind of quiet. It had been years since someone who wasn't a charged criminal was chosen as a Challenger in the Reclamation Run.

But now, it was me.

I climbed the steps onto the stage, the heat of the setting desert sun pressing down on me, sinking into my skin. It felt hotter up here. Maybe it was the lights, or the glare of the cameras, or maybe it was the thousands of eyes watching me from the safety of the ground.

Nova met me at the top of the stairs, her smile too wide, too practiced. She looped her arm through mine without missing a beat and dragged me across the stage. My feet barely kept up as she steered me into place beside the other Challenger.

Ezra Wynstone didn't even glance my way when I took my spot next to him. He kept his eyes forward, shoulders squared, calm as stone. I was grateful for it. I had enough people staring at me, I didn't need his gaze adding to the weight.

"Join me in congratulating your Challengers!" Nova's voice boomed, bouncing off the buildings and carrying through the tense, heavy air. "Your elected, Ezra Wynstone and your chosen, Brexlyn Hollis!"

Side by side. One facing the death penalty. One handed a death sentence.

I stood there, blinking against the lights, my breath catching in my chest as I looked out over the endless sea of people. So many strangers. So many faces. I wondered if anyone out there was memorizing mine.

CHAPTER TWO

BEX

The rhythmic movement of the train would have been soothing if I wasn't headed to my death. The last time I had ridden any sort of public transportation was when Damien Westhold won that trial nearly fifteen years ago. That was the last time the Canyon Collective ever placed first in anything. After his win, the train lines came back to life. Buses were delivered from Praxis and ran on constant loops, day and night, ready to take you anywhere you wanted. I used to hop on just to ride, no destination in mind, just because I could. I'd never known that kind of freedom before, and I haven't known it since.

People danced in the streets that year, their joy infectious. I don't think I've ever seen the Collective that happy. Damien never made it back to witness it, though, he died in the electricity trial. But for one year, we all reaped the benefits of his sacrifice.

We haven't won a trial since.

When we placed eighth in the transportation trial the next year, the buses vanished. The train still showed up once every three months, but no one boarded it, not unless they wanted to wait another three months to come back. So, for a moment I tried to ignore the twisting pain and fear in my gut and focus on the rhythmic hum and the gentle sway of the train beneath me.

Across the aisle, Ezra sat stiffly, his gaze fixed out the window as the desert of the Canyon Collective blurred by. He didn't flinch, didn't fidget, he just stared, unmoving. I took the opportunity to really look at him for the first time.

His hair was a mess of dirty blonde waves that fell onto his forehead and curled slightly above his ears. His jaw was sharp, tense, like he was clenching it to hold something in. He looked calm on the surface, but I could see the tight pull of his muscles, the way his hand twitched slightly against his thigh. His face was mostly turned away, leaving me to wonder, absurdly, what color his eyes were.

Before I could think too much about that, Nova appeared again, gliding down the aisle from the front of the train where she'd disappeared after we boarded. She wore a new outfit, just as shiny, just as metallic, but this time even more uncomfortable looking with spikes and beads.

"Well, well, well," she purred, her heels clicking against the floor as she approached. She had a silver case in her hands. "Leave it to your Collective to give us absolutely nothing to work with. Silent and boring as usual," she groaned, motioning for someone to follow in behind her.

The man who followed Nova onto the train car was tall. He had broad shoulders, and toned arms visible under the soft golden fabric of his short-sleeved shirt. It had the distinct shimmer of Praxis-issued gear, but his looked more functional, lived-in, nothing like Nova's performative glamour. Cords and equipment wrapped around him like some kind of tactical vest, camera slung at his side, gear clipped to his belt, thick headphones over his ears.

He had cropped red hair, pale skin dusted with freckles, and a face that could have stopped people mid-sentence. He was undeniably handsome, annoyingly so.

But whatever flicker of attraction sparked was instantly snuffed out by the twist of nausea in my gut. Because he was one of them. Praxis. And no matter how pretty the wrapping, he was part of the machine sending us to die.

"This is Zaffir Stark," Nova announced with a dramatic flourish, as if she were unveiling a prize instead of a person. "He's your Collective's designated cameraman for the duration of the Reclamation Run. He'll be filming nearly every waking moment in the desperate hope that one of you does something remotely interesting enough to make the final cut." She waved a dismissive hand in front of her face like she was already disappointed in us.

"He'll also be filming your talking head confessionals now that the vote's done." She nodded at Zaffir, tall, silent, all business, as he began unpacking his camera gear and setting up lights without so much as a glance our way.

"Who's feeling brave enough to go first?"

My head instinctively turned toward Ezra. He hadn't moved. He stared at Nova with the same cold focus I'd seen on his face since the announcement. No flinch, no twitch. Just stillness. If not for the slow rise and fall of his chest, I'd have believed he'd turned to stone.

After a long, pointed silence, Nova let out a sigh. "Fine. Ladies first, then."

Panic surged through me, hot and immediate. My palms dampened, breath catching in my throat.

"God, you look a mess," Nova said bluntly, stepping

forward and snapping open a sleek silver case that revealed an overwhelming array of makeup. "Zaffir, we'll take hers first. Get some B-roll of the train while I make her camera-ready."

Without a word, Zaffir obeyed, disappearing down the aisle with his gear.

Nova turned her attention to me, all efficient movements and sharp tuts of disapproval. She poked and swept and dabbed with brushes and powders I didn't recognize, luxuries the Canyon Collective hadn't seen in years. Hell, we couldn't even win the basic resource trials, let alone anything extra.

After a few minutes of relentless dabbing, brushing, and smoothing, my skin felt like it had been sealed beneath a layer of carefully curated lies. Nova finally leaned back, admiring her handiwork with a satisfied grin.

"There we go," she declared. "You might be the prettiest Challenger we've had from your Collective in a long while. They kept sending us homely looking men, who looked like they haven't showered in days." I didn't interject to say that most of them hadn't because they'd been sitting in a jail cell for days leading up to the election. "That face of yours will get us some screen time."

She practically buzzed with excitement, but I felt cold and tight with nausea. It didn't feel like the compliment she made it out to be. I glanced over, needing something solid to focus on, and found Ezra watching me.

Green. His eyes were green.

He studied me in silence, his expression unreadable, no smirk, no scoff, not even a blink. I couldn't tell if he thought I looked ridiculous or if he was just curious what Nova had turned me into. His poker face was ironclad.

"She's ready," Nova announced, snapping my attention back. She grabbed my arm with a little too much flair and steered me down the aisle to where Zaffir had finished setting up the shot.

Nova dropped me into the seat like a prop being set for a scene, then settled beside me with the elegance of someone who knew exactly how good she looked on camera. Zaffir, all quiet precision, adjusted the towering equipment in front of me. A blinding light clicked on, searing into my vision, and I instinctively winced. Without saying a word, he dimmed it slightly. I considered thanking him, but the words got stuck somewhere behind my ribs.

"All right," Zaffir said, his voice low and warm, like honey stirred into tea. "Just look into the camera and answer my questions, okay?"

I couldn't seem to make my mouth work, so I nodded instead, praying all the questions would be yes-or-no.

"What's your name and which Collective are you from?"

So much for that.

I swallowed hard, trying to summon enough spit to make a sound. "Um..." I cleared my throat. "My name is um...Brexlyn... Hollis, but Bex, actually. I'm Bex. I'm from the Canyon Collective." The words barely made it out. A whisper masquerading as a sentence.

"Oh for the love of....child, the camera's not going to bite," Nova snapped from her perch. "Wipe that look off your face and try again."

I met her eyes for half a second, just long enough to absorb the disdain, then turned back to the camera. "My name is Brexlyn Hollis, and I'm from the Canyon Collective," I repeated, only a shade more confident.

Nova scoffed, but didn't interrupt. It must've been passable.

Zaffir continued, voice still calm and neutral, as though

the question held no real weight. "Are you proud to represent your Collective in the Reclamation Run?"

The truth sat on the tip of my tongue, burning like ash. Proud? Of course I wasn't proud. I was being sent to a deadly competition with the hopes that I may manage to earn scraps of basic human necessities for the people I care about?

But they didn't want that truth in these confessionals. I've seen enough episodes of this wicked show to know that they want me to lie, to say I'm honored to have been chosen for such a momentous event, to tell them that Praxis has given me a beautiful opportunity. They want me to be grateful.

But I don't think I can do that.

"Speak, woman!" Nova screeched, frustration evident in her tone.

"Nova, why don't you give me a minute to talk to her alone," Zaffir said gently, his tone careful but firm.

I glanced up at him through the glare of the lights. Past the lens and into his eyes, golden, warm, and sharp all at once. He was watching me closely, like he could see the storm that was raging under my skin.

Nova sighed, loud and theatrical. "Fine," she muttered, rising with a dramatic roll of her eyes. She sauntered to the built-in bar at the far end of the train car, already pouring herself a glass of something amber and expensive-looking, like she couldn't possibly be bothered with my nerves a second longer.

Ezra stayed put, still perched in his seat twenty feet back, his unreadable gaze fixed on the spectacle before him.

And then it was just me and Zaffir.

A small red light blinked at the top of the camera. A quiet reminder that it was watching, recording. But Zaffir didn't stay behind it like he was supposed to. Instead, he slipped around the setup, crouching in front of me until we were eye to eye.

Up close, his eyes looked even warmer, more complex. Golden with flecks that caught the light like the sun through honey. For a moment, I forgot where I was.

"Look," he said softly, voice barely louder than the hum of the train. "I know you're scared. And I know you don't want to be here."

I opened my mouth to argue out of habit, but he raised a hand, stopping me with a gentle shake of his head.

"You don't need to pretend that's not the truth," he said. His gaze didn't waver. There was something there, just beneath the surface, compassion maybe, or pity. "My job is to get the most interesting content out of you and Ezra. The more screen time you get, the better."

I nodded. That much I already knew.

Zaffir glanced over his shoulder, checking to make sure Nova was still preoccupied at the bar before leaning in a little closer. His voice dropped to a whisper. "Look it's no secret... interesting Challengers? They tend to last longer."

Something in his tone shifted. He wasn't just giving me advice. He was warning me.

I stared at him, mind racing. I nodded again, slowly this time, as if that would help me make sense of the hundred questions swirling inside me.

"So, there's a couple ways you could play this," he said. "You could go the sympathy route. Audiences love a tragic backstory. Pull their heartstrings."

My thoughts immediately went to Jax, his laugh, his limp, the quiet pain we all pretended not to notice. To Ava and her brother. How much pain and loss she's been through. My stomach turned. I hated the idea of turning them into a strategy. But if it helped me make it to the medical trial...

I hesitated. "Or...?"

Zaffir gave me a heated look that made my skin prickle. "Or, you make them want you."

My eyebrows lifted. "Want me?"

"Nova's not wrong. You're gorgeous," he said, tone matter-of-fact, but it made warmth bloom in my cheeks. "You could lean into that, be flirtatious, mysterious, magnetic. Give the audience someone to obsess over. Make them want more of you."

A shocked laugh burst out of me, sharp and breathless. "You're not serious."

His expression didn't shift. "Dead serious."

The laugh died in my throat, and suddenly I felt the weight of what he was really suggesting. Of what I had to do. I shook my head, trying to process.

"No, I... I can't do that. I mean, I don't... I've never..." The words stumbled out, each one more awkward than the last. My cheeks burned. "I'm not... desirable. Not like that."

There was a pause, just long enough to make me regret saying anything at all.

His eyes flicked over me, a glance so quick I could've convinced myself I imagined it. But the heat that followed in its wake, lingering and sharp like the brush of a flame, was impossible to ignore. It curled against my skin, startling and oddly comforting.

"I beg to differ," he said, voice low and certain.

This time, I didn't have to imagine the heat in his gaze. It was real. Intense. Unapologetic.

I suddenly felt too bare beneath it. Too seen. So I dropped my eyes to the floor, hoping the flush in my face didn't give away just how much his words had shaken me.

"I can't," I replied.

He nodded like he'd expected it. "Okay. So, sob story it is, then?"

There was no judgment in his voice, but the question still hit hard. I hated that those were my choices. I hated that I was even considering them.

I looked away, pressing my lips together. Part of me wanted to scream. The other part, the part that needed to make it to the medical trial for Jax, was already doing the math.

And it made me feel sick.

"I don't want them to feel like I'm using them to get attention," I whispered, the fear in my chest finally finding shape.

"Who?" Zaffir asked softly.

"My best friend," I said. "And my brother, Jax." I swallowed hard, trying to keep the tears at bay, but my voice was already trembling. "He's six."

Zaffir leaned in just slightly, his expression gentle. "Tell me about them."

I tried not to look at the blinking red light perched on top of the camera. Tried not to think about how every word I said was being recorded, analyzed, broadcast. Instead, I focused on him, the strange, steady presence of the man sitting just a breath away. He didn't seem like Praxis. Not like the others. Not like Nova. He felt... quieter. Calmer. More human. I wanted to believe that.

"Ava, she lost her leg when we were younger. And then a few years later," I swallowed the lump in my throat, "she lost her brother." I didn't dare say that Praxis was the reason behind it. "I just hate that I had to leave her, too."

"Why?"

"Because she's already lost enough," I answered, feeling tears sting my eyes.

"What makes you think she'll lose you?"

'Because we always lose', was on the tip of my tongue, but I bit it back. "It's a dangerous game." Was all I said.

"Tell me about your brother," Zaffir prompted.

I narrowed my eyes at him, anger mixing with my sadness.

"My brother is the light of my life," I began, the words brittle in my throat. An undercurrent of fury at this red head's insinuation beneath each word. "My best friend. My person. You know that person who makes you feel like the world still has good in it?" I paused, blinking back the pressure behind my eyes. "That's him."

Zaffir reached out and took my hand, warm, gentle. His thumb brushed across the back of it like he was urging me forward without words. And I found comfort in it.

"He was born with a muscle disorder. At first, it was small things, he'd fall a lot, couldn't keep up with other kids. Now... he can barely walk some days. His muscles are wasting away, and there's nothing in our Collective to stop it. We don't have the medicine. The machines. Or the people who know how to help him." My throat closed again, but I forced myself to push through it.

"Every day, I watch him fade just a little more. I wake up wondering if today's the day he won't be able to get out of bed. Or worse, the day he just... stops breathing."

"Pretty honorable. Wanting to win those trials for your brother."

I didn't answer at first, simply trying to find the words to say.

"Fame and glory can't hurt either, right?" He asked.

I shook my head.

The tears spilled before I could stop them.

"I'm not interested in fame, or glory. The medical trials are the only way I might be able to help him. I have a chance to save him." I steadied myself and with a tone so fierce even I felt convinced, "I have to take it."

Zaffir reached up, brushing a tear from my cheek with the pad of his thumb. His touch was featherlight, careful, but it lingered just a second too long to be purely professional.

I should've flinched away. Should've pulled back, reminded myself who he was and what he represented. But instead, I froze, caught in the gravity of him. His eyes held mine, like he was seeing something more than a subject. And I looked back.

For a moment, everything else faded. The blinking red light of the camera, the stale scent of recycled air, even the gnawing ache of guilt in my chest. It was just him. Zaffir. Too close. Too warm. Too real.

I didn't want it. I didn't trust it. But I felt it all the same.

His fingers hovered near my cheek a beat longer, like he was reluctant to let go. And then, just like that, it was gone. He leaned back, and the cold settled in again, swift and merciless.

"Tears are really going to sell it," he said suddenly, his voice snapping back into something clinical. Cold. Detached.

I blinked, stunned, the spell of intimacy shattered. He leaned back, his expression unreadable, and reached over to shut off the camera.

"Smart move picking one of the later trials," he said, now fiddling with buttons and dials like I hadn't just poured my heart out in front of him. "Keeps the audience rooting for you. They'll want to see if you make it that far. Stroke of genius, really." His tone was dry and dismissive.

I stared at him, the weight of what he'd said settling in like a stone in my chest.

"Was any of that true?" he asked, barely looking at me.

"About your brother and your friend? Or did you make it up for the camera?"

"What?" I choked, the word cutting through the silence.

"Don't get me wrong," he said casually, still focused on the camera. "It played real. But this whole thing is just theater, right? Wouldn't be the first time a Challenger spun a story."

"I didn't make anything up," I snapped, my voice shaking with fury. "Every word was true."

He didn't respond.

I stood so fast the chair scraped loudly against the floor. Without another word, I turned and walked back toward my seat, blood pounding in my ears. I felt Ezra watching me. His gaze followed every step I took, but he didn't say anything.

Maybe he couldn't.

I slid back into my spot, hands clenched tight in my lap, jaw locked against the anger rising in my throat. I had almost trusted Zaffir. Almost let myself believe there was someone in Praxis who might actually see me. But he was no different. Just another piece of the machine.

"Alright, big guy," Zaffir called out cheerfully, like none of it had happened. "Get over here. Your turn in the spotlight."

Ezra stood, his eyes lingering on me for a moment longer before he made his way over to the set.

And just like that, it was someone else's story they were ready to exploit.

"Alright," Zaffir began, his voice clipped and tinged with impatience as Ezra finally claimed the seat in front of the camera setup. "What tactic are you gonna go with?"

Ezra remained still. Not a word. Not even a flicker of acknowledgment.

Zaffir exhaled slowly through his nose, irritation tightening the set of his jaw. "Okay then. Let's just begin, shall we?" He flicked the camera on with an annoyed little snap of his fingers. "What's your name and which Collective are you representing?"

Silence.

I shifted in my seat, watching the standoff unfold. Zaffir's fingers drummed against the arm of his chair. "Stoicism is great and all," he said, his voice sharpening, "but you're going to have to give me something. You don't have to pour your heart out, but if you don't make your first appearance interesting, the audience isn't going to care about you."

He was trying to be threatening, but I doubted Ezra gave a damn about making the audience care. In fact, the more Zaffir talked, the more I was convinced that Ezra's goal was the exact opposite.

"Ezra Wynstone, from the Canyon Collective," Zaffir finally prompted for him, clearly done waiting. "You've been elected to compete in the Reclamation Run. Tell us, what do you hope to do for the people back home who got you here?"

That's when it happened. Ezra leaned forward slowly, deliberate and dangerous. He stared down the barrel of the lens like it had personally wronged him. And when he spoke, his voice rumbled out low and rough, like it had been dragged across gravel.

"I'm gonna make 'em pay for it."

The words hit like a slap across the face. I felt the air in the room shift, charged, tense, electric. My heart stumbled in my chest, not sure whether it was fear or awe. Ezra's voice carried a weight that felt like it could break through walls. This wasn't for the sake of the show. This wasn't a strategy. This was a promise.

Zaffir let out a low whistle, clearly startled. "Bold move," he said, the edge of a grin tugging at his lips. "But it might just work."

Ezra pushed back from the chair and stood, no further

commentary offered. He returned to his seat beside me like nothing had happened, like he hadn't just dropped a live grenade into the room. I met his gaze as he sat down. His dark eyes locked with mine, and he gave me a curt nod, simple, matter-of-fact.

It wasn't warmth, not even friendliness. But it was... acknowledgment. A silent pact, maybe. He wasn't going to be my best friend, but at that moment, I couldn't help but feel like I might've just earned something rarer.

An ally.

And in this place, that could mean everything.

CHAPTER
THREE

ZAFFIR

"Do you have the cut ready?" Joree asked on the other end of the line, sharp and impatient, the same tone I'd come to expect from every producer, Architect, and executive up the chain at the Show Center. They never asked nicely. Never waited long enough to listen.

I pinched the bridge of my nose, letting out a breath through clenched teeth. "Just about," I replied, keeping my voice even.

I didn't hate the job. In fact, I liked a lot of it. Manipulating light and shadow, finding the right angles, pacing shots with rhythm and tension. It was an art form, and when I was behind the lens, when it was just me and the footage, I felt like an artist. But the editing booth was where the art bled out, where the work got warped into something false. That's what I hated. That's where they turned real people into characters and pain into spectacle. I especially hated that I was getting good at that part too.

I sat cross-legged on the thin cot bolted to the floor of the train car, computer perched in front of me. The footage flickered across the screen, paused on Ezra's face. Cutting his segment was hard, there wasn't much to work with, but I found a few shots of him on stage, arms folded, jaw clenched, eyes burning with something dark. He looked like a powder keg moments from going off.

That was good.

Praxis didn't love when Challengers showed open hostility toward the system, but this wasn't hostility. This was potential. And whether they wanted to admit it or not, viewers craved a villain as much as they craved a hero.

Now I was scrubbing through Bex's footage. The moment her name was called, the camera caught everything. She didn't hear it at first. Then I watched as her smile froze, her body stiffened, then she turned toward the crowd like she couldn't breathe.

The fear was palpable, but then there was resolve, focus, acceptance. She hid her fear from her brother's eyes. Trying not to scare him anymore than he already was.

The lens had almost missed her goodbye to her brother, the exchange was half hidden in the crowd. But when Bex knelt to say goodbye, the world disappeared around them. I watched her lips tremble with unspoken words, the desperate way she tucked a strand of his hair behind his ear, the quiet grief that pressed into her features.

And him...God, the closer I looked, the more obvious it was. The boy was sick. Pale, thin, fingers twitching slightly as he clutched her arm. I could see it now, the degeneration she spoke of.

I cursed under my breath. "Shit..."

I couldn't believe I accused her of faking it. Of using him.

The guilt gnawed at me now. She wasn't performing. She wasn't selling grief. That was real.

I dropped her confessional into the sequence, overlaying it against the goodbye, her voice soft but steady, the way she spoke of Jax with such reverence. "He's my best friend... my person..." she had said. I ended the segment on a close-up of her face, eyes bright with tears and fierce with resolve.

Those eyes. God, those eyes.

I froze the frame. Blue as a sparkling pool. Her face was soft, tanned, framed by windswept dusty blonde curls. She didn't need dramatic lighting or fake angles, the camera adored her all on its own.

I wasn't lying when I told her she was beautiful. I meant it. Every word.

Even if I shouldn't have.

Even if I knew better than to get pulled in.

But something about her tugged at me. Not just her looks, there was a gravity to her, a pull I couldn't quite name. Viewers would fall for her whether we played her up as the underdog or the symbol of hope.

"Zaffir?" the voice snapped again through the phone.

I blinked, shook off the daze.

"Yeah," I said, fingers hovering over the trackpad. "I'm done."

"Send it off. We're piecing the premiere together now," she snapped, her voice clipped and cold. Then the line went dead.

No goodbye. No thanks. Just a command and silence.

I stared at the frozen frame of Bex's face for a few more seconds, my thumb hovering over the trackpad. Then, with a reluctant breath, I closed the image and dragged the file into the transfer folder. Watching the progress bar crawl across the screen felt different this time for some reason.

Once it was gone, I set the computer aside and laid back

on the cot, arms folded behind my head as I stared up at the metal ceiling of the train car. A low hum of machinery vibrated through the walls.

Five years. That's how long I've been behind the camera, capturing the rise and fall of Reclamation Challengers like clockwork. I've filmed their introductions, their first confessional, their wins, their failures. I've cut together highlight reels of their deaths.

They all become stories. Then they become spectacles. Then they become memories.

I used to think I was desensitized to it. That maybe, over time, I'd built up some kind of immunity. But no matter how much I tried to convince myself that this year was just like all the rest, the thought of Brexlyn Hollis dying out there made my stomach churn. Maybe it's because before this, they'd always signed up for it. They campaigned for it. But not her. She was plucked from the crowd, ripped from her brother and she had no say in the matter.

I knew the odds. Most people didn't make it. Especially not from the Canyon Collective. Their track record was basically a death sentence.

And yet, God, I didn't want that to be her story. I didn't want to cut her eulogy six weeks from now with some overly dramatic piano music and a slow montage of everything we "loved" about her.

She deserved more than that.

If I couldn't keep her safe myself, I'd do the only thing I could. I'd make her unforgettable. I'd sculpt her image into something no one could bear to lose. I'd make the world fall in love with her, their underdog, their hope, their hero. I'd wrap her story in so much courage and meaning that the audience would demand her survival.

Because if they demanded it, Praxis would have to listen. Ratings trump rules. They always have.

That's how I'd help her. Not with weapons or strategy or even kindness.

With a story.

It was the only power I had

CHAPTER FOUR

BEX

I COULDN'T SLEEP.

Nova had told us we'd be arriving in Praxis by morning and that we should get some beauty rest. Her exact words were, "The cameras won't leave you alone from the moment we stop, so enjoy the quiet while you can." Easy for her to say, she wasn't the one about to be paraded like a prized animal for public entertainment.

I shifted on the stiff cot again, the thin blanket tangled around my legs like it was trying to keep me awake too. Every time I closed my eyes, I saw that cameraman—Zaffir—with his maddening smirk and accusatory tone.

How could he possibly think I was lying about my brother?

Did people really do that? Exploit their families, fake sob stories, just to win public favor? I thought about the Challengers I'd rooted for over the years, the ones I'd cried for, cheered for, believed in. Were they all just performing?

The thought made my stomach twist.

I already felt guilty enough for even speaking about my brother's condition. But it wasn't fake. It wasn't. And I wouldn't let myself become someone who lied just to win hearts and airtime.

I sighed and sat up, raking my fingers through my hair. Sleep wasn't coming. My mind was a hive of too-loud thoughts and too-late regrets.

I remembered the glint of amber liquor in Nova's glass earlier that night. Maybe a drink would help. It had been a long time since I'd had anything stronger than desert water, but the idea of a warm haze dulling the sharp edges of my brain sounded blissful.

I quietly slipped out of my traincar, pulling a knit cardigan around the frankly vulgar black silk night dress that Nova said was mine. I was suddenly terrified to see the rest of my Praxis issued wardrobe. But at least I had this thick sweater. The wool was soft and warm. I'd never owned anything like it. The train was quiet, humming and swaying gently in the moonlight. Shadows stretched long across the floor, and I padded softly, barefoot, through the narrow hallway toward the dining carriage.

I rounded the corner near the bar, the soft gleam of moonlight from a cracked window barely lighting the way, just enough to make out silhouettes.

And I collided with one. A solid, unmoving wall of muscle.

I stumbled back with a sharp breath, nearly yelping, but before I could make a sound, strong hands grabbed my arms, steadying me.

"Easy," a deep voice murmured.

I looked up and met Ezra's fierce, shadowed eyes.

For a second, neither of us moved. The moonlight painted

his face in half-light, outlining the sharp angles of his jaw. There was a faint scar along his brow, and quiet intensity in his expression.

His grip on my arms lingered, not tight, not possessive, just anchoring. Warm.

"I- sorry," I breathed, heart still hammering from the scare.

"What are you doing out here?" His voice was low, rough as gravel. This was already the most I'd ever heard him speak.

"Couldn't sleep," I admitted, my voice quieter than I meant it to be. "I was... going to get a drink."

He didn't let go right away. And I didn't step back. Something about the moment stretched. Stilled.

I was suddenly aware of everything, the way his fingers brushed lightly against my arms, the way his eyes searched my face. The fact that he wasn't wearing a shirt and his muscular chest was on full display didn't help.

"Me too," he said finally.

"What?" I responded, shaking my head and trying to focus.

"Couldn't sleep," he clarified. "Thought the bar might be less crowded at midnight."

A corner of my mouth lifted, a half-smile. "I guess great minds drink alike."

He huffed a quiet laugh through his nose, finally releasing my arms. "Come on then."

And for some reason, I followed. Maybe it was the promise of the liquor. Maybe it was that I didn't want to be alone anymore.

Or maybe it was just him.

I trailed behind him, studying the dark black sleep pants that hung low on his hips, and his toned back as we made our way to the bar, careful to keep a respectful distance this time. The last thing I needed was to barrel into him again like some nervous wreck. He didn't speak as we walked, but his presence filled the space between us like heat from a campfire, quiet and hard to ignore.

When we reached the bar, he pulled out a stool and gestured for me to sit. I hesitated, then climbed onto the seat, clutching the edge like it might steady the tremor of nerves humming just under my skin. Without a word, Ezra slid behind the bar like he'd done it a hundred times before, pulling two mismatched glasses from a shelf and lining them up neatly on the counter.

"What's your poison?" he asked, voice low and edged with a hint of dry humor.

I opened my mouth to answer, but stopped. Not because I didn't know, but because the question felt different coming from him.

My eyes drifted to the bottle he was holding, then to his rough hands. For the briefest of moments, I remembered what I knew about the other Canyon candidates. The criminals. The poison. The death. And now here I was. In the dead of night. Alone. With another convicted criminal pouring drinks.

It suddenly occurred to me that I should be afraid.

"You're wondering if I'm actually going to poison you," Ezra said calmly, not even looking up as he uncorked the bottle.

"No," I said, too quickly.

The corner of his lips quirked up into a smirk as he poured a finger of whiskey into one of the glasses. "You're not a very good liar."

I sighed, looking down at the worn wood grain of the bar. "I didn't mean it like that. I just... forgot, for a second."

"That I'm a criminal," he finished for me, his voice matter-of-fact. Not offended. Not angry. Just resigned.

He recorked the bottle and set it aside, then lined up three more bottles in front of me with a pointed look that said *you choose*. He picked up his own drink and took a sip, watching me over the rim of his glass like he could see straight through me.

I hesitated again. It wasn't fair, this creeping suspicion in my chest. He hadn't done anything to me. Hell, he'd caught me when I almost fell earlier. But the truth lingered in the back of my mind, unwelcome and sharp.

I didn't know what his crime was.

Even though he didn't look like a murderer... Do they ever?

I met his eyes then, green and unreadable, and suddenly the air between us shifted. I remembered where we were. What we were about to face. What this game required of us. Fear wouldn't help me here.

I didn't need another enemy.

I needed someone who might stand beside me when things got brutal. Someone strong. Capable. Someone like him.

My gaze dropped to the middle bottle, dark label, worn edges, something smoky maybe. I pointed to it silently.

Ezra raised a brow but said nothing. He took the bottle, uncorked it with a twist, and poured the amber liquid into my glass. Not a drop more than I'd need to sleep. Not a drop less than I'd need to quiet my thoughts.

When he handed it to me, our fingers brushed. I didn't pull away.

"Cheers," he said, with that same almost-smirk that made it impossible to tell if he was amused or just tired of the world.

"Cheers," I echoed, and lifted the glass to my lips.

It burned, but in a good way.

I watched the way his throat bobbed as he swallowed, his

Adam's apple shifting with the motion. There was a quiet tension in his shoulders that seemed to ease as the alcohol worked its way through him. He exhaled with a low, appreciative groan that rumbled in his chest.

"I'll admit," I said, breaking the silence, "I wasn't sure you were ever going to speak to me."

He turned his head, giving me a sidelong glance. "You're not the one who put me here," he said with a casual shrug. Then his gaze sharpened. "Or maybe you are. Who'd you vote for?"

"Rexen," I answered instantly, more honestly than I expected. I think I just really needed him to know I didn't vote to sentence him to death.

He nodded, almost as if he'd guessed. "You really wouldn't want to drink anything he handed you."

I let out a soft laugh, surprised by it. His eyes flicked to my face instantly, catching the sound like it was something rare.

"Don't know whether to thank you or be offended," he added, the corner of his mouth twitching in what might've been the beginning of a smirk.

"I knew you'd do well in the physical trials," I said quickly. "But I needed someone who stood a chance in the mental ones."

As soon as the words left my mouth, I winced. "Not that you couldn't stand a chance. I just meant Rexen had formal training, you know, schooling and-" I cringed. "Not that you need school to be smart. Obviously. I just-"I groaned and buried my face in my hands, mortified. "Please stop me before I say something worse."

A deep, warm chuckle rolled out of him, and I felt it like a pulse beneath my skin. I slowly peeked up from my hands to see him watching me with that same quiet amusement, his expression softer than I'd ever seen it.

"You're more afraid of offending me than you are of me," he said, still laughing quietly to himself.

"Yeah, well," I muttered, taking another sip of my drink. "I don't have a reason to be afraid of you."

He tilted his head, amusement flickering in his eyes as he lifted his glass in a mock toast. "Maybe you should be."

There was something in his voice, teasing, but edged with something darker. A reminder of the reason he was here. A reason I hadn't dared to ask about yet.

I held his gaze for a beat longer than I meant to, then raised my own glass and clinked it gently against his. "Maybe," I said, my voice quieter now. "But I'm not."

"Good."

Something about the way he said it, low, unbothered, maybe even a little impressed, sent an unexpected warmth to my core. Not the alcohol this time. Something else.

And I didn't know what to do with that.

"You wanted Rexen to place in the medical trial. That's why you voted for him," Ezra said, not accusing, just stating it like it was already obvious. "For your brother?"

The truth hit harder coming from him. Not because it wasn't my little secret anymore, the entirety of Nexum probably knew by now, but because hearing it aloud made it real. Tangible. And painful.

I clenched my jaw, trying not to let it show. "Yeah," I said through gritted teeth. "His condition is treatable... if we had anyone back home to treat him."

I could feel the anger rise like an unrelenting wave. I hated how easily it surfaced, but I was tired of apologizing for it. Tired of what we were forced to live without in the Canyon Collective. What my brother had to live without.

Ezra took a drink, watching me. "Who was the girl you

were speaking to? The one you left your brother with. She looked familiar."

"Ava," I said, my heart skipping a beat. "My best friend. She's practically Jax's big sister too. You might recognize her because her brother was our Challenger a few years back."

Ezra's brows lifted in recognition, and he made a low sound in his throat. "Yeah... yeah, that's it. He's the one who..."

He trailed off, the rest of the sentence hanging between us like smoke.

Killed himself.

That's what he was going to say.

"Yeah," I murmured, the word tasting bitter. "That one."

The grief came creeping back in like a tide, slow and heavy. It always did when I thought of him. What he went through. What the Run did to him. He came back with a body intact but a spirit broken. He hadn't placed above last place for a single trial, and somehow to the people who'd sent him, that became unforgivable.

The cruelest part of the Reclamation Run was how the rewards were structured. As long as all ten Challengers remained alive and competing, the resource prizes were tiered. First place earned a full year's supply, enough to sustain an entire Collective. Second and third place still walked away with a meaningful share. Fourth and fifth got something, though it was barely enough to stretch. But sixth place and below? Typically nothing.

And that system only got harsher as competitors started to die off, which they always did. Fewer survivors meant fewer rewards. If only five were left standing, only the top three received anything at all.

Ava's brother had been one of just three Challengers who made it out alive that year. He placed third in the last few trials. But with only three left, that also made him the last, and last place, no matter how brutal the odds or how hard the fight, meant going home empty-handed.

The night he got back to Canyon, they were waiting, people who had voted for him to die, then cheered for him. All of a sudden they hurled their hatred like knives. Night after night. At his door. At his name. The Collective that sentenced him to death didn't welcome him home alive, they blamed him. As if failure to bring back resources meant he didn't deserve to breathe.

The threats. The harassment. The utter isolation.

It was too much for him. And Ava. I saw the toll it was taking on them first hand. They both lost so much of themselves in those weeks following the Run.

He proved to me, in the most heartbreaking way, that survival wasn't the same thing as freedom. That making it home didn't mean you were safe.

Didn't mean you were whole.

Didn't mean you'd been spared.

Ezra nodded slowly, mulling that over. "You don't have any other family that could look after your brother?"

I looked down at my drink and swallowed hard, thankful for the change in subject, but not all that comfortable with the newest line of questioning either. "Nope. It's just the two of us."

There was a beat of silence where my guilt felt suffocating. How could I just leave him like that? I hated myself. But then I tried to remind myself that I was doing this for him too. To get him the resources he needed. I guess both things could be true at once. I could be doing the right thing, and still hate myself for it.

Ezra sat quietly waiting for me to exit my shame spiral. No prying, no follow-up. Just the quiet clink of glass as Ezra uncorked the bottle and poured another splash into my glass without asking. A silent gesture that made my chest tighten.

I gave him a small, grateful smile, and we sipped in comfortable quiet for a moment.

"What about you?" I asked. "Do you have anyone back home?"

He exhaled through his nose and stared off over my shoulder, his voice turning flat. "Not anyone who's rooting for my return."

I winced. "I'm sorry."

He shrugged, but didn't look back at me. Just drank.

The silence hung between us again, heavier this time. Then, after a beat, he spoke. "You can ask, you know."

I glanced at him. "Ask what?"

"What I did. Why I'm here. What I was convicted of."

My heart thudded. My fingers tightened around the glass. I could ask and finally know what the whole Collective had been clamoring about. Finally discover if any of the wild rumors held any truth. Find out what danger I might really be in by trusting him during the Run.

But a part of me didn't want to. Didn't want to take the trust I already somehow felt for him and ruin it with something that was in the past and frankly didn't matter.

Not tonight. Not ever.

"I know," I said softly. "But I don't want to."

His brow arched slightly, clearly surprised. "You're not even a little curious?"

"Curious?" I nodded. "Of course. But I don't need to know. If we're going to make it through this, I just need to know one thing." I looked up at him, holding his gaze. "Will you have my back in there?"

He studied me for a long moment. His eyes scanned my face, then flicked, just for a breath, down to my lips before meeting mine again. Something shifted in his expression. A softening.

"Yeah," he said at last. "I've got your back, Bex."

"That's all I needed to know." I smiled, and lifted my glass. We clinked, then I downed the rest and pushed myself away from the bar.

"I should probably try to sleep," I said, turning to go.

"Bex?"

I stopped and turned over my shoulder.

Ezra had stepped out from behind the bar and was already closing the distance between us. He came to a stop right in front of me. Close. Close enough that I could feel the warmth of him, smell the whiskey on his breath, sweet and sharp. Goosebumps rose along my arms and my nipples pebbled, hardening to painful peaks.

He looked at me, his gaze dipping down, not to leer, but to notice. And then, gently, his hands came up and drew the sides of my cardigan closed over my thin nightdress, shielding me from view.

My breath caught in my throat. My cheeks burned. Had he just seen my body's reaction to him?

His touch lingered just a second longer than it needed to, then he stepped back.

"Goodnight," he murmured, voice low and rough.

And then he turned and disappeared down the aisle, leaving me standing there with my pulse thudding in my ears.

CHAPTER
FIVE

EZRA

Nova's god-awful screeching woke me before the sun had fully risen. Her voice pierced through the cabin walls, shrill and merciless, yelling something about it being "time to get up," as if any of us had slept well enough to deserve that tone.

The morning light was beginning to slip through the slats of the blinds, casting sharp, golden stripes across the floor. Beneath my feet, the train's momentum shifted, slowing, easing us into the final stretch. Praxis was close.

I groaned, dragging a hand over my face before tossing the covers aside and hauling myself upright. The cot in this glorified closet of a cabin wasn't built for someone my height, and my spine reminded me of that fact with every reluctant pop and crack. I took my time stretching, dragging my arms overhead and twisting until the ache dulled enough to stand without grimacing.

I moved toward the outfit Nova had laid out for me the

night before, black dress pants and a slate-grey button-down. Standard Collective issue. Dull. Lifeless. A walking eulogy to the system that chewed us up and spit us out. Meanwhile, Praxis would greet us in their flashy metallics like God descending from the heavens. We looked like the shadows they left behind. And that's exactly how they liked it.

For a second, I considered putting my old clothes back on, the ones from the vote. But after days in a cell, those clothes were more grime than fabric. The shower on the train had been a gift, and I wasn't about to ruin the feeling of being clean again. No matter how badly I wanted to tell Praxis and their issued clothing to fuck off.

So, despite the stubborn part of me that didn't want to make anything easy for Nova Lockeley, I slid into the outfit she'd provided. Might as well look like her perfect little Challenger, even if I had no intention of playing the part.

I didn't plan to speak during my confessional. I really didn't. But the cameraman just had to ask *that* question, 'what did I hope to do for the people of my Collective'?

The same people who convicted me. Who heard the evidence against me and locked me away anyway. Who sentenced me to die.

I wasn't going to stay silent after that.

I didn't care about dying. Hell, at this point I'd probably welcome the sweet release of death. But I didn't want them to think they'd gotten away with it without a fight.

I watched the segment last night. One of the lounge cars had a mounted TV, and I needed something to dull the growing fire in my chest. I saw the lineup, each Collective parading their picks like prized livestock. The same Collectives that always won had strong, polished candidates who gave the camera a proud smile and fed the masses bullshit about "duty" and "honor." I rolled my eyes so hard I almost gave myself a headache.

Then came the lottery picks. That was a different story. Fear practically oozed off the screen. I saw elders with fragile hands and sunken eyes, children barely old enough to tie their shoes. Now, being sent to die for their Collectives. The camera zoomed in on their trembling fingers, their darting eyes.

One Collective got a whole segment because their elected Challenger's twin brother was chosen in the lottery. They did their confessional together, the elected was a little more reserved, a soft smile on her lips. But her brother? He was full of swagger and confidence.

A lucky family, they called it.

I called it losing both children in one fell swoop.

And then... It was Canyon's turn.

And there I was.

The brooding silent type. The wildcard. The candidate with the dark attitude and even darker past. They painted me like I was some creature to be tamed. The red-haired cameraman worked with barely a scrap of footage and spun it into prime Nexum propaganda. I almost had to applaud the bastard for it.

Almost.

Up until last night, my plan was simple... fail the trials. Let Canyon lose. Let them feel every ounce of the consequences for casting me aside. If I was going to die, at least I'd drag their precious hope down with me.

But then...

Then she happened.

Bex.

Now I had a reason to make it to the medical trial. A reason to fight, if not for Canyon, then for her. Maybe I needed to survive long enough to give her a shot at getting home.

Maybe I had to play the game.

Last night as I watched the screen, I tried not to focus on her. I didn't want to get involved. Didn't want to think about the person from my Collective who'd be just as dead as I was in a few weeks.

But then her face filled the frame, eyes like the sky. Haunted. She got more screen time than anyone, clear shots of her tearful interview, and her touching goodbye with her brother. That was good. She'd need to rely on that kind of sympathy when it all turned to blood and smoke.

I couldn't listen to another second of the Nexum-fed lies, so I slipped away for a drink. Something to silence the noise in my head.

And that's when I found her.

I groaned, trying to ignore the way the thought of her standing there in that thin fucking silk nightgown made my cock stand at attention. I saw the way her breasts heaved as I neared her, the way her nipples jutted through the fabric of that night dress. I had to force myself not to bend down and taste them right then and there.

Any kind of relationship would only complicate things. The last thing I needed was for Nexum to twist whatever feelings I might, or might not, have into some kind of headline. A tragic romance. A betrayal. A narrative they could sink their claws into.

So I shoved that strange pull I felt toward her deep down, buried it beneath layers of grit and resolve, and locked it away where no one, not even me, could touch it.

Then I stepped out of my cabin, face blank, heart walled off and headed to the main cabin.

Nova's high-pitched and annoying voice met me before I

even rounded the corner. She was buzzing around like a deranged hummingbird, hunched over who I assumed was Bex, applying makeup with the same obsessive fervor she'd shown yesterday.

She was painting her face again, no doubt with dark, smoky eyes, rouged cheeks, lips likely bleeding red. It did something to her features, giving her a striking, almost dangerous beauty. But I found myself preferring the way she'd looked last night. Barefaced. Blushing. Real.

Get a grip, I told myself, jaw tightening as I dropped into one of the seats that faced away from them. I needed to focus. Not on her. Not on that face. Not on the memory of her sleepy voice or the softness of her cardigan brushing against my bare chest.

Zaffir, the ever-present shadow with a lens, was already moving around the cabin, filming everything like the voyeur he was. I saw the camera shift toward me before I even heard his voice.

"Good morning, Ezra," he said.

I didn't answer.

"Are you looking forward to seeing Praxis today?" Still nothing from me.

He pushed again. "And are you excited to meet the other Challengers?"

I flicked my eyes up to the lens, then back down, saying nothing. I could hear the tight breath of his frustration, which almost made me smile. Almost.

Play the game, I reminded myself. *For her.*

But the words wouldn't come. I didn't know how to play it, not in a way that didn't make me feel like I was slicing off parts of myself just to fit into their frame.

Zaffir gave a low huff and turned his attention toward the real star of the show...Bex.

"You're just about ready," Nova chirped. "And... there." She stepped back like a painter finishing a canvas, admiring her work.

I couldn't see past her at first, but I felt it. That tug in my chest, the tightening of something I didn't want to name. My neck craned against my will, hungry for a glimpse.

And then Nova shifted, and there she was.

Bex sat in the center of the cabin like she didn't even know she'd stolen the air right out of it. Her blonde curls were swept into soft waves that kissed the edges of her cheeks and spilled over her leather-clad shoulders. A black corset cinched at her waist, structured and elegant, flaring out into a skirt that teased movement with every breath. Her eyes were lined in deep, smoky black, and her lips, god, those lips, were painted in a red so rich I couldn't stop the thought of seeing them stretched over a thick hard part of me.

It hit me low, hard, and sudden. A surge of heat, a hunger that had no business affecting me this much.

And I didn't realize how badly I'd slipped until I caught the movement to my right.

Zaffir.

His camera.

Pointed directly at me.

He'd caught it. Every flicker of lust, every pulse of weakness. It was all on film now. My big, stupid, traitorous reaction.

Fuck.

I forced my expression to harden, turning away, jaw clenched tight enough to ache. This couldn't happen. I wouldn't let it. Not with her. Not like this.

Not with them watching.

"She's gorgeous, isn't she?" Zaffir's voice slid in like a knife disguised as silk, low and baiting.

I glanced up.

He wasn't even looking at me. His gaze was on her. Bex. His mouth hung slightly open, that dazed, awestruck look on his face as if he forgot, for just a second, where he was.

A flash of jealousy shot through my chest like a live wire.

"Don't look at her," I growled, the words coming out sharper than I intended.

Zaffir's head turned toward me slowly, the corner of his mouth twitching like he'd just won a bet with himself. "It's my job to," he said, with a shrug that tried for nonchalance, but I saw the heat still simmering behind his eyes.

"No," I snapped, voice low and dangerous. "It's your job to film. Not to stare."

He cocked his head, lens still trained on me, and his voice dipped into something far more calculated. "Well you certainly were.. Staring, I mean." He said, pointing to the camera which was still firmly fixed on me.

My fists clenched at my sides. I tried to keep my tone level and firm. Not begging. Threatening. "Don't use that footage."

"Why not?" he asked, clearly enjoying himself now. "Too real? Too honest?" His camera didn't budge.

"Because I don't need you turning this into something it's not," I hissed through clenched teeth, glancing to the side to make sure Nova still had Bex distracted. She was fussing with a stray curl near her shoulder and droning on about how excited she was for the food she was going to scarf down at the welcome party.

Zaffir raised a brow, mocking interest dripping off him. "Oh?" He turned his head back toward Bex, giving her a once-over. "She's a pretty girl. Can't say I'd blame you if you were developing feelings."

I moved before I could stop myself, rising from my seat and stepping in, right to the edge of his precious shot. My shadow blocked part of his light and the lens tilted slightly upward to compensate.

"Shut the fuck up," I muttered, venom in every word.

Zaffir didn't even flinch. If anything, his smile widened like he'd finally struck gold. "Did I hit a nerve?"

His tone was smug, a thread of pride woven through the faux innocence. This was what he wanted. A reaction. A spark. Something to spice up the show between segments of Nexum propaganda and sanitized interviews. And I was giving it to him.

I stared at him and something clicked. Maybe this was how I played the game. By letting him take control.

Let him film the glare, the growl, the tension between us like it was some new subplot for the masses to eat up. Let him shape me into whatever caricature he needed for his little show. Let him make me so interesting that they wanted me to stick around long enough so I could keep her safe.

Let him "produce" me.

"Leave her alone," I said, stepping back deliberately, just far enough to be sure I was framed cleanly in his lens.

Zaffir's eyes narrowed like he knew what I was doing. He could feel the shift. "You're awfully protective of Miss Hollis," he said, the words practically laced with bait. He was setting the stage, and handing me the script.

"Because if anyone deserves to win the Reclamation Run and return home to their family... it's her." The words came out easy. Honest. And that was the worst part, it was the truth. But the slow, satisfied curve of Zaffir's lips told me I'd just bought myself a spotlight.

The camera's light blinked off, and he lowered it with a click before stepping in. His voice dropped to a whisper.

"Good work," he said with a hint of praise.

"I don't know what you're talking about," I replied flatly, eyes locking with his.

But he wasn't fooled. He gave me that smug, knowing smirk. "Sure you don't."

Then he glanced past me. I didn't have to follow his gaze. I could feel her behind me like a beacon. Bex. She didn't even have to speak for the room to tilt toward her.

"You and I want the same thing," he said carefully.

Another flicker of jealousy lit through my chest but I bit it back before it burned through.

"I want her to win," Zaffir went on, voice surprisingly sincere. "I want her to get what she needs for her brother. I want her to make it out."

I studied him. Hard. The way he said it. The way his eyes softened when they landed on her again. He wasn't lying. Or if he was, he was a damn convincing actor.

"Since when does Praxis care who wins the trials?" I spat.

He met my gaze for a brief moment, he looked like he was going to say something, but then stopped himself. Finally, he spoke. "We're always rooting for our favorites." It was a Praxis response, but it seemed... wrong. Like he didn't really mean it.

I glared at him. "And so what, you're going to help her?"

"No," he said, shaking his head. "*We* are."

I folded my arms, jaw clenched, waiting.

"I can't fight in those trials with you," he continued. "But I can shift the narrative. I can make the world fall in love with her. I can turn her into a fan favorite, give her momentum."

"And me?" I asked, voice like flint. "What do you expect my part to be in all this?"

Zaffir's eyes gleamed like he'd been waiting for that question.

"I can make you into the quiet soldier. The brooding protector. The guy who doesn't give a damn about the cameras or the glory, only her." He looked at her again, and for a split second, I wasn't sure who he was pitching the story for, me or himself. "If we play it right, the viewers will eat it up. They'll root for her. Fight for her. They'll want you there to protect her."

He stepped a little closer, lowering his voice again. "And maybe... that'll be enough to keep her alive."

My breath slowed. The possessiveness hadn't faded, but it was tempered now by something colder. Smarter.

The more people who cared about her, the more shields she'd have in this game.

Still... "What's in it for you?" I asked, watching him like a wolf watches another circling too close to the kill.

That glimmer in his eyes returned. That look, lust tangled up with fascination. "I just want her to survive this."

"You like her," I said, quietly.

He gave a half-shrug, unapologetic. He didn't deny it. Didn't even try. "Can you blame me?"

Jealousy twisted again in my gut, but it didn't settle. It burned itself out with the realization that the more allies she had meant more chance for her safety. And the truth was...no, I couldn't blame him.

"Fine," I said, quietly. "Tell me what I need to do."

CHAPTER
SIX

BEX

THE TRAIN CAME to a screeching halt, and for a moment, all I could hear was the rapid pulse in my ears, drowning out the usual noise. My body tensed, a mix of anticipation and dread wrapping around me. The fabric of my outfit clung uncomfortably to my skin. It wasn't the usual loose-fitting comfort I was accustomed to, everything felt tighter. Every curve of my body was on display, and there was no escaping the way it felt, especially when I could feel my own breath hitch in the tight corset around my torso. My chest felt like it was being pushed forward, and my face, once again coated with layers of thick makeup, seemed almost foreign to me. I hated it. I hated the way it made me feel like an object, something to be admired and scrutinized.

I would have argued, protested the way they'd dressed me up, how they'd painted me into this character, if I hadn't seen the looks Ezra and Zaffir gave me when they thought I wasn't looking. I caught the way their eyes lingered, scanning my body like it was a prize they were trying to figure out how to claim. I pretended not to notice, keeping my gaze averted, but their stares burned into me. It was subtle, but undeniable. The heat in their eyes was clear, and full of appreciation, desire, and lust. And suddenly I didn't want to shrink away from it, to protest, but rather indulge in it.

It had been so long since anyone looked at me like that. Since anyone noticed me with that kind of hunger in their gaze. Maybe I shouldn't feel the way I did, considering the situation, but I couldn't help it. That didn't stop the rush of warmth their gazes elicited in me. I could feel myself soaking it in, almost greedily. How much longer would I even be alive to feel it? To be looked at? To be desired? I may never feel that kind of affection again. And that thought made me sick with longing.

"Now, when we step off the train, there will be a warm welcome. I advise you to make a good impression," Nova's voice was cheerful, almost overly so as she led me toward the exit. Her steps were quick, her heels clicking against the metal floor of the cabin, but I couldn't shake the feeling that everything was about to change. "Nexum saw you last night during your segments, but they need to get to know you now. Really get to know you." Her smile was wide. "Just smile, wave, and follow me. We're headed to the welcome party for all the Challengers." She clapped her hands with enthusiasm.

I could hear the bustling crowd just beyond the door, the chatter, the laughter, the low hum of excitement. My stomach twisted. I wanted to take a deep breath and mentally prepare myself, but I couldn't seem to focus.

I glanced at Ezra, whose eyes were locked on me. He leaned in closer, his shoulder brushing mine, grounding me in this moment. His touch was solid, like an anchor in the chaos of this manufactured world around us.

"You okay?" His voice was low and gentle, a stark contrast to the manic energy of Nova's commands.

I looked up at him, a soft smile tugging at my lips despite myself. "I'm not sure," I answered honestly, my voice betraying the nervousness I was trying so hard to hide.

He nodded slowly, his expression falling into the stoic mask he wore during the vote. But in his eyes, there was a fleeting glimmer of the warmth he'd shown me last night, tucked away in the quiet darkness of the train car.

For a moment, I felt a strange sense of pleasure. There was something oddly satisfying about knowing that the softer side of him, the part of him that was open, vulnerable, and real, was something I was getting to witness when no one else could.

Without saying a word, he lifted his hand, palm open, and held it out toward me.

"Together?" He offered, his voice steady, but there was an unspoken promise behind it. His gaze didn't waver, meeting mine with a quiet intensity that made my heart skip a beat.

I hesitated, a thousand thoughts running through my head. The cameras, the producers, the way they'd twist any action for the drama. Every fiber of my being screamed at me to think twice, to pull back, to keep my distance. But when I looked into his eyes, I saw something different. No masks, no games, just the same honesty that had been there last night.

"The cameras..." I challenged softly, unable to keep the edge from my voice.

Ezra just shrugged, unfazed. "Fuck them. They can think whatever they want. I told you I had your back. And I meant it." His words were fierce.

Something in his tone made it impossible for me to hold back. He meant what he said. I could feel it, and maybe I wanted to believe him.

I let my reservations slip away, the protests in my head quieting as if they had no place here. Ezra was right. To hell with them. I reached out and gripped his hand, fingers intertwining with his. The connection was immediate, warm, steady, and comforting. It was a simple gesture, but it brought a wave of relief that washed over me, calming the storm in my chest. For a fleeting moment, it felt like there was nothing else in the world except the quiet strength of his presence.

Together, we walked toward the chaos beyond the door.

The roar of the crowd was a violent, deafening wave that crashed over me as soon as we stepped off the train. The air was thick with excitement and energy, the sea of people dressed in gleaming silver, copper, and gold, their makeup extravagant and their clothing even more outlandish. Jewelry glittered like gaudy treasure, and their eyes gleamed with an almost frantic desire for attention. The anticipation was palpable, the crowd was hungry and restless, just waiting for us to make our way through.

Ezra's hand tightened around mine as we stepped onto the golden carpet, its plush surface stretching out before us like a path through the madness. The crowd parted around us like water around a stone, but they surged at the rope barriers, their voices crashing together in a chaotic symphony of shouts and calls. "How's your brother?" "Why are you holding his hand?" "What's wrong with your brother?" "Why are you so angry, Ezra?" "Are you two together?" "Are you single?" "Where are your parents?"

Each question felt like a needle, sharp and invasive, probing into places I didn't want anyone to see. My mouth was plastered into a smile, the kind of smile that was forced and fake, but I could hear Nova's voice in the back of my head saying *'Smile, wave, and make an impression.'* So, that's what I did. One hand lifted, and I waved. But it was too much. Too fast. My heart was pounding in my chest, my skin crawling with the weight of their gaze.

Ezra's grip on my hand was steady and unwavering. I looked over at him, finding that familiar softness in his gaze. He was watching me, his eyes saying more than words ever could. Without a single word, he silently begged me to stay focused, to keep my eyes on him and not on the madness around us. And so I did. I tuned out the world, focusing on the warmth of his hand in mine and the steady rhythm of our footsteps.

We moved through the crowd together, Ezra a solid presence by my side, and Nova leading the way, reveling in the attention. I could see Zaffir in the corner of my eye, the lens of his camera following every step we took, capturing our every movement.

Finally, we reached the long stretched vehicle. The moment I slid inside, a small breath of relief escaped me, and I leaned back, closing my eyes for just a second. The noise, the questions, the press of people. But just as I was about to release a full sigh of relief, Zaffir slipped inside right behind us, taking the seat opposite us without a second thought.

The red light on his camera flashed, and the tension in my chest knotted tighter. I wasn't free. Not at all. The cameras were still rolling. The show wasn't over.

Ezra pressed closer to my side. "It's okay," he whispered, his voice low and steady. I turned my gaze toward him, finding solace in the warmth of his touch.

But as I glanced over to where Zaffir was seated, camera in hand, I noticed something flicker in his eyes. A flash of something sharp, as his gaze briefly lingered on the way Ezra's hand held mine.

Before I could dwell too much on it, Nova's voice cut through the tension like a knife. "Well, that was fun!" she exclaimed. She knocked on the partition between the cabin and the driver's seat. "We're ready," she added, clearly eager to get to the welcome party.

The car lurched forward, jerking me from my thoughts. I wasn't prepared for the sudden movement, and before I could steady myself, I felt myself tipping forward, my balance off-kilter. But then, in an instant, Ezra was there. His arm shot around my waist, pulling me back against him, keeping me from crashing forward into the seat. His face was inches from mine, his breath warm against my skin. I could feel the steady beat of his heart beneath my palm where it rested against his chest.

"I've got you," he promised. I found myself leaning into him.

Nova's voice droned on, explaining what we could expect at the party, her words a blur as they passed through my ears. My mind felt like it was in a whirlwind, spinning in every direction. I watched as trees with bright pink flowers framed the street as we passed. I wanted to focus on that, but I felt drawn to something else instead. Ezra's sudden shift in demeanor had thrown me off. One moment, he was nothing but a scowl toward the cameras, keeping a cool distance. The next, he was openly showing affection, his hand in mine as if it were the most natural thing in the world. If it hadn't been for the quiet, intimate moment we'd shared last night at the bar, where everything felt real, stripped of the cameras, I might have thought he was messing with me, trying to toy with my emotions, playing some game.

Finally, the car came to a halt, and we arrived at our destination. The doors opened, and I stepped out into a world I couldn't have imagined even in my wildest dreams. There, in front of me, stood the center of Praxis itself.

I stared up at the grand structure, my breath catching in

my throat. The sight of it was overwhelming. I had never seen anything like this, anything this pristine. The buildings in our Collective, the ones that we considered beautiful, were battered by time, faded from years of neglect and lack of resources. This beautiful home was the opposite of that. Pristine, untouchable, as if it existed in a world where the pain and hardship the rest of Nexum had endured had never even touched it. The bright white walls gleamed in the sunlight, contrasting against the deep green of the lawn that stretched out in front of it. Elegant pillars rose up at the base of the house, supporting the grand structure above, while sweeping staircases led up to the massive entrance.

It was a symbol of everything Praxis claimed to uphold, the power, the wealth, the untouchable beauty that we, the lowly Collectives, could only dream of. Untouched by time, untouched by the desperate and dark history that Praxis liked to remind us of every single day. It was a thing of beauty, yes, but it also felt like a reminder of just how far away the people who lived inside this place were from the rest of us.

I swallowed hard, trying to focus as we made our way up the steps, but the sight of the gleaming home looming over me kept gnawing at the back of my mind. This was their world, beautiful, cold, and impenetrable. And we weren't their guests. We were their entertainment.

Ezra was still holding my hand and I tried not to read too much into it. He was offering comfort, and I needed it. Simple as that.

Nova stopped just before the grand front doors and turned to us with a sharp look. "Alright, time to go in." She glanced at our joined hands, her gaze lingering for a second too long. "One at a time, I'm afraid."

I nodded, slowly pulling my hand from Ezra's, more reluctant than I cared to admit. "Ezra, you first," Nova instructed, giving him a small push toward the door. He shot me one last encouraging look before disappearing inside.

I stood there for a moment, my fingers nervously playing with the fabric of my skirt. The sound of footsteps approaching interrupted my thoughts, and I looked up to find Zaffir standing next to me, his camera now off.

"You don't have to be nervous," he said, his voice almost too casual.

I scoffed, raising an eyebrow. "Of course I do. I'm about to walk into a room full of people who have no idea who I am, except for whatever they saw in a two-minute segment. People who are either cheering for my success or praying for my downfall. Or both."

Zaffir gave me a small, knowing smile. "I'm sure they already love you. Your story really resonated with them."

I frowned. "You mean the story you thought was made up?"

He winced, the smirk slipping for just a second. "Okay, not my finest moment." He paused for a beat, eyes scanning my face with something softer than usual. "You're not playing a game, Brexlyn. I get that now. You're just... honest. And that's rare around here. I wasn't expecting it."

I crossed my arms, trying to mask the vulnerability his words stirred. "Doesn't exactly make for good TV."

Zaffir chuckled, leaning against a pillar casually. "You'd be surprised. People like the truth. They like to watch someone who doesn't hide behind a mask, who isn't obviously on a show. That's why you'll stick around, because you're not pretending."

I narrowed my eyes at him, not sure whether to be annoyed or... grateful. "And you think that's enough?"

"To win? No, probably not," he replied, his tone a little more serious now. "But it'll get you pretty far. If you're smart enough to learn how to play the game once you're in it, that is."

I snorted, but there was a hint of humor in it. "I thought I was already in it."

He smirked, his eyes twinkling with humor mixed with sadness. "I guess you are."

I stared at him for a beat, letting the silence settle heavy between us. "So what now?" I asked. "You gonna give me a tutorial on how to lie to the camera? Sell a story? I'm guessing you're a seasoned pro."

Zaffir's grin curved, sharp and amused. "No," he said. "My advice? Be honest, don't lie...show Nexum exactly who you are. Just don't expect anyone else to be."

"Be what? Honest?"

"Yeah, you'll be better off if you just assume everyone is lying," he added. An unreadable expression crossed his face.

I huffed a short laugh, crossing my arms. "So, then why should I trust you?"

"Because," he said, without missing a beat, "I'm behind the camera, not in front of it. I've got no reason to lie to you."

"Actually," I said, tilting my head, "I think that gives you plenty of reason."

He smirked at that, eyes glinting like he enjoyed the verbal sparring. "I don't gain anything by feeding you bullshit, Brexlyn. I'm not here to manipulate you, I just document what happens."

"Isn't that what producers do? Manipulate?"

His smile didn't quite falter, but something in it cooled. "Touché."

There was a pause, just long enough for me to feel the static shift between us. Then he added, "Look, this whole thing, it's a giant show. You wanna survive? Be real. But don't lay your cards out for everyone and then expect them to play fair."

I studied him, unsure if I wanted to take that as wisdom or warning. "You're awfully invested for someone who's supposedly neutral."

He shrugged. "Maybe I'm tired of watching my Challengers fail every year. Or maybe I just want to see someone who deserves it win for once."

That hit harder than I expected. My throat tightened, but I didn't let it show. I rolled my shoulders and forced the mask back into place.

"I'm rooting for you, Brexlyn Hollis." His eyes latched onto mine. Focused. Pleading.

I raised a brow. "Because you care, or because if I go down, your gig goes with me?"

His gaze flicked over me, serious now. "This has nothing to do with the job."

There it was again, that flicker of something real behind his careful facade. And just like that, the air between us felt heavier, charged.

I didn't trust him. Not entirely. But part of me wanted to. "How do I know you're not lying to me too?"

He pointed to the camera at his side. Off. "Because nobody else is listening."

"Alright," I said finally, voice low. "I'll keep that in mind."

"Do," he replied, stepping back with that same infuriating, unreadable smirk. "Because you're not as much of a wild card as you think."

I swallowed, trying to keep my focus. But before I could respond, Nova's voice rang out from inside. "Bex, it's your turn."

I nodded, ready to go, but as I stepped forward, my foot caught on the threshold. Before I could catch myself, I tumbled forward, expecting to face-plant right onto the marble floor. But Zaffir's arms shot out, quick and steady, catching me effortlessly before I could hit the ground.

He looked down at me, his hands still gently gripping my arms, and a teasing glint flashed in his eyes. "Careful."

I blinked up at him, my heart racing in my chest from the sudden proximity. I gave him a small, reluctant smile before pushing off his chest and standing up. My skin still tingled where his hands had been, and I quickly smoothed my skirt to distract myself.

With a deep breath, I turned to head inside, but just before the door clicked shut, I heard Zaffir's voice again, softer this time, with a touch of sincerity I didn't expect.

"Good luck, Brexlyn."

The door closed behind me, but his words lingered in my ears, like a quiet promise.

Nova led me toward the entrance of a grand hall, and I suddenly felt exposed all over again. My body still tingled from the encounter with Zaffir. I couldn't quite figure out why I was reacting like this to him. He was Praxis, after all, he wasn't on my side. But there was something about him, something magnetic, that drew me in. Then, of course, there was Ezra. His mysterious aura, the way he made me feel when he showed me that softer side of him. I couldn't deny the pull, but I also couldn't ignore the fact that both of them were, in their own way, obstacles in my path.

I needed to focus. I was about to walk into a room full of competitors, people who were all vying for the same goal, for the same chance. And if I wanted to save my brother, and return to him alive, I couldn't afford to be distracted by schoolgirl crushes. This was serious.

The door opened, and my name was announced. A wave of noise swept over me as the crowd's attention focused in my direction. The ballroom was breathtaking, the guests from Praxis in shades of gold, gowns and suits that shimmered like something out of a dream. In stark contrast, the other Challengers stood out like sore thumbs, their dark blacks and grays clashing against the opulent surroundings.

I stepped forward into the crowd, trying to smile graciously as I made my way deeper into the room, but my mind kept returning to Ezra. When I finally spotted him across the room, I hesitated. I couldn't go to him. Not now. I needed to stay focused.

I navigated the sea of guests, answering polite questions, smiling, and doing my best to keep Zaffir's warning on repeat in my head. Everyone's mask was on. Painted grins. Words polished to a shine.

Eventually, I found myself drifting to the edge of the room, away from the spotlight. I let the crowd blur, my gaze sharpening as I watched them move. My eyes tracked gestures, shifts in posture, lingering glances. I didn't care about what they said when they knew I could hear them, I cared about what they gave away when they thought I couldn't. Praxis guests would clamor around a Challenger, fawning over them, then slink away to boast, tease and chat about the exchange. Like gossiping little children.

"Always a pleasure to meet a fellow people watcher," a voice called from behind me.

I turned, expecting another Praxis lackey desperate to interact with the entertainment. But the woman standing there wasn't Praxis. She was a Challenger.

She wore a tailored black suit that hugged her curves like it had been made with her in mind. Her skin was sun-warmed, smooth, and golden. Her hair was pulled back in a low, tight bun. Her dark brown eyes burned into my skin. They trailed over me, curious, slow.

I blinked. My throat dried up. I swallowed hard.

"I must be doing a pretty poor job of it if you noticed me," I said, a half-smirk tugging at my lips. "I'm supposed to be the one watching, not being watched."

She smiled, just enough to let it be dangerous. "Not your fault," she said. "You're just... noticeable."

My pulse spiked. I held her gaze, refusing to be the first to drop it.

"I prefer the edges too," she said, then finally broke eye contact to glance out over the crowd again. "I find you learn the most about people when they let their guard down."

I stared at her profile, watching and her keen eyes surveyed the room.

"Remind me to keep my guard up then," I responded.

She smirked, eyes flicking back to me, clearly entertained by my response, and held out her hand. "Briar Grey, Darkbranch Collective."

I raised an eyebrow but took her hand, shaking it firmly. "Brexlyn Hollis, Canyon."

"Oh, I know," she said smoothly. "I watched your segment last night. But I have to admit, the screen didn't do you justice."

I felt a flush creeping up my neck and quickly cleared my throat. "What do I owe the pleasure of your flattery?" I asked, trying to keep the mood light.

She tilted her head slightly, her smirk turning more mischievous. "Can't a gal get to know her competition?"

I gestured toward the rest of the ballroom. "Sure. There they are."

She chuckled, low and enticing. "You don't consider yourself competition?"

I flexed my nonexistent muscles for effect, earning a laugh

from her. But then she stepped closer, invading my space in a way that made my breath catch.

"You and I both know," she said, her voice low and almost purring, as she trailed a single finger along my upper arm, sending a jolt of electricity through me, "that these muscles," she traced a finger down my arm, "aren't the only strength you need in these trials."

I froze, unsure how to respond. There was something about her, something dangerous in the way she looked at me, like she knew everything about me just by staring into my soul. Something that sent a wave of warmth rushing through my chest, and to my core.

"I guess we'll see when the trials start, won't we?" I responded, trying to mask my reaction with a feigned smile.

She leaned in, her smirk widening just slightly. "We will," she said, her voice dark and inviting.

"So," I said, tilting my head toward her, trying to sound casual, maybe a little aloof, but the flirt crept in anyway. "Have you learned anything useful about your competition yet?"

It came out more sultry than I intended. I told myself it was a strategy. A tool. Just another way to get her talking. It had nothing to do with how sinfully unfair her eyes were.

"Tons," Briar said smoothly, a smirk tugging at her lips. "Why, you curious?" She leaned in, warm and teasing, eyes glinting like she already knew the answer.

"If you're willing to share," I said, my voice barely above a breath. Her gaze dropped to my lips, and for a split second, everything else in the room dulled.

Something sparked behind her eyes. Not just heat, something darker. Lustful. And I felt it coil low in my stomach. I pressed my thighs together, hoping to regain even a sliver of composure.

"Hollis," she murmured like a velvet secret, lips brushing close to my ear, "I think you'll find that I love to share."

A humiliating shiver rippled down my spine.

"Saltspire's elected, Devrin, is aiming for the electricity trial, but he plans to place in as many as possible," she said, straightening up slightly and nodding toward a massive guy posted near the far wall.

I followed her gaze. "Saltspire? But don't they run mostly on hydropower?" I asked, recalling images from books and old transmission reels, coastal cliffs, crashing waves, and massive turbines.

"They do," Briar replied. "But their main plant's half-dead. Infrastructure's failing, so they need a backup source."

"They need electricity," I finished for her, nodding slowly.

Her smirk softened into something more thoughtful. "The Wildfold elected and Oasis elected both want Air Filtration. Apparently, the last few years have been rough, standing water, and pollutants. People are getting sick."

"Sick?" This was the first I was hearing of this.

She nodded. "Wildfold's also got their eyes on medical supplies, they need more masks."

My brows furrowed. "They're wearing masks?" I asked, a chill crawling up my spine.

"Outdoors, almost constantly," she said, her voice lower now. "Something's tainted the air. Could be mold, chemical runoff, or worse. They're not sure."

She paused, and her gaze locked on mine again, no smirk this time, no flirtation.

"Which is why Wildfold's lottery pick, Lark, is also aiming for the medical personnel trial." And there it was. The one resource I needed more than anything else. She didn't say it aloud, but we both knew what hung in the air between us. She knew what I wanted.

Of course she did. Even if I hadn't said it with my whole chest in my interview, she would've figured it out. She was sharp like that. She seemed like the type to find anything out. My mind reminded me to be careful when divulging anything to her. No matter how charming she may seem.

"That's unfortunate for me," I replied, looking over at the Wildfold chosen Challenger. He was thin, but muscular, a sort of frame that screamed 'athlete'. He had an almost laser-focused look on his face and I tried not to let the fear seep in, but it was here anyway.

"It's a mental trial," Briar continued. "From what I gather, he doesn't have any formal schooling." There was a silver lining at least. I smiled up at Briar, genuinely, even if it was a little stiff.

"Thank you."

"So, Hollis," Briar said, my name rolling off her tongue with that same easy confidence. "I wanted to tell you that I'm sorry about your brother. His illness. That you had to leave him."

My eyes narrowed instinctively. Of all the things people had said about my brother today, his condition, his circumstances, no one had expressed any sympathy for *me*, for the fact that I left him just when he needed me most. A nagging voice, that sounded a lot like Zaffir, in the back of my head reminded me not to trust it entirely.

I must have looked surprised because she added, almost like an afterthought, "I've got a brother, too."

I sighed, trying to keep my tone light but failing to hide the edge. "It must have been hard leaving him to come here." After all, I knew the feeling.

Briar shook her head, and there was something raw in her eyes, something I didn't expect. "I wish I got to leave him behind," she said, a dark twist to his words. My eyebrows rose, and eyes widened in question. "The unlucky bastard just had to go and get himself chosen in the lottery."

My breath hitched, unable to stop the shock from registering on my face. "Your brother's here, too?" I asked, my voice a little breathless.

She nodded, but there was a strange, bitter edge to the motion.

"Yes, he is. And he's not unlucky. He just got a free all-expenses paid vacation to the capital of Nexum," another voice interrupted from behind us, dripping with sarcasm.

I turned quickly, eyes widening at the new figure standing there. He was a near mirror to Briar, with tanned skin, dark hair, eyes that gleamed with an intensity that matched his sister's. But this man's hair was shorter, cropped and shaggy just above his ears, and his features were a little sharper.

"Thorne Grey," the man said smoothly, offering me his hand.

I blinked, caught off guard by the unexpected introduction. His presence was as commanding as his sister's. I hesitated for a moment, then shook his hand.

"Thorne and Briar?" I asked, sending a cheeky look back over my shoulder.

Briar shrugged, moving to stand next to her brother. "Our Ma was real outdoorsy," she said as if that was answer enough for the woodsy nature of their names.

"Brexlyn Hollis," I said, turning back to Thorne. "You're Briar's brother, then?"

"Nah, no relation" Thorne said, his lips quirking into a half-smile.

Briar elbowed him in the ribs and Thorne let out a hearty laugh.

"Alright, alright. Unfortunately, I am." He gave his sister a glance that spoke volumes, a complicated mix of familiarity, irritation, and something else I couldn't quite put my finger on. Then, turning back to me, he leaned in slightly, as if sharing some secret. "But don't let her fool you. She may have gotten the votes, but I'm the far superior twin."

Briar rolled her eyes, clearly used to this dynamic. "Maybe you should go get something to drink, Thorne."

But Thorne wasn't having it. He waved a hand dismissively, his voice teasing. "Oh, and miss out on meeting this gorgeous creature? Look, if the universe wants to play its cruel joke on me, at least let me enjoy it."

There was a flicker of something in Briar's expression, something like regret, maybe even a hint of defensiveness. But before she could respond, Thorne gave her a shove, turning back to me with a wry grin.

"So, love, can I call you love?" he said, his tone shifting again, "You're here to win the medical trials right? "

I stood a little straighter, feeling the weight of their gazes on me, and crossed my arms. "Maybe I'm here because the universe is playing some cruel joke on me," I said, borrowing from Thorne's description. He offered me a smile. "But while I'm here, yeah, I hope I can win those trials. Or at least place high enough to get my brother some help."

Thorne's grin widened, his eyes twinkling with a cocky glint that made my stomach flip. He looked like he was about to say something more, but before he could, the anthem of Nexum blared through the speakers, its booming, triumphant notes echoing through the grand hall. The entire room fell silent in an instant, all eyes drawn to the elevated platform where Archon Evanora Veritas had taken her place.

I swallowed the sudden lump in my throat as I looked up at her. There, standing above us all, was the epitome of power. Archon Veritas, tall and imposing, with a presence that seemed to dwarf everyone in the room. Her gown was an elaborate masterpiece of gold and silver. The flared edges of the skirt created a solid few feet of space around her, a deliberate gesture that kept anyone from getting too close. A barrier designed to remind us of her untouchable position.

The room's collective attention shifted entirely to her as the anthem reached its peak, and then, with a calm, commanding voice, she spoke.

"By the will of the Praxis, you are welcome," she exclaimed.

"For the will of Praxis, we arrive," the room boomed. I'd never heard the response quite so full and eager. But I guess when in Praxis...

"Welcome, Challengers, to the Reclamation Run!" Her voice was smooth, laced with an undeniable edge of authority, but there was also something strangely captivating about it, like she could command a room without lifting a finger. The crowd responded with a loud cheer, a chorus of admiration and anticipation.

As she spoke, her gaze swept over the gathered crowd seeking out the Challengers scattered amongst the privileged, lingering just a moment longer on each one of us. Her eyes passed over Briar and Thorne briefly, but then I noticed her attention flicker in my direction, just for a split second. I didn't know if it was because she recognized me or if it was simply the way she had a knack for making everyone feel like they were under her watchful eye. Either way, my heart skipped a beat.

I wasn't the only one to feel it. The entire room seemed to hold its breath as she continued, her posture regal and unwavering.

"Tonight, we mark the beginning of the Run. Those of you who survive the trials will be given the chance to reclaim what's been lost. Your prize? Resources. Honor. And for some of you...salvation."

The applause that followed was deafening, but I felt a sudden unease crawl up my spine. Evanora's gaze never wavered as she stood there, studying us.

The crowd slowly started to settle, but there was an unspoken weight in the room.

Thorne leaned in slightly, his voice low but teasing as he murmured to me, "Well, it's official now. Let the trials begin." His words were almost a dare, and the corner of his mouth twitched as if he were enjoying this far more than I was.

Briar gave me another appraising look, her expression unreadable but her eyes sharp. I nodded, forcing myself to breathe deeply and shake off the unsettled feeling in my chest. I didn't want this. But now that I was here, I wasn't going to waste the chance. I would fight, claw, and outsmart whoever I had to in order to make it out alive and bring what my brother needed back with me.

The Reclamation Run wasn't built for the brave, it was built for the brutal. One wrong move, one misplaced trust, and it could all be over. I had to be smart. I had to be careful. I had too much to lose.

Archon Veritas raised her hand, signaling for the crowd to quiet once more. The room fell to a heavy silence, all eyes locked on her. "Tonight, you feast, you celebrate, you dance. But tomorrow, the first trial begins."

My heart thudded in my chest, and I knew this was just the beginning.

Archon Veritas lifted her crystal glass high, her voice ringing with hollow warmth as she declared, "To unity, preservation, and progress!"

A sweeping cheer followed, polite and practiced, as the Praxis elite mirrored her movement. Golden arms raised in near-perfect unison. The air shimmered with the clink of glass and the rustle of silks and satins.

I glanced around at the rest of the Challengers, those of us dressed in black and gray, standing like shadows in the midst of a celebration in our names but one we didn't feel invited to. None of us lifted our glasses. Some didn't even hold one. We stood still, watching them, because toasting this might be a lie too far.

Because what were we toasting, really?

Their unity wasn't ours. Their progress had cost us everything. And as for preservation... we were barely surviving out in the Collectives, what exactly were they preserving?

So we stayed still.

And I felt it then...that divide. Us versus them. They were here for a show.

We were here to survive.

The crowd exploded into lively and jovial excitement, as the music resumed and they slipped onto the dancefloor to take a turn about the room.

"Wanna dance, love?" Thorne asked, holding his arm out for me to take.

"I don't dance," I replied.

"Then follow my lead," he said, gripping my hand and dragging me toward the dance floor.

"See you around, Hollis," Briar promised with a genuine smile. Thorne spun me, and my feet moved on their own accord, when I was pulled back to him, he circled my waist and held my front pressed to his. I looked up breathless at him.

"So, fuck that lottery, am I right?" he said, breaking the tension and I couldn't help but laugh.

"Not sure I would say it quite as brashly, but I can't say I disagree with the sentiment," I said back with a soft smile. "I can't believe you were chosen in the lottery after your sister was elected. I mean what are the odds of that happening?"

Thorne let out a low laugh, his voice smooth with just a hint of smug. "Roughly zero-point-zero-zero-one-zero-two percent. One out of an eligible population of 9,792." He tilted his head, looking far too pleased with himself. "You'd have better odds of catching a snowflake on your tongue in Wild-fold in the middle of summer. Blindfolded."

I gave him a dumbfounded look.

"I'm really good at math," he whispered, his voice almost too smooth, like he was revealing a secret only meant for me. I shouldn't have felt the heat rush through me, but I did. Maybe it was his cocksure attitude, or maybe the way his intellect practically radiated from him, but something about it had me thrown off balance.

"I can see that," I replied, my voice a little more breathless than I intended as he spun me out and then pulled me back in. My head was spinning, not just from the dance, but from everything else. I couldn't help but wonder if someone with his level of sharpness would be my biggest competition. To save my brother. That thought was always there, in the back of my mind, lurking.

"Well, now that you're here," I said, trying to keep my voice steady and free from the nerves that were coursing through me, "what trials are you hoping to aim for?"

The question hung in the air, and I felt a tightness in my chest. I didn't want to admit how scared I was of facing him, someone who could probably calculate his way through any obstacle without breaking a sweat. Me? I could memorize equations, sure, but actually applying them? That was a different story entirely.

"Don't worry, love," Thorne said with a crooked grin, that mischievous glint in his eyes sparking like lightning. "You won't have to worry about me and my incredibly impressive brain getting in the way of you and your precious medical trials."

I huffed a laugh, a small knot of tension loosening in my chest. But before I could reply, his voice shifted.

"Truth is..." He trailed off, glancing sideways, his gaze flicking toward the far corner of the room where a pair of Praxis guards leaned against the wall, half-bored but always watching. "I'm not entirely sure I'm aiming for any trial at all."

That made me pause. "You're not going to compete?" I asked, more startled than I meant to sound.

Thorne didn't answer right away, spinning me around the dance floor, then pulling me tight to his chest. "Let's just say," he murmured, so low I had to lean in to hear him, "if Praxis is going to force me to play their game, I might enjoy playing one of my own."

I frowned. *Was he serious?* Speaking against Praxis, even in a half-joking way, was the kind of thing people disappeared for. The kind of thing that made people 'examples.'

"Thorne," I whispered, glancing toward the guards.

He finally relaxed, his smirk softening at the edges. "Relax," he said, voice light again. "What's a little venting between friends. We are friends now, right?"

I didn't know what to say. He made it sound like a joke, but it wasn't. Not really.

"Just... be careful," I managed.

He chuckled, reaching out to tuck a strand of hair behind my ear. "Worried about me, love?"

I rolled my eyes with a scoff. "I just...you should watch what you say. I wouldn't want my...friends to get hurt."

That earned a real grin, quick and sharp. But then, his voice softened again. "Don't waste a moment worrying about me. The stars..." He paused, catching himself, then smiled sadly. "They've got a habit of shining on those who earn it."

"Can I cut in?" a familiar deep voice whispered from behind me. I felt his presence before I turned.

Ezra was standing there, expectantly, his eyes locked on mine. I smiled instinctively when I saw him. My heart fluttered softly.

"See you in the trials, love," Thorne said with a sly grin, bowing deeply and pressing a soft kiss to the back of my hand. His lips burned against my skin, sending an unexpected wave of heat racing up my arm. I stood there for a moment, watching him walk away, before I turned back to face Ezra.

My heart skipped. Was Ezra upset? Did he think that just because I danced with someone else, it meant something? We had held hands, sure, but was that enough to make him think we were... something more? Did I want to be? Would he be angry if he knew that my body reacted to those handsome strangers just as strongly as it did to him? The thought gnawed at me.

I shook my head, trying to silence my racing thoughts. But then, just as I began to settle my nerves, Ezra stepped closer to me. His presence was commanding, protective, so intense it almost felt like the air itself thickened. Before I knew it, his strong arms were around me, pulling me into him as we began to sway. For a moment, we moved in complete silence, just the sound of our breathing filling the space between us.

"I didn't know you could dance," I murmured, surprised by the ease of his movements.

Ezra gave a quiet huff of amusement, barely a sound, but enough to make my chest tighten.

"I never have," he said. "I guess you're just a good partner."

I tilted my head slightly, studying him in the low light. His jaw was tense, like he was holding something back, like letting this moment happen went against every instinct he had. He didn't look at me right away, just kept his eyes somewhere over my shoulder.

"Why are you being like this?" I asked quietly.

That got his attention. His gaze flicked to mine, searching. "Like what?"

"Like this," I said, gesturing between us with a slight shift of my hand. "Open. Affectionate. Dancing with me. Holding my hand."

He hesitated. The weight of his silence pressed against me harder than his arms ever could.

"Forgive me for pointing it out, but this is a far cry from the guy who was silently staring down the barrel of the camera yesterday." I hated saying it, but it was nagging at me.

"I don't typically let people in," he said finally, voice rougher now. "Anymore."

"So why me?" I asked, barely more than a whisper.

"You make it feel worth the risk."

My breath caught, my fingers tightening slightly at the back of his neck. Ezra's eyes flicked to my mouth, just for a second. Barely. But I felt it like a spark lighting a fuse.

He didn't pull away. If anything, he drew just a little closer, not enough to cross a line in front of the onlookers, but enough to make me *ache* for it.

"I don't know what to trust," I whispered, the words slipping out before I could decide if I meant to say them aloud.

"You can trust me," he replied.

"Yesterday," I began, "you said your only goal was to make Canyon pay for electing you."

"Yesterday, that *was* my only goal," he said. His thumb moved along the curve of my spine, slow enough to feel deliberate. "Then you came along and ruined it."

I gave a short, breathless laugh, but it died in my throat when our eyes met again. There was nothing guarded in his face now, just heat, and something that felt dangerously close to longing.

"I don't want to ruin you," I said.

His gaze dropped to my lips, lingering this time. "Too late."

I didn't move. Didn't breathe. My whole body felt suspended in that space between decision and surrender.

"You look like you want to kiss me," I whispered because I couldn't focus on anything else.

He didn't deny it. "Tell me not to," he said. But his voice was already unsteady.

I didn't. I couldn't.

Our eyes locked, and the world around us faded. It was as if there was no one else in the room but the two of us. The only thing that existed was the heat rising between us, the electric pull that threatened to consume us both. His hand slid lower, drifting gently along the small of my back, pulling me even closer. I felt the heat of his touch sear through my dress, the longing inside me intensifying with each passing second.

By the time the song ended, I was burning with need. Heat pooled between my thighs, an ache I couldn't ignore. But Ezra didn't pull away. He just held me there, as the music shifted into another song. And then another. The minutes passed, but neither of us seemed to care. We simply moved together, lost in the rhythm of each other's presence, and the growing hunger in my core.

When the final notes of the third song rang out, Ezra took my hand, his grip firm and steady. He led me from the dancefloor, through the crowd, and toward the quiet edge of the ballroom. The eyes of the onlookers faded into the background, and my pulse quickened as we left the safety of the crowd. He didn't say a word as we moved deeper into the hall, away from prying eyes. He turned a corner, then another. Traveling through a maze that no camera could follow.

As we stepped into a shadowed hallway, the music became nothing more than a distant hum. The air here was cooler, quieter, more intimate. I could feel every nerve in my body tense with anticipation. Ezra stalked toward me, his eyes dark with desire, chest heaving with each sharp breath. My heart pounded as I stepped back, my shoulders brushing against the cold stone wall behind me. The low sounds of the ballroom faded further, leaving only the sound of our ragged breaths.

He didn't hesitate. His hand shot out, resting on the wall above my head, effectively caging me in. I swallowed, staring up at him. I was desperate for him to touch me, to kiss me, to break the tension that was threatening to snap.

His eyes flicked from my lips to my eyes, the heat building between us so thick it was almost suffocating. I didn't know what would happen next, but at that moment, I didn't care. All that mattered was him, and the way he was making my entire body ache for him.

"Please," I breathed into the darkness, my voice barely a whisper.

In an instant, his lips were on mine, fierce and demanding. His hands cradled my face, fingers digging into my skin as I clutched at his neck, pulling him closer, desperate for more. His kiss was relentless, deep, and as he teased the seam of my lips with his tongue, I couldn't help but open to him, letting him take control. A moan escaped me, the pleasure building between us, a perfect balance of giving and taking.

I felt weightless, as if the world had disappeared around us, but at the same time, his body pressed against mine, grounding me with its heat and strength. It was as if everything else had ceased to exist, and the only thing that mattered was the electric connection between us.

Instinct took over, pure unbridled mindless passion, and I hitched a leg over his hip. One of his hands slid down to hold it in place and he drove his hips forward. I felt the hard evidence of his arousal pressing against my center and I groaned at the pleasure and simultaneous anger that we had so many layers of clothing separating our needy bodies from each other.

"I need to touch you," he whispered against my lips and the cry I released was nothing short of desperate.

"Then do it," I exclaimed as our lips locked together.

His fingers danced along my thigh, pushing the flared skirt up and up until it bunched around my waist exposing my panty covered core to him. His fingertips brushed along the sensitive skin on my inner thigh and my head fell back against the wall, my mouth falling open on a pleasure-filled sigh. I didn't know where to put my hands, I wanted them everywhere all at once. I wanted to explore him, to keep him, to pleasure him. I gripped his hair, holding his lips to my skin. His mouth took advantage of my exposed neck, and he began peppering hot, needy kisses to the skin there as his fingers continued to travel higher and higher on my thighs.

I had only a brief moment where I wondered if what I was doing was reckless. Naive, or indulgent. I should be focused on surviving this, on making it out alive and getting back to my brother. It was selfish of me to feel this much. To lose myself, however momentarily, in the feel of this relative stranger. But just as the doubt came, the resolve washed it away. Tomorrow wasn't guaranteed. I may not walk out of here alive, and if I do, I may not walk out as myself. So, I would take what little pleasures life offered me, and I would indulge. I deserved to be a little reckless since my life was on the line.

The first brush of his finger along my panties sent a jolt of pleasure through me, the second drew out a thick moan. The third had my stomach clenching and my mouth seeking his.

When our lips crashed against each other again, I whispered into his kiss, "Touch me, Ezra. Please."

His eyes flared, pupils blown with white hot desire consuming him. He was just as lost to this sensation as I was.

He slid the edge of my panties aside and in a delicious, quick thrust, two fingers entered my soaking wet pussy. I almost screamed out, but his lips silenced mine, drinking my scream in his kiss. His teeth captured my bottom lip and bit down, offering a twinge of wonderful pain to perfectly pair with the overwhelming pleasure he was drawing from me with his talented fingers.

His thumb pressed against my clit, and as he fucked me with his hand, I felt mindless, weightless, breathless.

I'd never experienced something so blinding, never felt passion this consuming before. We weren't even done, and already I needed so much more.

"You're so fucking wet, Bex," he praised which only made my core clench around his fingers tighter as I rocked my hips, chasing the pleasure he was offering. "That's it, baby. Fuck my hand."

So I did. I held onto his shoulders and bounced my body against him, feeling his fingers hook within me and hit me where no person has ever reached before.

"Ezra," I cried out as I felt my pussy clench and my release begin to crest.

"Come for me," he demanded, his dark eyes watching my face. I leaned my head back against the wall, my mouth wide open as a string of needy eager moans slipped from my mouth.

I felt the pressure build and build as he slammed his fingers into me, his thumb working my clit expertly in time with his thrusts. It was all too much, until the release shattered, wracking my body. I clung to him as I rode out wave after wave of pleasurable relief. His fingers stilled within me, no longer seeking to draw pleasure, but rather to soak up every second of the release he earned from me.

When my breathing returned to normal, I let my eyes find him again as he slowly removed his fingers from my throbbing core. With his gaze locked on mine, he lifted them and placed them on his tongue, closing his mouth around them. I watched with rapt attention as he drank my release from his skin with a dark, vibrating groan.

"Delicious," he vowed, and I was suddenly ready for another orgasm.

Before I could reach for him again, the soft sound of footsteps echoed down the corridor. Ezra immediately stepped back, his hands quick to smooth down my dress, and a knot of panic tightened in my throat.

Zaffir rounded the corner, and to my relief, he wasn't holding his camera. Thank god, because if he had been, the evidence of what had just transpired would have been glaringly obvious. His gaze flicked between us, noting our expressions, the slight disarray, and I couldn't quite read him. He was good at masking his thoughts, whatever they were. I suddenly found myself hoping he wasn't upset. Which was absurd. Why should I care what he thought?

"Nova says it's time to head to our lodgings," he said, voice calm and almost too casual. "We can take the back way." As he passed, I could have sworn I caught a glint of amusement in his eyes, perhaps a wink, though it could've just been my imagination.

Ezra offered me a small, reassuring smile before extending

his hand. Without a word, I took it, our fingers intertwining as we followed Zaffir down the hall.

CHAPTER
SEVEN

BEX

The blessing, and curse, of having a memory like mine is that I remember every face I've ever seen. Every detail, every flicker of expression, every glance. It's useful... usually. But not at three in the morning, when I should be asleep, resting up for the first trial. Instead, my mind kept looping through the last few days like a fever dream I couldn't wake from. The faces of the brazen people I'd crossed paths with etched into my brain like scorch marks. Every flirtatious wink, every half-smile dripping with trouble, every glance that lingered just a moment too long. Every lingering, fiery glance from Zaffir. Every gentle and charged whisper from Briar. Every romantic spin along the dance floor with Thorne. Every swipe of Ezra's fingers against my body. I could feel them all, see them all, and it was like they were here, breathing against my skin. My body flushed with heat, traitorous in its reaction. This was not the time or place for selfish desire. And yet... it stirred in me like a second pulse. My fingertips traced the curve of my collarbone, my breath coming in ragged, uneven spurts.

The cool night air didn't seem to help steady me as Zaffir led us away from the ballroom and into what felt like a different world. We found ourselves standing in a large circular driveway, surrounded by ten rustic but beautiful cabins, their wooden exteriors glowing softly under the pale moonlight. It almost felt like a campground, though there was an undeniable luxury to it that made the place feel more serene than rugged.

Zaffir guided us toward one of the cabins, which he casually mentioned would be ours for the duration of the Reclamation Run. Ezra, Zaffir, and I, our little team, or whatever it was.

I couldn't help but feel a little out of place as we approached the cabin. When I'd asked Nova if she'd be staying with us, she had laughed, a sound that seemed to echo in the night. "Like I'd ever sleep in one of these rundown little huts," she'd said, as if the very idea was laughable. It looked more than fine to me.

I looked around and shook my head, comparing it to the dilapidated state of Canyon. This cabin was pristine by any standard, a far cry from the crumbling buildings I had grown up with. The disparity between the two worlds couldn't have been clearer.

Once inside, I quickly withdrew into myself, trying to get distance from the whirlwind of emotions still buzzing through my body. My mind kept drifting back to the hallway, the feel of Ezra's body against mine, the electric tension between us, and the pulse of his kiss still lingering on my lips. Then, of course, there was Zaffir, who had walked in on us. I couldn't stop wondering if he'd heard everything, and even more absurdly, I found myself hoping that he had.

It was these thoughts that were keeping me awake, and there was a desperation lingering beneath my skin that I simply had to chase. My fingertips brushed across my peaked nipples and I bit my lips to stifle the moan that slid through my lips. My bedroom shared a wall with one of the men, I wasn't sure who because I locked myself away pretty quickly after returning, but I heard movement over there as whoever it was readied themselves for sleep.

I needed to stay quiet, but I couldn't ignore the burning in my core or the aching need in my blood. I needed another release like I needed another breath.

I slid one hand under the silk fabric of my sleep dress, and pinched my nipple between two fingers, groaning quietly at the delicious bite of pleasurable pain. Then my other hand trailed lower, and lower to my bare pussy. My legs slid open to accommodate my needy fingers as they pressed delicately against my throbbing clit.

I stifled another moan and I pressed circles against the bundle of nerves. My body was a live wire, burning beneath my touch as my mind flashed through memories of the four stunning near strangers who'd affected me this way. Pressing in, I let one finger hook inside of me, which drew a thick moan from my lips, one I couldn't quite stifle quick enough. I paused for a few moments, remaining still. Hoping I didn't draw any attention. After a few silent moments, when I was sure I didn't wake anyone, I continued. Sliding a finger in and out of my heat, taking care to rub my clit and pinch my nipples in time to maximize my pleasure. I arched off the bed as my fingers drew me closer and closer to release.

Then I heard a soft knock at the door.

"Shit," I cursed, drawing my fingers from my core and the cresting orgasm that was nearly there drifted away. I felt equal measures of frustration and embarrassment as I ensured my body was covered by the silk dress and padded across the floor toward the door.

The door creaked open, and there stood Zaffir, leaning casually against the doorframe. His pupils were dilated, his hair tousled as though he'd just rolled out of bed. He wore nothing but tight sleep shorts that hugged his muscular thighs, and his bare chest was on full display. Even in the darkness, I could see the outline of his cock straining against the material. My gaze lingered over the freckles scattered across his skin, and, embarrassingly, I had the absurd urge to trace each one with my lips.

His eyes locked onto mine, intense and smoldering, and I could see the rise and fall of his chest, the way he was breathing just a little too hard. The air between us thickened, and for a moment, the world outside that door seemed to vanish.

"Zaffir..." I whispered.

"I heard you," he replied, and a flash of white hot desire shot through me.

"You heard me," I repeated. His eyes scanned my body, which was draped in that thin silk dress that was low enough to show most of my breasts, and short enough that one wrong move and he'd get an eyeful of my bare pussy.

Or maybe one right move.

"I'm sorry," I added, even though I wasn't. Which was shocking and surprising to me. He was Praxis. So why the hell did I want him to come in?

He looked pained, like he was desperate to reach out, but was fighting against his instinct. "Did you..." he began, but then cleared his throat. "Did you come?"

I felt my body warm, and my needy core clenched.

"Not yet," I replied and he groaned, running a hand along his face. We stood there, watching each other, our breathing heavy and thick.

"Show me," he finally demanded. And I felt the inferno consume me.

"I-" I started to protest, but he stepped inside, crossing the threshold of my room. His presence enveloping me in a heat that wasn't entirely unwelcome.

"Please," he added, voice quieter now, but no less intense. I searched his face for the smug bastard who'd once accused me of lying, or the one who told me not to trust anybody, but he wasn't here. This wasn't that man. This was someone else entirely, a man unraveling at the seams. A man made of need. Of want.

"Why?" I asked, my voice barely above a whisper.

"Because I think your body craves mine the way mine craves yours."

My breath caught. "Are you lying?"

He shook his head, slow and certain. "I will never lie to you, Brexlyn."

I bit my bottom lip, heat pooling in my core. "I don't believe you."

His eyes locked on mine. "I know."

"You're Praxis," I said, softer this time. I didn't know if I was reminding him... or myself.

"Do you want me to leave?" he asked.

And the worst part was that somehow I knew he would. If I said the word, he'd walk away. Just like that. He'd take all this heat and hunger and ache and disappear with it.

But I couldn't say it. My lips wouldn't move. I wouldn't trust him with my mind, and definitely not my life. But maybe I could trust him with my body.

On one hand, Zaffir was Praxis. The epitome of everything I was supposed to resist, the polished face of the regime that had taken so much from all of us and gave us nothing but scraps in return. On the other, my body reacted to him before my brain had a chance to catch up. And there was a chance I'd be dead this time tomorrow.

I was being selfish. Indulgent. Reckless, maybe. But for once, maybe that was okay.

I took a step back, allowing him to enter the room fully. He shut the door behind him, and with a swift motion, he locked it. Our eyes never left each other as I continued to retreat, my steps slow and deliberate. When the backs of my thighs hit the edge of the bed, I lowered myself onto the mattress, careful to keep my legs pressed tightly together. The space between us seemed to shrink, the tension thickening in the air. He leaned against the wall, crossing his arms across his bare chest and eyes glistening as he watched.

Slowly, I spread my legs.

He groaned, thick and deep as I revealed my core to him. His eyes scanned my body and I watched as his tongue darted out to lick his lip. I wanted to taste him...After he'd tasted me. The thought was strange. And wrong. But I couldn't stop it.

"Show me how you pleasure yourself, Brexlyn," he ordered quietly and I felt compelled to do everything he asked.

I let my hand trail across my stomach again until it reached the glistening apex of my thighs. I spent a few tortuous moments swiping a single finger through the wetness at my lips without dipping in, and with each swipe my body convulsed and Zaffir's eyes darkened.

Then I dipped a finger inside and moaned. The pleasure was heightened because of his eyes on me.

I pressed my finger in, slow at first, trying to savor every inch, and every moment of this charged interaction. I used my other hand to press against my throbbing clit and my two hands worked in tandem bringing me to a delicious blissful peak.

"Is this how Ezra touched you?" Zaffir asked. My head shot up, and my fingers stilled.

"What-" I began. Suddenly worry was all I could feel, even above the cresting pleasure.

"Did he press his thick fingers into your greedy cunt, Brexlyn?" he asked, tilting his head and darkening his eyes. It wasn't anger or jealousy in his gaze. It was heat. And I think I liked it.

"Yes," I answered softly.

"Did he make you come all over his hand?" he asked, his voice wavering slightly, telling me that he didn't have quite as strong a hold on his control as he'd want me to believe.

"Yes, he did," I replied. The worry slipped away, replaced again by the overwhelming sensation of my fingers and the memories his words were eliciting.

"Show me how he fucked you," he ordered and my pussy clenched with his dirty words. God, what were these people doing to me?

I slid another finger inside and rolled my head back as I slammed them into me while rolling my clit with the other hand.

"Hmm.. two fingers?" Zaffir noted. "And he paid attention to your clit? Good boy," he praised and even though it wasn't directed to me, I felt it in my entire body.

I heard him let out a soft groan and when I lifted my head to look at him, I saw that he had his cock out and was running it through his hand. I bit my lip to stop from begging him to let me taste it. Or feel it replacing my fingers deep inside of me. As much as I was lost in this moment, I couldn't forget who he was. I couldn't go that far.

"Do you think you can come before I do, Brexlyn?" he challenged, breathlessly.

I nodded. Feeling my body already reaching the peak

again, desperate for release that's been interrupted a few times already.

"Show me," he ordered, as his hand worked his cock faster. I watched him closely, my eyes glued to his pleasure as I slammed into my pussy, imagining it was his cock that was reaching those dark desperate parts of me.

I felt the orgasm build and build, until I erupted, my core soaking my hand as I rode out the explosive release. I heard Zaffir curse under his breath as he came too, and I watched as his thick hard cock twitched with release.

There were a few quiet moments in the aftermath, and for the briefest of seconds, all I felt was pure pleasure, bliss even, but it was fleeting. It slipped away as quickly as it came, replaced by the sharp sting of shock and overwhelming embarrassment. I pressed my thighs together, my body tense, and sat up, unable to meet his eyes. I turned my gaze away from him, trying to regain control over my chaotic breathing.

What had just happened? How had I let myself fall into this with someone from Praxis?

I felt his presence before I saw him, his warmth wrapping around me, swallowing me whole. He approached quietly, and his fingers brushed my chin, tilting my head up so that I had no choice but to meet his soft, honeyed gaze. "Tell me where you just went," he whispered, his voice a gentle command.

"Y-You're..." I faltered, my throat tight, the words getting stuck. "You're Praxis."

His expression softened, and I saw something almost painful flicker across his face. His thumb caressed my lower lip, and for a moment, I almost gave in, wanting to dip my tongue out to taste him. But I stayed still, watching him instead.

"I know," he whispered, his voice heavy with something I couldn't place.

A slow sigh escaped him, like he was fighting with himself, and then, without another word, he turned and left the room.

What was I doing?

I collapsed back onto the bed, my arms folding across my eyes in an attempt to block out the confusion swirling in my mind.

I was getting distracted, and I couldn't afford that, not now, not with the trials starting tomorrow. I had to survive. I had to find a way to help my brother. The last thing I needed were the burning gazes of handsome, confusing men clouding my thoughts. But with a memory like mine, I knew I wouldn't forget any of it anytime soon.

CHAPTER
EIGHT

EZRA

THE SCENT of her lingered on my skin and the taste of her was still there on my tongue as I drifted into a restless sleep. Zaffir had interrupted us, and I was desperate to continue what we'd started. I wanted to sink my cock into her wet heat and claim her as mine. Which was not only a terrifying thought, but a dangerous one.

There were real threats heading our way, and soon enough, our entire lives would be broadcast to all of Nexum. The TV in the room I'd been assigned was the only source of entertainment, sitting on the far end of the house from where Bex slept. The room next to hers had already been claimed, something the smug, red-headed asshole had no problem reminding me of more than once before we both retreated into our respective rooms for the night.

I found myself watching the coverage of the welcome ball for a while, and as Zaffir had predicted, and planned, there was plenty of intrigue surrounding my connection with Bex. The screen flashed to moments I couldn't erase from my mind, me whispering something to her and her skin flushing in response, the way I held her hand as we walked, how I kept her close in the limo, the protectiveness I showed as I danced with her across the ballroom. That was the narrative Zaffir had crafted with his edits, and it was exactly the story they were devouring.

The host, a tiny, blonde woman with garish silver eyelashes and a wardrobe that looked like it belonged to a metallic nightmare, droned on about "the brooding man from Canyon Collective and his dark protective streak." She called it... swoon-worthy.

I wanted to throw something.

It made me sick how easily they took something raw, something real between Bex and me, and turned it into a cheap spectacle for their own amusement. I clenched my fists, watching the screen.

But at the end of it all, I reminded myself that this was the game we were in. If this was the image they wanted, so be it. I just had to play along long enough to keep Bex safe. That was the only thing that mattered now.

Then I heard the tell-tale sounds of my girl's moans. A sound so new, yet so finely tuned to me already. I shot straight up, and was out of the door before I could even stop to think of a reason not to. As I approached her door, the sounds of her gentle sighs of pleasure grew. She was trying to stifle them, but I could hear them plain as day. My hand reached for the doorknob, but then a voice stopped me in my tracks.

"Is this how Ezra touched you?" It was Zaffir. His voice was low, challenging, tempting. I half expected jealousy to flare in my chest, but instead, I felt heat curl in my lower abdomen.

"What-" Bex whispered, with an edge of shock. Her voice was low and sultry. Seductive. She was lost in passion, and desire. I heard the soft sounds of fingers moving through her wetness. I didn't know if it was her hand or his eliciting that noise from her.

"Did he press his thick fingers into your greedy cunt, Brexlyn?" I gasped, but quickly covered my mouth with my palm, feeling my cock harden and press uncomfortably against my pants. His words, so vulgar, so dirty. I should have felt jealous, but for some reason, I didn't.

"Yes," she vowed, breathlessly. And I felt a flash of pride.

"Did he make you come all over his hand?" Zaffir asked, his voice authoritative, brash, and fuck... hot as hell.

"Yes, he did," she answered and I couldn't stop myself from reaching for my straining cock. Releasing it from the fabric prison and stroking it gently. I let my thumb dance along the tip, spreading the precum. I bit my lip hard to keep quiet as I chased my pleasure to the sounds of Bex feeling pleasure while Zaffir drew sinful little admission from her lips.

"Show me how he fucked you," Zaffir ordered, and fuck. I felt my balls tighten as my own release built in my core.

"Hmm.. two fingers?" Zaffir noted. "And he paid attention to your clit? Good boy." The praise did something completely unexpected to me, sending shivers of unexplained ecstasy through my body. I felt my cum soak my hand as I rode out wave after wave of my orgasm.

I heard Zaffir groan, the tell-tale sound of him chasing his own pleasure, and for a brief, unexplained moment, I wished I could watch.

"Do you think you can come before I do, Brexlyn?" he challenged, and I listened intently, breathing heavily. "Show me."

Then there was a soft symphony of completely vulgar and downright sinful sounds slipping from under the door. My cock nearly twitched back to life ready for round two when the two of them found their releases. I breathed hard and heavy, suddenly worried that I'd be caught out here. I slipped away quietly heading to the bathroom to clean myself up.

Glancing in the mirror, I didn't recognize the man staring back at me. His pupils were wide, still caught in the aftermath of his release. I splashed cold water on my face, hoping it would help clear my head. When I slipped out of the bathroom, I found Zaffir walking toward me.

I stopped dead in my tracks, and he did the same. He looked... different. Disheveled, satisfied, but underneath it all, there was a flicker of something sad, something I couldn't quite place.

"Oh, um, I didn't know you were up," he said, his voice awkward, the usual cocky edge gone. He sounded almost... uncertain.

I let my gaze travel over him, taking in the sight of his bare chest, his shorts tight and low on his hips. It left very little to the imagination.

"Like what you see, Ezra?" he teased, but the words were laced with something that felt more serious than playful.

I shifted uncomfortably, trying to push the heat in my chest down. "So, who won?" I asked, my voice sharper than I intended.

His expression tightened, a flicker of confusion crossing his face. "What do you mean?"

"Did she come before you did?" I whispered and his eyes widened in shock. If I wasn't so trapped in a haze of desire, I might have laughed at his reaction.

"You-" he swallowed the words. "You were listening?"

I nodded, and watched as his eyes trailed my body, lingering on my lower half for a half second too long.

"Are you going to kick my ass?" he asked, raising an eyebrow.

"Still thinking about it," I replied, but that wasn't the

truth. In fact, it didn't even cross my mind. Yes, I was starting to feel some real, and scary, things for Bex... but the thought of more people in her corner. More people willing to do whatever they could to protect her through this... That didn't affect me the way I would have thought.

And plus, hearing those two do what they did was hot enough to have me erupting like a volcano, I couldn't stop myself from imagining what would happen if I could watch.

"I like her," he whispered, like it was an admission, but also a promise. To me. To prove that he wasn't doing something out of some weird manipulative tactic. I nodded, pleased to hear him say it, but I already knew it was true.

"I do too," I replied.

We were quiet for a few moments, a silent understanding passing between us. The pact we'd made just this morning somehow found a deeper, more intimate meaning.

"I'll let you get some sleep, you have a big day tomorrow," he said, sidestepping to let me past. I slipped by him, and didn't miss the way his body shivered as my shoulder brushed against his chest.

"Zaffir," I said, turning to see him just as he was disappearing into the bathroom.

"Yeah?"

"Did you get to taste her?" I don't know why I asked. Maybe it's because I still have her taste on my tongue and the thought of getting more right from the source was making me blind with desire. His eyes flashed darkly.

"Not yet," he vowed.

"When you do..." I whispered, shocked by the words I was going to say next. "Let me watch."

He groaned and I had to turn and leave down the hall to stop myself from doing something stupid like leaning in to taste the sound on his lips.

When I locked myself safely back in my room, I struggled to control the pounding heart and ragged breaths.

What the fuck was I doing?

And why the fuck did I like the idea of it?

I closed my eyes and drifted off to sleep to my mind filling in the blanks of what happened behind that door.

PART TWO

THE TRIALS

CHAPTER
NINE

BEX

MY PALMS WERE clammy as I gripped the straps of the pack strapped to my back. A shiver ran down my spine, and I couldn't help but feel a wave of gratitude for the thick wool coat Nova had tossed at me earlier that morning when she came to collect us for the first trial.

Now, here I was, sitting on a plane, shoulder to shoulder with the other Challengers, completely blindfolded. My other senses were heightened, and although I couldn't see anything, I could feel Ezra beside me. His presence was unmistakable, like a quiet anchor. That was a small comfort, at least.

The plane jolted, shifting slightly in the air. I'd never been on one before, and I was already hoping to never ride in another one again. My stomach twisted in knots, and my ears throbbed, desperately trying to pop and adjust.

"You're okay," Ezra's voice broke through my anxious thoughts, soft but reassuring. His words helped steady me, even if just a little, allowing me to focus on what was coming next.

If they were following the typical structure of the Reclamation Run, this one would likely be a physical challenge. Tasks normally designed to test endurance and resilience.

I felt the telltale warmth of lights switching on, heating my face and confirming what I already knew...cameras were rolling. I forced my expression into calm neutrality and tried to steady my breathing. If Jax was watching, I wanted him to think that I was brave.

"Good morning, Challengers, and welcome to the first trial of the Reclamation Run!" The chirpy voice echoed from overhead speakers, too cheerful for the moment. Annalese Wyley. The host of the Run. I used to think her voice was annoying, high-pitched and overly girlish, more irritating than intimidating. But now, it sent a shiver down my spine.

"Your first trial will be for the resource of..." she paused dramatically, milking the tension. "Transportation!"

I let out a slow breath. Transportation. It wasn't the end of the world to not have it, it just took more time to get around. But, Canyon could benefit from a few working buses back in the Collective. Even one could change things for the better. And maybe, just maybe, Ezra stood a fighting chance in this one.

"Right now, our Challengers are being transported over one hundred miles away from our bustling Praxis. In honor of the value of transportation, and the vital role it plays in survival, our first trial is simple....make your way back home."

I flinched at her phrasing. *Home,* she'd called it. Praxis wasn't home. Not to me. Not to any of us on this plane.

Then the reality of the challenge hit me. One hundred miles. On foot. No maps, no paths, no clues. Just forest, terrain, and time. My stomach dipped, nausea curling tight in my gut. I felt Ezra's leg press reassuringly against mine, grounding me again. I leaned ever so slightly into it, grateful.

"This is a race to the finish line!" Annalese continued brightly. "The first person to re-enter Praxis city limits will win the trial."

I felt Ezra's leg press harder against mine. Almost like a promise.

"And to accommodate the double participants, and to show Praxis' honor and integrity..." I had to force my scoff to remain silent. "The top thirteen competitors will be awarded rations based on placement." That meant that the remaining seven would receive absolutely nothing.

Nothing.

Just days of pain and surviving the elements, and the possibility of returning with nothing to show for it. My heart pounded like a drumbeat in my chest.

And that was *if* they returned at all.

Who knew what waited out there?

The land surrounding Praxis was a stretch of dense, unforgiving forest known only as *the Wilds*. When resources dwindled and the wars erupted, that territory devolved into lawless chaos. And when Praxis rose to power, they didn't bother reclaiming it. They didn't try to tame it. They just... let it fester. Let it grow wild and ruthless.

Now, miles upon miles of that overgrown wasteland stood between Praxis and the nearest Collective, like a natural shield, or a deliberate wall.

And I knew almost nothing about what lived within it.

Only that it was unwelcoming.

Uninhabitable.

And dangerous as hell.

I could only hope the pack they strapped to my back held some sort of tools or equipment I might be able to use.

"Now, to explain the rules, here's General Sharpe," Annalese's voice rang out.

A heavy pair of boots echoed down the center aisle of the plane. Each step closer sent a spike of tension through me.

"You each have a body camera strapped to your chest," the General's voice was deep, sharp-edged, and unyielding. "It's been charged to last one week of continuous recording."

My stomach dropped. A week? They expected this might take a *week*?

"You are permitted to turn it off for up to four hours a day," he continued. "But the other twenty must be recorded. Is that understood?"

A few scattered grumbles answered him.

"I said, is that understood?"

This time, we all responded in unison. "Yes, sir."

"You will begin the trial alone, but you are allowed to work in teams if you choose."

A harsh exhale left me. Alone. I'd be starting this alone. Maybe Ezra would find me, but even if he did, I'd only slow him down. And I couldn't ask him to do that. Not if it meant costing Canyon a chance at rations. At survival.

"Any survival tactics you deem necessary," the General added, his tone turning even colder, "are considered legal and acceptable."

The air around us seemed to drop ten degrees.

Any tactics.

We didn't need him to spell it out. He meant violence. He meant bloodshed.

It wasn't unheard of, some of the most desperate trials in past years had ended with Challengers dead by one another's hands. Especially when the prize was something critical.

I could only hope that, since this trial was simple transportation, no one would be willing to go that far.

At least... not yet.

"When I call your name, stand. Your trial will begin."

General Sharpe's voice sliced through the cabin, followed by the heavy thud of his boots as he made his way down the aisle.

Begin? We were still in the air...what did he mean?

"Devrin Marx."

A shuffle of movement came from farther down the row as someone stood. Devrin. The elected from Saltspire, the one gunning for the electricity trials this year, as Briar mentioned.

More rustling. He was being guided away. Then the temperature shifted, an icy draft swept through the cabin. Something was opening. My breath caught in my throat as I heard it, the roar of wind, growing louder by the second.

I tightened my grip on the straps of my pack, fingers trembling. Panic curled deep in my gut.

"I've got you," Ezra whispered, his voice nearly drowned by the howling air. His hand found my thigh, grounding me for a second. But even his touch wasn't enough to quiet the rising fear.

A moment passed, thick and tense, then—

The General shouted something, but I couldn't catch the words. Then came the scream. A raw, startled yelp ripped through the noise, disappearing into the distance.

Devrin had been pushed out of the plane.

"Avrin Schone," the General cried out. With each new name, and each new scream, I felt my whole body tense and shake. I'd only known fear like this once before. On a night Jax had lost control of his limbs and stopped breathing. I don't know how, but I managed to keep him with me that night, but even as I held him in my arms, feeling his chest rise and fall, I knew I couldn't do that alone forever.

I'd take this fear over that ever again.

I'd take this fear if it meant getting my brother the help he needs.

"Briar Grey," the General called out, and I didn't miss the way my heart fluttered remembering her kindness. I hoped she'd be okay. And when her twin was called after her, I sent a prayer after them. I didn't do it often, but I felt they deserved it.

I wanted them to be safe.

After the Grey siblings were sent on their way, they called the Challengers from Ironclad Collective. Then it was our turn.

"Ezra Wynstone," the General called.

Ezra stood beside me, close enough that I felt the brush of his arm. He leaned in and whispered, "I'll find you, Bex."

I shook my head instinctively, but of course, he couldn't see me. My mouth opened to protest, to tell him not to, but before I could say a word, he was gone.

I swallowed hard. I didn't want him wasting time looking for me or trying to protect me. But still... the thought of someone having my back out there, it wasn't the worst thing.

I strained my ears, waiting for a cry, a shout, something that would betray his fear. But it never came. Ezra wouldn't give the cameras the satisfaction. And at that moment, I decided I wouldn't either.

"Brexlyn Hollis."

The sound of my name made my stomach lurch. My legs felt like stone, but I forced myself to stand. Numb. Unsteady.

Hands gripped my upper arms and guided me forward, closer to the roaring wind that now sounded like the mouth of a beast waiting to swallow me whole. The blindfold made everything worse, my balance skewed, my perception warped. I kept waiting to step off into open air by mistake.

I was grateful for the grip on my arm, even if it was rough and cruel.

"You can remove your blindfold when you hit the air," the General yelled into my ear. I nodded, unsure if he could see it.

He took my hand, rough fingers guiding it up to a strap near my shoulder and curled it around something solid.

"That's your parachute," he said. "Don't pull it too late."

I opened my mouth, the question already forming 'What counts as too late?' but the answer never came. Instead, a sharp shove to my back sent me careening into the void.

The world vanished, but I didn't scream.

There was no up, no down. No wind or sound, just a gut-wrenching sense of falling, like the universe had yanked me out of itself.

I scrambled, fumbling with the blindfold. My fingers trembled and slipped against the knot, panic rising in my throat. *What if I'm already close to the ground? What if I pull too late? What if I'm dead before I even begin?*

Finally, the fabric tore away, and I forced myself to keep it clenched in one hand. Out here, even a scrap could be useful.

The world exploded into color and movement.

Below me there was endless green. A vast sea of trees, dense and wild, broken only by twisting rivers and the occasional clearing. It was breathtaking, and terrifying.

I wasn't in immediate danger of crashing into anything, but I could feel the pull of gravity intensifying, my descent speeding up.

I scanned the sky, heart pounding, searching for other parachutes. Ezra's maybe. No...focus. I'd never have this vantage point again.

I turned my eyes toward the horizon.

There. A glint. Praxis.

A tiny shimmer in the distance, like a jewel tucked

between the trees. I burned it into my memory, then traced the curves of rivers, the gaps in the trees, the layout of hills and valleys. If I didn't have a map, I'd become one.

And then, I pulled.

The force of the parachute deploying yanked me upward with a brutal jolt, snapping my body back and slamming pressure into my shoulders where the pack's straps dug in deep. Pain radiated through the joints and I cursed instinctively, then immediately clamped my mouth shut.

The camera. Strapped tight against my chest. I could practically feel its lens blinking, watching, recording. Jax was watching. Everyone was.

I'd never used a parachute before. When would I have? I didn't know how to steer or slow or aim. All I could do was clutch the straps and try to make educated guesses based on nothing but gut instinct and fear.

The trees were coming up fast.

Really fast.

The fear surged again, hot and sharp in my throat. If I landed in the river, I'd be drenched and chilled to the bone. One night in soaked clothes and I could be dealing with hypothermia. But if I hit the rocks... Well, that was a shorter kind of problem. A final kind. My mind raced through every worst-case scenario like a skipping stone.

I adjusted the straps, trying to shift my weight....maybe if I leaned a little left? Slowed the spin?

No time to overthink it. The treeline was right there.

Branches slapped at me as if nature herself took offense to my intrusion, scratching my arms, ripping at my clothes. I cried out as something sharp nicked my cheek, then yelped again as my chute snagged suddenly on a branch above, tearing slightly with an awful *rrriiippp*.

And then...nothing.

I fell. Tumbled through the branches like a ragdoll, slamming through leaves and limbs, reaching out in vain for something, anything, to grab. My fingers scraped bark as I slipped.

The world was a blur of green and motion and pain.

And then my chute caught on something solid.

I jerked violently, the momentum wrenched to a halt, and I swung midair like a pendulum. Everything went still. My breathing, the leaves, the drop. All of it. Still. I hung there. Alive. Twenty feet off the forest floor, tangled in a parachute that had for some reason decided to spare me.

My heart thundered in my chest. I couldn't help the hysterical laugh that bubbled up in my throat, half relief, half terror.

Now came the hard part.

Getting down.

I writhed and twisted for a moment, tangled in the web of chute strings that clung to my limbs like spider silk. Branches that had snapped in my fall jabbed at me from all angles, some dug into my side with sharp, splintered insistence. Pain radiated along my ribs. They were definitely bruised, maybe worse. My cheek throbbed with a fresh sting, and when I pressed trembling fingers to the skin and pulled them back, they came away smeared with blood.

"Great," I muttered under my breath. As if dangling twenty feet in the air wasn't enough.

I took a moment to scan my surroundings, well, as much as one could while hanging from a half-shredded parachute. The tree I was tangled in wasn't giving me many options. But the tree next to it? That one had a thick branch jutting out not far from where I hung, complete with plenty of rugged bark and smaller limbs I could maybe use for the climb down.

If I could push off hard enough, I might be able to grab hold of that branch, swing over before the chute snapped completely. The cords might give me just enough time to make the leap, but there was no guarantee I could free myself fast enough.

My pack weighed heavy against my spine, but there was no way I was ditching it. Not unless I absolutely had to. Whatever they gave us, food, supplies, maybe tools, if there's anything in there at all, I'd need it all. And if I could salvage the parachute too? It could serve as a makeshift blanket, shelter, or even rope. Out here, everything had a use. And something I learned in Canyon was you didn't dare waste a single resource.

"One step at a time," I breathed. My voice was small, steady, and broadcast to every watching eye on the live feed.

I braced my feet against the tree trunk, heart hammering in my chest, and launched myself toward the other branch. Pain tore through my side as I twisted midair, arms outstretched—

I missed.

My fingers scraped bark and air as I swung back, slamming into the original tree with a thud that rattled my bones. The chute groaned overhead, then tore a little more, and suddenly I dropped another few feet, jerking to a stop like a marionette yanked by a spiteful puppeteer.

No more chances. If I didn't get out of this now, I'd be ripped down with it.

"Come on, Bex," I hissed through gritted teeth.

Again, I pushed off, gritting past the pain, flinging my body toward the branch like my life depended on it, because it did. My fingers connected this time. Clenched. Held.

Just as my grip locked tight, the chute gave out behind me with a vicious rip and fell, now dangling from my body like dead weight. It pulled at me, but I hugged the branch with everything I had, muscles trembling.

Carefully I tested each branch before shifting my weight. Downward, one move at a time. The wind stirred the leaves around me, and every crack of wood or rustle made my heart leap into my throat. But I didn't let go. Didn't falter.

Eventually, my feet met solid ground. I dropped the last foot or two with a grunt and let myself collapse onto the wreckage of my parachute, splaying out on the fabric. For one breath, I just lay there, staring up through the canopy at the sliver of sky above me. Clouds drifted lazily past like they had no idea the world was watching. I exhaled.

"Let the first trial begin," I whispered.

I allowed myself only a few more precious minutes to catch my breath, lying flat on the shredded parachute and feeling the ache in every inch of my body. Then, I sat up and forced my hands to get moving, digging through the pack they'd strapped to me before the drop.

The contents were underwhelming at best, infuriating at worst. A metal canteen, empty, of course, a single stick of dried jerky, and a small, battered book of matches. Seven, I counted. Seven matches. Seven chances at warmth, light, or survival before I had to rely on sticks and desperation.

No knife. No compass. No medkit. Not even a thread of kindness.

I muttered a curse under my breath, then turned my attention to my injuries. My side throbbed, but after a careful inspection and some tentative prodding, I was relieved to find nothing seemed broken. Just bruised. Badly. It would slow me down, but it wouldn't stop me. The cut on my cheek still burned, the blood having dried into a sticky smear. I'd need to clean that soon in order to avoid infection. Water first. That had to be the priority.

Once I cataloged everything in the pack, mentally noting weight, usefulness, and what I might need to ration, I stood and closed my eyes, forcing myself to visualize the map I'd built in my mind while falling. The winding river, the ridgeline, the jagged cliffside to the east. I'd gotten a little turned around crashing through the canopy, but if I was right, and I *had* to be right, then a river should lie about a mile to the northeast. Toward Praxis.

A mile. Battered, bruised, blind without a true landmark. But it was the only option.

I packed up the torn chute, folding it down tight and securing it under the pack's flap. It made the bag bulkier, but I wasn't leaving it behind. Not yet. Slipping the straps over my shoulders, I adjusted the weight and took one last look up at the treetops I'd tumbled through.

Then I picked a direction, set my jaw, and started walking.

One step at a time.

CHAPTER
TEN

BEX

I HAD BEEN RIGHT about the direction, a small, victorious thrill sparked in my chest as I dropped to my knees at the edge of the riverbank. Relief came fast and strong, nearly knocking the breath from me. Cool, clean water rushed past, and I wasted no time splashing it onto my face, rinsing the dried blood from my cheek and gently cleaning the cut. I worked carefully, mindful not to soak my clothes and risk a chill later. The breeze already had a bite to it.

The sun hung midway through the sky, a little westward now. Mid-afternoon, maybe. That gave me a few more hours of light, and I needed to make every minute count.

I filled my canteen and splashed a bit more water on my arms and neck, letting the cold soothe the ache in my muscles. Then I stood, adjusted my pack, and kept going.

Most people would follow the river if they found it. Praxis rested near a body of water, and all rivers eventually led some-where, so people without a compass or a map would cling to the edge of this river and ride it all the way to the finish line. But I knew better. I'd seen it with my own eyes as I fell. This river would wind and twist for miles through The Wilds before ever leading near Praxis. Following it would guarantee arrival, sure... but far too late.

I needed to cut through if I wanted to make it home before I starved to death, to hell with winning.

Now that I had my bearings again, the mental map I'd crafted during the fall reoriented itself in my mind. I could see it clearly. I started walking with something unfamiliar blooming in my chest, something that felt a lot like confidence.

But after the first hour, that bloom began to wither. My ribs were screaming with every step. After a few more, my feet throbbed in protest, my head pulsed with a dull ache, and the emptiness in my stomach became impossible to ignore.

Still, I kept going.

I was no stranger to hunger. I'd gone without plenty of times, always making sure Jax had enough first. I knew I could push through until at least midday tomorrow before it started affecting my focus, though that was without bruised ribs and physical exertion.

And worse, I had no idea how to hunt. With or without a weapon. The woods were still and unnervingly quiet, save for the occasional rustle of leaves or chirp of a distant bird. A few squirrels had darted past earlier, but nothing big enough to give me a fighting chance at food.

The sun was dipping low, and with it, the forest changed. What had been pretty and peaceful during the day now felt... wrong. Twisted shadows stretched through the trees, and every innocent rustle of leaves made my skin crawl. It was like the woods were holding their breath, waiting for something.

I glanced around, trying to find somewhere safe enough to

hunker down for the night. It took a few minutes, but I found a small alcove, barely big enough for a person, but the entrance had a natural overhang. If I used that as my back wall and stretched the chute over it, maybe I could feel safe enough to close my eyes.

I worked carefully, weighing down the edges of the chute with rocks and fallen branches. It was full of holes, sure, but it was something. I sat back and stared at it for a long moment, debating. Fire would give me light. Warmth. Comfort. But I only had seven matches. And if I could get through tonight without using one, I would. No matter how cold it got. No matter how loud the forest became once it was fully swallowed by night.

I reached for the camera and flipped the switch, watching the little red light fade to black. And even though it left me in near-complete darkness, I felt lighter. Like I could finally breathe.

So I did.

I let it all come out.

Tears, silent but steady, slipped down my face as I curled in on myself beneath the torn chute. With no one watching, I didn't have to pretend to be fine. I didn't have to hold it together for the audience, or for Jax. I didn't have to keep up the act.

For the first time since the drop, I let myself feel it all.

Only once the weight started to lift did my thoughts shift to the others, the rest of the lottery picks. The older woman. The little boy. Just eight years old. Somewhere out here in the dark, trying to do the same thing I was. Survive. That is, if they even made it to the ground in the first place.

I swallowed hard, forcing that thought down.

There was nothing I could do for them. Not tonight. Right now, surviving was all I had space for.

I flicked the camera back on, the red light blinking softly in the dark. Then I curled tighter beneath the chute and let myself drift off into a restless, uneasy sleep.

Morning brought a sharp pain in my side and a breath of relief that I was still in one piece. My ribs were furious about what I'd put them through yesterday. I couldn't really blame them. I felt the same way.

I packed up quickly, drank a few sips of water, and set out again. I didn't know exactly how far I'd traveled, but when I reached the base of a large cliff, one I'd seen from above yesterday, I knew I was making good time. There was still a long way to go, though.

I wondered, just for a moment, if Ezra was nearby.

He'd said he'd find me. Maybe I should've tried to find him, too. But I didn't want to waste what little resources I had on backtracking or guessing. I was lucky enough to have the map burned into my brain. Maybe Briar had been right about the kinds of muscles it takes to survive these trials. Even the physical ones. My mental map was already proving invaluable.

I kept a steady pace for most of the morning, but by midday, my body started to cave beneath me. My head was light, my legs heavy. Hunger was hitting harder than I'd expected.

I found a spot on a fallen log and dropped my pack, rummaging through it until I pulled out the jerky. If I could make it last, eat it in thirds, it might be enough to keep me moving without blacking out.

The first bite was heavenly. Dried jerky had never been my favorite, but right now, it tasted like magic. I moaned around the mouthful, letting the flavor linger on my tongue before I took another bite. When I'd eaten about a third, I forced myself to stop. My stomach protested, loud and angry, but I wrapped it back up and tucked it into my pack.

That's when I heard the rustling.

I froze, heart skipping, head on a swivel.

It was louder than the squirrels I'd seen yesterday. Heavier. My heart leapt with a flicker of hope, maybe it was Ezra pushing through the trees.

But the longer the rustling went on, the more that hope turned into dread. My chest tightened.

Then, out of nowhere, a cat-like creature burst through the treeline and lunged at me.

I screamed and dove, barely avoiding its first strike. Grabbing my pack but not bothering to sling it over my shoulder, I ran. As fast as I could.

Behind me, the beast snarled and crashed through the underbrush. I jumped over fallen logs, tried to weave between trees, but it was faster. And gaining.

I turned just in time to see it leap again, and this time I didn't have time to dodge. I raised my pack between us as we hit the ground. The creature landed hard, pinning me beneath its weight.

I kicked. Thrashed. Shoved the bag into its mouth as it snapped and snarled. Teeth tore through fabric, missing skin, for now. But it wouldn't be long.

I screamed and fought, kicking as hard as I could, but it was relentless. Wearing me down.

Jax's face flashed in my mind. Then Ava's.

Ezra. Zaffir. Even Briar and Thorne.

One by one, they passed through my memory, in brutal clarity, as the creature clawed for my end.

And then a hot spray hit my face. The weight on my chest went slack.

Blood soaked through my shirt and dripped down my neck, warm and wet. The creature slumped.

Dead.

Fear clamped around my heart like a vice as I struggled to crawl out from under the creature's weight. But it was too heavy. I couldn't move. Panic rose sharp in my throat.

"Hey, hey, Hollis, don't worry," a voice said, low and gentle. Familiar. "We got you."

The pressure lifted as the creature was heaved off of me. I scrambled upright, heart pounding, and found myself staring at Briar and Thorne Grey.

They looked like hell. Mud streaked their faces, their clothes were torn and smeared with dirt and dried blood. But I'd never seen anything more perfect.

I lunged forward and wrapped both of them in my arms. Briar let out a surprised gasp, but then melted into the hug. Thorne gave a dark little chuckle right in my ear.

"Thank you," I whispered, pulling back, wiping at my face. "I really thought that was it."

"Not a problem, love," Thorne said with a crooked grin. He bent down and picked up a blood-slicked rock, his makeshift weapon. When I looked back at the creature, I saw the dent in its skull.

"Not bad for a little improvisation, huh, sis?" Thorne said, tossing the rock once in the air and catching it.

How he could still joke and find humor out here was beyond me. But I was grateful for it. Grateful for both of them.

"Yes, yes, you're the almighty hunter, and we should all sing your praises," Briar deadpanned, crouching to examine the body of the creature. She glanced up at me, eyes tired but warm. "So, Hollis. What do you say?" She grinned. "Let's eat."

BRIAR

THE MOMENT I heard Devrin's startled yelp as he was shoved from the plane, I knew what was coming.

I leaned toward Thorne and whispered, "I'm going to pull my chute right away. It'll slow my descent. By the time you jump, you might still see me falling. Aim for me. Don't waste time when they call your name."

"Chute? What do you mean?"

I rolled my eyes, not that he could see it through the blindfold. My brother was brilliant. Logic, math, science? A prodigy. But sometimes he was alarmingly slow on the uptake.

"They're making us jump," I said. "Out of the plane."

He tensed beside me.

"Don't think. Don't panic. Fear's useless here."

I reached out, laying a hand on his shoulder. His muscles were tight, coiled, ready to spring or snap.

"Look for my chute. Aim for where I land. Got it?"

Silence.

"Thorne."

"Yes," he said quickly, voice rough. "Yeah. I got it. I'll follow your chute."

"Briar Grey," the General barked. I squeezed Thorne's shoulder once, firm and quick.

"Find me," I said, and then I was moving, guided to the open hatch, wind screaming in my ears.

The General's voice was little more than noise as he muttered something about not pulling too late. Joke's on him. I was going to pull the second I hit open air.

A hard shove against my back, and I was free-falling.

The sky opened up around me, a rush of wind and chaos. I twisted in the air, searching for stability, and when I finally found it, I yanked the cord.

My chute burst open with a violent jolt. I grunted, breath knocked from my lungs, and tore off the blindfold.

My descent slowed.

The world stretched wide and vivid around me, blue sky like a painting, trees below thick and lush, endless. I turned slightly, scanning the horizon. I couldn't see anything above me except the wide extended chute. No sign of the plane. No sign of Thorne.

But I had to trust. Had to believe he was falling toward me now. Watching my chute, lining up his drop.

I adjusted the cords, steering the best I could with zero training. A break in the trees caught my eye, a small clearing. Perfect. I swore softly, trying to hold my course as the wind fought me for control.

Closer. Closer.

My feet hit the ground running, catching the momentum before stumbling to a stop. The chute collapsed behind me in a heap of fabric.

I didn't waste a second.

I looked up.

A figure was plummeting through the air, chute tangled, twisting violently in the wind, refusing to catch. My heart leapt into my throat.

"No. No, no, no," I whispered, then screamed, feet already moving beneath me as I ran toward the falling shape. "Come on, untangle, untangle, please."

The chute I'd abandoned dragged behind me, and just as I gained speed, it caught on something. My body jerked back.

"No!" I howled, ripping at the harness, tears stinging my eyes. But it was too late.

The figure fell fast, too fast, and then vanished into the treetops with a sickening crash that echoed in my bones.

My knees buckled. I hit the ground hard, sobs tearing through me as I pressed my forehead into the dirt.

"No. No. No."

Thorne. My twin. My other half.

Gone.

He knew why I campaigned for this. Knew why I fought so hard to be chosen. I always knew I'd have to watch my own back in the Run, but when they called his name, out of nearly ten thousand...I felt real fear for the first time.

And now... he's gone.

"Whoa, shit! Are you hurt?" a voice called from the edge of the clearing.

I froze. My head jerked up.

Thorne.

Jogging toward me. Alive.

I dropped my pack, sprinted to him, and threw my arms around his shoulders. Relief crashed into me like a tidal wave.

"I thought you– how did you..." I looked over my shoulder, to the place I'd seen the body fall. "I thought you were dead," I whispered, my voice breaking.

"Hey," Thorne murmured, holding me close, one hand cradling the back of my head. "I'm here. I'm okay. We're okay, sis."

I pulled back just slightly, enough to speak. "Someone didn't make it. Their chute didn't open right. They landed just over there. I thought it was you."

"Shit," Thorne said, turning to look. His throat bobbed as he swallowed hard.

A new, sharper fear hit me.

What if it was Brexlyn Hollis? The captivating clever girl from Canyon.

No, no, she hadn't been called yet. It had to be someone from Ironclad. It had to be.

I nodded, forcing myself to breathe. Reminding myself that he was alive. He was okay. He was with me. We packed up my chute, stuffed it into the pack, and started walking, toward the place where someone had fallen. Toward whoever hadn't been as lucky.

It took us about ten minutes to reach the place where I'd seen the Challenger fall. The path was easy to trace, snapped branches, scuffed bark, a trail of destruction carved through the trees.

A tangled chute hung like a ghost in the canopy, trailing down through the limbs. Below, half-buried in a pile of broken branches and leaves, a leg jutted out at an unnatural angle.

Thorne let out a low sigh and took a step forward, but I caught his shoulder, stopping him.

We could see there was a body. What we couldn't see from where we stood was their face, and I didn't want Praxis to see it either.

I couldn't stomach the thought of them using the footage

from my camera to splash this death across the screens, turning it into entertainment. The first casualty of the Run.

I switched my camera off. The red recording light blinked out.

Thorne didn't say a word. He just reached up and did the same.

Only when both lights were dark did we step forward.

It was the chosen Challenger from Ironclad, Dominic Shallow. I'd spoken to him briefly at the ball the night before. He had a wife and a kid waiting for him back home. He told me he was scared.

I was good at getting people to open up, to feel safe around me. He'd confided that he didn't care about winning or bringing home resources for his Collective, he just wanted to survive. To make it back to them.

My throat tightened, and tears blurred my vision again. At that moment, I was grateful for it. It softened the image of the broken body in front of me.

I stepped forward, and Thorne instinctively moved with me. Together, we gently pulled Dominic from the wreckage of twisted branches and splintered wood, laying him on a patch of even ground.

Thorne slid Dominic's pack from his back, while I climbed up and tore the chute from the branches. We spread it out and draped it over him like a shroud. When he was finally covered, I turned my camera back on. I only got four hours of uninterrupted time a day.

At least now, his family wouldn't have to see the pain frozen on his face.

Thorne picked up Dominic's pack and slung it over his shoulder. It felt wrong, taking from the dead, but if it meant keeping my brother alive, I'd carry the guilt.

"Come on," I said softly. "We've got a lot of ground to cover."

I gave one last look at the form beneath the chute, then turned and started walking toward Praxis.

———

THE FIRST NIGHT WAS BRUTAL.

We found water in a winding river that was carving through the forest like a silver scar. For a while, we followed it, Thorne insisting we stick close. "Rivers always lead to civilization," he'd said. But after hours of hiking, it started curving south and looping back.

We'd reach Praxis eventually if we stayed on that path, but it would take forever. Time we didn't have.

We filled our canteens, even the one we found in Dominic's pack. Then Thorne finally did what we'd been putting off and consolidated all the useful supplies into his own bag and ditched the extra pack.

Leaving it behind felt like leaving Dominic all over again. God forgive me.

We fought over it, loud, bitter words in the silence of the forest. But eventually, he agreed to veer from the river and cut directly through The Wilds. It was a risk, but it would get us to Praxis faster. And if anyone was equipped to make the journey, it was us.

Darkbranch was built on terrain like this, with thick forests, jagged cliffs, restless wildlife. Thorne and I had been hunting since we were old enough to hold a bow. But this time, we were unarmed. No weapons, no traps. Just instincts and desperation.

We needed food, and soon.

Thorne, idiot that he is, ate his entire jerky stick the moment he found it. Like it was a snack, not survival rations.

Now we only had half of mine and whatever Dominic had in his pack. Not nearly enough to get us through the Wilds.

"We'll have to hunt," I said, scanning the undergrowth.

"You even seen anything out here?" Thorne asked, a little too casually, but I could hear the edge of hunger in his voice.

"Not the animals themselves. But there's signs." I crouched, brushing the dirt aside with my fingers. "Look."

A paw print. Broad, deep. Still fresh.

"Bobcat," I muttered.

Thorne whistled low. "Big one?"

"Big enough to feed us for a couple days, if we're careful."

He looked down at the print, then up at me. "So we track it?"

I nodded. "We track it."

We slipped into old rhythms, falling into step like we were back in Darkbranch woods back before Pa died when he taught us how to track. Thorne was a pattern-reader, he could look at broken twigs and displaced moss and tell you which way something turned, how fast it was moving. I was tuned into the terrain itself, listening to the rhythm of the forest, feeling the shift in energy when something nearby moved.

We followed the trail, paw prints, broken branches, scraped bark. Silent. Focused.

Then we heard it.

A scream. High-pitched. Terrified. Feminine. It was cut off by a snarl, low, guttural, and unmistakably feline.

For a split second, Thorne and I locked eyes. Then we were moving, sprinting through the trees, leaping over roots and ducking under branches.

We didn't say a word. We didn't have to.

Someone was in trouble, and this time I was going to get there before it was too late.

The cat had someone pinned, its claws digging in as the figure beneath it thrashed and screamed, fighting like hell. Whoever it was, they weren't giving up easily.

Thorne didn't hesitate. He surged forward, instincts sharp and deadly, and brought a rock down hard on the creature's skull. The crack echoed through the trees. The cat gave a final twitch, then collapsed in a heavy heap.

I exhaled sharply, the tension in my chest unraveling all at once.

Then I saw her face.

Bex.

Relief crashed over me so hard my knees nearly gave out. If we'd been even a minute later...if we hadn't heard that scream...

I shoved the thought down as I rushed to her side. She was still struggling, still panicked, pinned beneath the weight of the cat's body. Her limbs flailed, breaths coming fast and shallow.

"Hey, hey, Hollis, don't worry," I said, keeping my voice low and steady despite the adrenaline still burning in my veins. "We got you."

Thorne and I hauled the dead, bleeding creature off of her, and the moment its weight was gone, she shot upright, wild-eyed and breathless.

And then, God, she looked at me.

Hair tangled, cheeks flushed, dirt and blood streaking across her jaw, and I swear, I forgot how to breathe. Even covered in grime, she was luminous. Unshaken spirit blazing behind her eyes.

Then she launched herself into us, arms thrown around our necks. I let out a sharp breath, startled, but then I melted into the warmth of her. My arms found her waist almost on instinct.

Thorne, ever the devil, chuckled. I didn't have to look to know he'd caught the stunned look on my face. And sure enough, the moment she pulled back, wiping her eyes, he shot me a knowing wink over her shoulder.

"Thank you," she whispered, and I could still feel the ghost of her touch on my chest. "I really thought that was it."

"Not a problem, love," Thorne said with that infuriating grin, already bending to snatch up the blood-slicked rock he'd used to bash the creature's skull. My brother, ever the improvisor.

He turned to me with a smirk. "Not bad for a little improvisation, huh, sis?"

I rolled my eyes, crouching beside the creature to get a better look at it, anything to hide the smile tugging at my lips.

"Yes, yes, you're the almighty hunter, and we should all sing your praises," I muttered. He snorted, pleased with himself.

Then I looked up at Bex again. She was watching me, long golden hair catching the sunlight through the trees, something unspoken lingering in her expression. My chest tightened.

"So, Hollis," I said, meeting her gaze, letting the corners of my mouth curl up just a little. "What do you say?"

I gave her my best grin, heart hammering beneath my ribs. "Let's eat."

"Alright, I'll get it ready," Thorne said, already crouching beside the feline's body. "You go start a fire somewhere."

"Get it ready?" Bex asked, brow raised.

"Gotta prepare the meat, love," Thorne replied with a grin that had far too much innuendo packed into it as he began tying the creature's legs with cords from the chute. I shot him a glare, but when I caught the way her cheeks flushed pink, the irritation melted into something warmer.

"Wanna keep me company?" Thorne asked, cocking his head with that stupid smirk.

"While you skin an animal?" she said dryly. "Thank you, but no."

And then she stepped toward me. I couldn't help the grin that spread across my face. I cast a smug glance over my shoulder at Thorne. His answering glare said *'game on'* loud and clear.

"Come on, Hollis," I said, voice softening as I placed a hand at the small of her back. "Help me get the fire going."

She didn't pull away. My hand stayed there, light and careful, guiding her away from the bloodied scene. It felt like something small, but significant, like trust was settling between us. And I wanted her to trust us. I needed her to. Because something in me had already decided that I'd do whatever it took to make sure she survived these Wilds.

I found a small clearing, open enough that the fire wouldn't catch on anything nearby. Safe. Controlled. When I started gathering kindling, I glanced up and saw her doing the same. No complaints. No hesitation.

Of course she was like that. Brave. Steady. I felt that in her when I watched her interview. And I could sense it when I spoke with her.

And dammit, I was already in trouble.

"Thanks," I said, as we gathered the firewood into a pile. I crouched beside it, arranging the pieces in a way that would catch easily. Bex sat on a hollowed-out log nearby, watching with quiet focus, like she was memorizing every move. Maybe she was. I noticed she did that. Watched people, studied things. I had been watching her for a few minutes before I spoke to her at the ball. Her eyes darted around like she was committing everything to memory. Taking a mental snapshot of the world around her.

I collected the kindling, struck a match from the small pack I kept tucked away, and coaxed the flame to life. I didn't need the match, I could've done it without them, but this was quicker. Within moments, the fire crackled, steady and bright.

When I was sure it would last, I looked over at her. She was still watching me.

"How did you know how to do that?" she asked.

"Darkbranch is a lot like The Wilds," I said, brushing ash from my fingers. "We grew up in the woods. We're comfortable here."

She nodded thoughtfully. The flickering light played across her features, beautiful and bloodied. Splatter from the cat still marked her skin, dried in small, harsh flecks across her cheek and temple. I hated seeing it there, marring the face that had already started to haunt my thoughts.

I pulled my pack over and sat beside her on the log. The wood groaned under our weight. From inside my bag, I retrieved my canteen and the strip of fabric that used to be my blindfold. I poured a little water onto the cloth, then turned to her.

"Let me help?" I asked, voice low.

Her eyes, clear, bright, and impossibly blue, met mine. Something passed between us in that silence, then she gave a small nod.

Gently, I reached up and began to clean the blood from her face. My fingers moved slowly, careful not to startle her. Careful not to linger too long, even though every brush of the cloth against her skin made me want to memorize the feel of her. I was aware, acutely, of how much water I was using, how stupid it was to waste it, but I didn't care. Not right now. She deserved to feel like herself, without the remnants of the attack splattered across her features.

As I moved toward her cheek, she winced. I immediately pulled back, heart lurching.

"Are you okay?" I asked, concern tightening my voice.

"I cut myself in the landing," she said. Now that the blood was gone, I could see the thin slice beneath it. Not deep, but raw. Angry.

"I've got it," I said softly. I returned to the task with even more care, dabbing gently, making sure I didn't hurt her again.

After a moment, I let the silence stretch, then said, "So... how's it been so far? You know, aside from the whole bobcat trying to eat you alive, part."

Her mouth curved into a crooked, tired smile, and she laughed. The sound went directly to my core, but I forced a breath to calm my thoughts.

The fire crackled between us, sending small, fleeting sparks into the night sky. The warmth of it felt oddly comforting, like a shield against the wildness of the world outside the circle of light we'd created.

Bex stared into the flames, her expression distant, but I could see the tension still pulling at the corners of her face. She seemed to be sorting through something in her head, gathering the words she needed before speaking.

"I got stuck in a tree about twenty feet up on my way down," she started, her voice soft but with a hint of amusement. "Was about three seconds from failing this trial before it even began."

Her eyes never left the fire, but I could see the way her brow furrowed, that tight crease between her eyes that told me just how close she'd been to a fate similar to Dominic's. I felt a small pang of protectiveness for her.

I let out a low sigh, my voice low but playful. "I landed in a clearing, lucky for me. I'm not much of a tree climber."

She looked up at me then, a smirk playing on her lips, though I could still see the remnants of the nerves beneath her eyes. "But I thought you were a woodswoman. Shouldn't climbing be one of your skills?" she teased.

I couldn't resist. "Well, you know, I'm better at falling," I replied, the flirtation slipping into my words so easily.

Her eyes softened, but she didn't break eye contact. I hoped I hadn't pushed her too far. Flirty innuendos were more my brother's expertise, but something about her made me want to rise to the challenge.

After a moment, she spoke again, almost as though she was letting the air settle. "How did you find Thorne?"

I paused, pulling my thoughts back to that moment. "I pulled my chute as early as I could to slow my fall. Told him to aim for me when he jumped right after me."

She raised an eyebrow, clearly impressed. "That was... clever."

I grinned, feeling a rush of pride. "I'm glad it worked. I wouldn't have been able to focus on getting back to Praxis if I was worried about trying to find my brother out here. Not that he couldn't handle it on his own. But..."

"You can focus when you know he's safe," she finished for me, her voice soft, understanding. Her gaze held mine, steady and warm.

"Yeah, exactly," I said quietly.

"It was a good plan, I'm glad it worked," she offered, and there was something in her tone that made me feel like she genuinely admired me, and I wasn't used to that. I felt my chest puff out a little in pride.

"Told you the kind of muscles you need to survive these

trials aren't all right here," I teased, giving her a playful nudge on the upper arm.

The moment my hand touched her arm, I felt the subtle shift in her body, a tiny catch in her breath that made something deep inside me stir. Her eyes flicked to mine, and for a moment, I could see the way her pulse quickened ever so slightly, the softening of her features. She inhaled softly, and the sound did something to my insides, making it impossible to ignore the way my heart started to race.

"I'm glad you're safe" I said, my voice suddenly thick with something I couldn't quite name.

She gave me a look, one that sent a shiver down my spine. "I'm glad you found me."

"Me too," I whispered in return. Our faces were close enough that I could feel her cool breath on my lips. My eyes flicked down to her lips, then back to her eyes to find she was studying me too, breath shallow.

I sat back then, needing a little space before I did something stupid, like kiss her. I leaned back, watching the fire dance in front of us, its flames reaching for the sky. Her gaze followed the movement, and soon we were both silently mesmerized by the flickering light. Without realizing it at first, I began to hum softly, a gentle sound escaping my lips. The hum turned into words, and before I knew it, I was singing quietly into the night.

"I walk the path where the wild things grow,
Where the pine trees whisper and the rivers flow,
With each step, I feel the earth beneath my feet,
In the woods, I find my heart's steady beat."

I felt her eyes on me, but the spirit of the song had taken over. I couldn't stop, not now that the words were flowing freely.

"In the woods I am, and the woods are me,

A part of the leaves and the sky so free.
The wind in my hair, the sun on my skin,
In the woods I'm where wild things begin."
The last note lingered in the air, and for a moment, silence fell between us. The crackling of the fire was the only sound.

"That was beautiful," she whispered, her voice soft and sincere. I looked over at her, finding her leaning forward, her arms resting on her knees as she watched me. "What is that song?"

"Something my Pa taught me, once upon a time," I replied, my voice quiet but steady.

She nodded slowly, her gaze thoughtful. "I haven't heard music in..." she paused, trying to find the words. "I don't even know how long. Well, aside from the Praxis anthem."

I nodded in return, understanding.

"Darkbranch hasn't placed in the entertainment trial in a long time either," I added, trying not to let the weight of that truth show on my features. "It's been a while since we've had music there too."

She shook her head, her grip on my hand tightening. Her face leaned closer to mine, the warmth of her breath mingling with the cool night air. "You *are* the music, Briar."

My chest tightened, the words stirring something deep inside me. I felt the sting in my eyes, the threat of tears lingering just beneath the surface.

She saw it. "Do you have anyone waiting for you back in Darkbranch?" she asked gently, her voice a soft whisper in the quiet.

I shook my head. "Thorne's all I got left... You?"

"I have Jax," she replied. "And Ava." My chest tightened with a sad sort of jealousy.

"Your partner?" I asked, trying to keep my voice even. I had assumed there was something between her and Ezra, anyone could see the way they looked at each other at the Welcome Ball, but I guess a selfish part of me had hoped there was room for me.

"Best friend," she replied, with the slightest bit of a knowing smirk. I grinned, unable to resist the pull between us. I leaned toward her slightly, keeping my gaze on her, watching the firelight flicker in her eyes.

"Ah," I said, meeting her eyes again. The tension between us pulled taut and thick.

I pulled my bottom lip between my teeth, trying to force myself not to claim her lips with mine, and her eyes hungrily tracked the movement.

"Hollis.. I..."

"Good evening, and welcome to *Restaurante de la Grey*!" Thorne exclaimed dramatically, carrying the prepared meat piled on a thin slab of stone into the clearing with the flair of a seasoned chef.

I gave Bex a quick smile, before gifting my brother with an exaggerated eye roll. I sat back, putting much needed space between her and I.

"On the menu tonight, you'll find my specialty. Big cat a la... uh... delicious."

Bex laughed, the sound light and carefree, as she snickered at my brother's ability to turn any moment into something fun and airy. Honestly, I'd be jealous of his charm if I didn't get to bask in the way her laughter sounded like music in my ears.

"We recommend pairing this delectable meal with some of our finest water, straight from the dirty-ass river, with minimal filtration," Thorne continued, his grin widening as he set the meat down by the fire with an exaggerated flourish.

Bex's eyes sparkled as she watched him, a playful smile

tugging at her lips. "Sounds perfect," she replied with a teasing glint in her eyes.

Thorne, ever the flirt, slid into the seat next to her with all the casual confidence of someone who knew exactly how to make an entrance. He pressed his side against hers as if it were the most natural thing in the world. I rolled my eyes at my brother's antics but couldn't help the way my chest tightened as I saw how easily he made her smile.

I'd never felt jealous of the people Thorne gave his affection to, probably because our tastes rarely overlapped. And when they did, it never felt like competition. It felt... natural. Back home in Darkbranch, some people raised eyebrows when we dated the same girl, but to us, it made sense.

After we lost our parents, there were parts of us that never quite healed. Big, jagged spaces that no one person could fill. Loving someone together wasn't unconventional, it was about making sure that person never had to carry the full weight of either of us alone. We shared that responsibility, that tenderness, because we knew what it meant to be broken. And neither of us wanted to let someone we loved feel that way.

I never found it strange, if anything, I found comfort in it. I liked knowing that the girl I cared about was also cared for by someone I trusted.

For a brief, dangerously tempting moment, I wondered if Bex would mind letting us care for her.

Shaking the thought from my mind, I got to work on cooking the meat, making sure it was perfectly seared over the fire. The sizzle and crackle of the flames filled the air, and I did my best to focus on the task, even though the low hum of Thorne and Bex's banter kept pulling at my attention.

When the meal was ready, we all dug in with eager hunger. We pressed our hands against our stomachs when we'd eaten our fill, groaning in contentment.

"Five stars," Bex said, her voice light but warm, and I felt a small flicker of pride that my brother had managed to make the evening feel almost normal.

Thorne grinned, his eyes glinting mischievously. "Would you like to see our dessert menu?" he asked, his voice dropping to a low, tempting pitch.

I couldn't help but glance up at them, just in time to see Thorne lean in closer, his breath teasing her neck. The way her body reacted sent a jolt through me, her breath hitched softly, her cheeks flushed with a delicate pink that made something deep in me stir. I couldn't help but notice the way her thighs pressed together ever so slightly.

I could think of a desert I'd like to taste.

I think she knew where my mind had gone because she met my gaze with a fiery expression.

I felt the temperature around the fire rise, my heart rate picking up, but then my eyes flicked to the cameras strapped to Thorne and Bex's chests, and I knew I needed to get it together before we gave them more of a show than they'd signed up for.

"Let's set up camp for the night," I said, trying to sound casual, "We'll hit it hard tomorrow."

Thorne grinned like a mischievous child. "Yes, we're very good at hitting it hard," he replied, his voice dripping with feigned innocence.

Bex, mid-sip of water, choked and spat it out, her cheeks turning a shade of red that I couldn't help but notice. I threw my pack at Thorne, he caught it with a huff. I groaned and ran a hand down my face, exasperated, but I couldn't suppress the smile that crept onto my lips. Maybe a few days hike in the woods wouldn't be all that bad with her by our side.

CHAPTER
TWELVE

BEX

I COULDN'T SLEEP.

The ground was too hard, the air too cold, and every time I closed my eyes, I saw Ezra's face. The worry clung to me like a second skin, itching at my nerves, refusing to let go.

I glanced over at Thorne and Briar, both asleep, their breathing even and steady in the dark. I envied them. Carefully, quietly, I slipped out from under the thin blanket of our makeshift shelter. I didn't go far. I wasn't stupid, the Wilds might be calm now, but they could turn in an instant. Still, I needed space. Room to think. Room to breathe.

I switched off the camera strapped to my chest. Four hours a day. That was the rule, our one scrap of unsupervised time.

I wandered a few paces and found a fallen log. Perched on it, leaning back, I tipped my head toward the sky. It was clear tonight, dark and endless. No storm clouds, no heavy winds. Just a blanket of stars above us. Out here, with the trial paused and the cameras off, the Wilds didn't feel like the threat they were. They felt... still.

A rustle behind me snapped me back to reality.

I shot to my feet, my heart pounding as I reached instinctively for the nearest object.

But it was Thorne.

He stepped into view with his hands raised in mock surrender. "Easy, love," he said, the edges of a grin playing on his face. "Didn't mean to interrupt your brooding."

I let out a breath, my muscles unclenching. "I wasn't brooding."

He shrugged. "Could have fooled me."

I sat back down, and after a beat, he dropped onto the log beside me. I heard the soft *click* of his own camera shutting off, and a peculiar hush settled over us. The kind you only got when nobody was watching.

"You doing okay?" he asked, softer now, his voice carrying none of his usual teasing edge.

I hesitated, then admitted, "I'm worried about Ezra."

"Yeah." Thorne raked a hand through his hair. "If I hadn't found Briar when I did, I'd be losing my mind too." He glanced sideways at me. "You really care about him."

It wasn't a question. Just a quiet observation.

"I do," I said, the words heavier than I expected them to be.

He huffed a humorless laugh. "A confession without a camera rolling. Take that, Praxis," he muttered. His grin returned for a flicker, but it didn't reach his eyes this time.

I tensed a little. Even with the general distaste for Praxis in Canyon, I wasn't used to people talking about them like that. Not so plainly.

"You're... very vocal about your feelings," I said carefully, meaning it both as a compliment and a warning.

Thorne shrugged, his gaze returning to the stars. "Well, my Ma always said if you don't speak your truth, someone else'll write it for you. And trust me, Praxis has one hell of a pen."

There was a somber twinge in his voice then, a note I recognized. The kind you didn't learn unless you'd lost something you weren't ready to lose.

"I'm sorry for your loss," I murmured.

His head turned, surprise flashing in his eyes. "How did you—"

"Grief recognizes grief," I whispered. "And Briar mentioned you two didn't have anyone waiting back home."

The quiet stretched between us. Thorne took a long, steadying breath, then let it out like a man who'd been holding it for years.

"She's been gone almost ten," he admitted.

I swallowed. "Seven for me."

He reached out, gripped my hand, and gave it a gentle squeeze. No theatrics. No smirk. Just warmth.

"I'm sorry," he said quietly.

"Me too."

For a moment, there was nothing but the sound of the wind in the trees and the distant hum of the Wilds. His thumb brushed against mine, and when he spoke again, his voice was barely more than a whisper.

"You ever wonder what it'd be like... if it wasn't like this?" His gaze stayed on the stars. "If we didn't have to fight for scraps, or bleed for a system that treats us like... this?"

I didn't answer. I wasn't sure what to say.

But Thorne wasn't really asking. He was remembering. Or maybe imagining.

"Not sure we're allowed to imagine that," I replied.

"Yeah," he said, smiling up at the sky.

"You said something once to me," I said. "Something about the stars."

He smiled at me, a glint of mischief in his eyes.

"I sure did," he replied.

"What did you mean?" Ava had once said something similar, and I couldn't help but be curious.

"Funny thing about stars," he murmured. "You can't see 'em in the city anymore. Praxis burned out the sky with their towers of lights and their technology. But out here? They're still shining." He tilted his head, a faint, almost wistful smile playing at his lips. "Even all the glitter and gold can't stop them."

I thought it was just another one of his poetic turns of phrase, but something in his voice made me look at him a little longer.

"I should get some sleep," I said quietly, not sure why my throat felt tight.

"Yeah," Thorne agreed, but he didn't move.

Neither did I.

"Goodnight, Thorne," I murmured as I stood, brushing the dirt from my hands.

He didn't look away from the sky. "Goodnight, Brexlyn," he replied, his voice softer than I'd ever heard it.

I made my way back to the tent, the chill settling heavier around me now. I crawled inside, curling up on the cold ground, but sleep still refused to come. I waited... for what, I wasn't sure. For his footsteps, maybe. For the familiar weight of him beside me. I told myself it was for warmth. Just that.

When he finally returned, I felt him settle down nearby, the faint shift of fabric and breath in the dark. I didn't move, but I knew he knew I was awake.

A moment passed.

Then his hand brushed against mine. A tentative,

lingering touch, skin meeting skin in a way that sent heat rushing through me despite the cold. Slowly, his fingers laced with mine, his thumb tracing slow, deliberate lines along the back of my hand.

We didn't speak.

Didn't need to.

For a few stolen minutes, it felt like the world outside the tent walls didn't exist, no trials, no cameras, no Praxis. Just us and the stars.

Then, without a word, he lifted my hand to his lips. His mouth was warm against my skin, a ghost of a kiss. A promise, or a goodbye, or maybe just a little indulgence.

He let go.

The air shifted again.

I heard the soft *click* as his camera flicked back on. And a breath later, I turned mine on too.

Our brief, star-filled escape vanished and I felt Praxis' eyes fall on us again.

BRIAR WAS GONE when I woke up the next morning. Thorne lay curled in his blanket, softly snoring, his face peaceful. I slipped out from the edge of the campsite and stretched my legs, the early morning air cool against my skin.

Thorne's words from last night circled in my head.

I should remember what Zaffir told me. Don't believe a word they say. And maybe he was right. Maybe I shouldn't have believed a thing that came from either of their mouths. But... I did. Or I wanted to. Maybe that was naïve. Maybe it was stupid. Or maybe, I could just read them. They didn't feel like liars. They felt real. I liked them.

And I think I trusted them.

"Morning," Briar's voice came from behind me.

I jolted, heart leaping into my throat.

"Shit, you scared me."

She smiled, all slow amusement. "Didn't mean to sneak up on you."

"You walk so quietly in the woods, it's either really impressive or really terrifying. I haven't decided which yet."

She gave a small chuckle and held out her hand, palm open. Handing me a piece of fruit, deep red and round. Ripe. Juicy.

"Breakfast?" she offered.

I glanced at the fruit, then up at her. "Where'd you find this?"

She stepped over to a stump and dropped down onto it, pulling another one out from her pocket. I joined her.

I noticed then that the camera at her chest was off. I flicked mine off, too. I kind of liked being able to be alone with them. Even just for a little while.

"A lot of this area used to be rich with fruit trees," she said, turning the fruit over in her hand. "Most of them died out, but there are a few still hanging on. If you know where to look."

I stared down at the one in my palm, its skin dappled with gold. I couldn't remember the last time I'd held something this fresh. Have I ever? I didn't even know what kind of fruit it was. Didn't know how it would taste.

When I glanced up, Briar was watching me.

"You do that a lot," I said quietly.

"Do what?"

"Watch me."

Her lips twitched with a soft smile. "Sorry."

"It's okay," I said. "I just... I can't imagine I'm that interesting to look at."

That made her laugh, quiet and under her breath, like I'd told a joke without meaning to.

"What?" I asked.

She shook her head slowly. "You really have no idea, do you?"

"About what?"

"How special you are."

The words landed with a quiet thud in my chest. I looked at her, and she didn't look away. My breath caught, and I didn't know what to say. So I bit into the fruit instead.

The taste exploded on my tongue. Tart, sweet, fresh, so fresh it nearly hurt. A moan slipped out before I could stop it. Juice ran down my chin, sticky and sweet, and I turned my head, embarrassed. But when I looked back, Briar's eyes were on me, hot and dark, like I was something to devour.

I licked the juice from my bottom lip slowly, instinct more than intention. Her gaze tracked the movement. I felt another drop slide down my chin and went to wipe it away, but she beat me to it, her fingers brushing gently across my skin. She caught the juice with her thumb, then raised it to her mouth.

And licked it off.

I stared, stunned and speechless, heat blooming in my chest.

I wanted to kiss her.

But I didn't.

Couldn't.

Shouldn't.

I shook my head, trying to shove the thought away, the desire curling under my skin like fire.

"So," I said, voice rougher than I meant it to be, "how'd you get so good at reading people?"

She shifted, gaze falling to the trees beyond.

"It's not a fun story," she warned.

"I don't mind," I replied.

"When we were kids," she said, voice distant, "Thorne and I were almost taken."

The breath caught in my throat. "Taken?"

"There was a man in our Collective. He was... well, he was stealing children. Killing them. Dumping their bodies in the woods."

The air around us changed. Went still.

"He murdered ten kids in three months."

"Oh my god," I whispered.

"Ma and Pa warned us. Said don't trust anyone. Don't walk home alone. Don't stray from the path. All the usual stuff."

I nodded. My stomach felt cold.

"There was this old man who lived just past the woods," she went on. "We used to bring him small game, squirrels, rabbits. He'd give us coins. He was kind. Sweet. He'd smile at us. Told jokes. He remembered our birthdays."

She paused. Swallowed hard.

"We were there every day that summer. Laughing, joking. And the whole time, he was out there, taking kids."

I reached out, found her hand, and held it.

"He tried to take us one day," she said, voice barely above a breath. "But he'd never taken two at once before. Might be why he waited so long to try. We never went alone. We fought. We got away. We ran."

She didn't look at me, just stared ahead, like she could still see the moment unfolding in front of her.

"He got caught. Sentenced to death."

She was trembling.

I slid closer and wrapped my arm around her, pulling her in.

"I saw him every single day," she whispered, breaking. "I

smiled at him. Laughed at his dumb jokes. And I never saw it. I never saw it. Ten kids died. Because I never even looked close enough."

"No," I said, firmly. "Briar. You were a kid. That wasn't your fault."

She shook her head. "He fooled me. He fooled everyone."

"You're the one who got away. Who turned him in. You saved lives."

She looked up at me, eyes wet. "That day, I swore I'd never be caught like that again. If there's something to know about someone, I will find it. I will see it."

I reached up and cupped her cheek, thumb brushing away the tears. To hell with what Zaffir said, I trusted Briar at this moment. I knew she was telling me the truth. I knew this was raw honesty. This was her story, and she felt comfortable enough to share it with me.

"Thank you for telling me," I whispered.

She leaned into my touch just slightly. "Thank you for listening."

A few hours later we were packed up and back on the trail. Briar had been modest when she mentioned that she and Thorne were comfortable in the woods. Watching them move through the trees, navigate the terrain, and hunt with the precision of seasoned experts, I almost felt like a useless third wheel. They moved like they were part of the wilderness, not just in it, and I was just trying to keep up.

"Not that way," I called, as Thorne began to track down a hill to the northeast.

"Praxis is that way, love," Thorne replied, his voice calm and unbothered, as though it was a simple correction.

"Yes, but at the base of this hill is a lake," I said, pointing. "And we're not going to be able to swim it."

Both of them stopped, blinking at me in unison.

"Can you hear the water or something?" Briar asked, lifting an ear, trying to catch whatever it was I was hearing.

I shook my head. "No, I saw it."

The two of them exchanged a puzzled glance.

"When I was falling from the plane," I explained, shrugging like it was nothing.

"That was three days ago," Briar said, her voice tinged with disbelief.

"And you were falling from a plane..." Thorne added, as if he was still processing it. "Are you sure?" he asked, genuinely shocked, but not accusatory.

"Yeah, I'm positive," I replied, not bothering to explain the details of my fall. They didn't need to know everything.

There was a long pause where I wasn't sure if they would believe me or trust me. I didn't totally blame them, if I was wrong, I'd be taking them hours out of the way. "Lead the way, love," Thorne said with a smile, a sense of ease in his voice that made me relax a little. It felt really good to know that they trusted me.

I turned us due north, guiding us down the hill. We'd reach the northern edge of the lake, then follow it along the shore for a few hours, cutting east once we were past it. It felt strange to be the one leading, especially after watching them both navigate so expertly.

A few hours later, we spilled out onto lower ground just north of the large, uncrossable lake.

"Damn, Hollis," Briar said, her voice low as she whistled. "You just saved us hours of backtracking."

"Other muscles, I guess," I said with a grin, glancing at her. She met my smile, and the warmth in her expression made me feel something flutter inside my chest.

"Alright, how'd you do that?" Thorne asked, meeting my gaze with an excited spark in his eyes. "How'd you remember the lake? We're probably seventy miles away from the drop site at this point."

I hesitated, then took a breath, reaching up to switch off my camera.

They followed suit, their cameras clicking off with a quiet sense of solidarity. It felt like a weight had lifted. No longer were we under the gaze of the cameras, with the world watching our every move.

I promised myself I'd keep my little 'superpower' to myself so I didn't make myself a target. But somewhere between being chased by a bobcat and this moment, I grew to trust these two, and I found that I wanted to tell them.

"My memory is... really good," I said, keeping it simple, even though I knew the truth was more complicated.

"Good..." Thorne repeated, furrowing his brow.

"Like eidetic?" Briar asked, her gaze sharp and inquisitive.

I nodded.

"That's wicked," Thorne exclaimed, clapping his hands together with a grin. "So what, you just saw the lake and remembered where it was?"

I shook my head. "Well.. sort of."

Briar's smirk grew, a knowing look crossing her features. "You made a map, didn't you?" she said, her voice filled with impressed amusement.

I couldn't help the small surge of pride that bloomed in my chest.

"I did," I admitted, a quiet confidence settling in. "I mapped out the whole trip in my head while I was falling. It's all right here."

Thorne's eyes widened, his jaw dropping slightly. "You're incredible."

Briar chuckled, but there was a softness in her expression,

a rare warmth that made my heart race just a little faster. "That's impressive, Hollis. Really impressive."

"Hell yeah it is. Who knows... maybe we actually stand a chance at winning this damn thing," Thorne said, sauntering onward with that cocky swagger of his.

I tried to ignore how his use of the word "we" hit me. How it made my chest tighten in ways I wasn't prepared to deal with. As we pressed forward, the weight of it stayed with me, but I kept my focus on the path ahead.

By the time nightfall came, we were working like a well-oiled machine. The tasks had become second nature. I gathered firewood, Briar ventured off to hunt, and Thorne set up the chutes between the trees, turning them into makeshift tents. If it weren't for the fact that we were in the middle of the Reclamation Run, I might have even enjoyed myself. Being in nature, alongside them, it was a surprisingly peaceful feeling.

Briar had a deep reverence for the forest that I couldn't help but admire. There was an artistry in the way she moved through the woods, as if the trees whispered to her and the breeze carried stories only she could understand. She taught me to listen to the birds, not just to hear them, but to decode their songs, to recognize their calls like a hidden language. She read the tracks of animals with that same kind of reverence. It was a deep thoughtful connection, a bond between her and the forest.

I watched her, captivated, and saw how she hummed to herself as she worked, her voice so quiet it was like a breeze among the leaves. It wasn't something she did consciously, I don't think. It was just a part of her, like breathing. The melody seemed to flow from her without effort, a soft tune that blended with the rustling of the trees and the distant calls of wildlife. It was as though the forest itself was making music, and she was simply giving voice to it. I began to realize that this was her art. Her gift was not only her connection to the land, but the way she could pull harmony from it, without even trying.

I found myself longing to hear her sing again. The night around the fire, I was captivated by the rawness of it, the emotion woven into every note. There was something so real, so genuine in the way she sang, it was beautiful.

Meanwhile, Thorne was a walking encyclopedia of the wilderness. He eagerly pointed out different species of plants and creatures, explaining their unique properties, and his enthusiasm was contagious. I had always been good at learning quickly, but Thorne's mind, his knowledge, it was incredible. And in those moments when he let his expertise shine through, there was something undeniably beautiful about him.

The fire crackled between us, and I couldn't help but notice how the flickering flames cast shadows across their matching, yet entirely different faces, how their dark eyes sparkled with excitement as they spoke and playfully teased each other. It was strange how, even in the middle of this chaotic trial, these small moments made everything feel like it was going to be alright.

My heart tightened at the thought of Ezra, a wave of missing him crashing over me. I forced myself not to let the fear take hold. The fear that he wasn't okay. Briar had told me about the man from Ironclad who never even made it to the ground alive, and I pushed the image of Ezra meeting a similar fate out of my mind. But at night, when everything was quiet and we were all drifting to sleep, his face was the only thing I could think about.

A selfish part of me hoped he was still looking for me, but I also hoped he hadn't stayed behind to do so. Maybe we'd run into him soon. We hadn't encountered any other Challengers yet, but we had stumbled across a campsite earlier that day. The embers of the fire were still warm. Whoever it was had gotten ahead of us, but not by much.

I tried to convince myself it wasn't Ezra to stop myself from using what Briar had taught me about following tracks and racing after him.

"If all goes right, we'll probably reach Praxis by midday tomorrow," I whispered, my eyes closed as I updated our location on my mental map.

"How desperate are we to get out of these woods?" Thorne asked, his gaze expectant.

"What are you suggesting?" Briar replied, raising an eyebrow.

"Well, I don't know about you two, but I'm getting pretty tired of sleeping on the ground. Not that your company hasn't been delightful," he added, sending me a quick wink. I smiled back, appreciating how he always seemed to lift the mood with his words.

"You want to hike through the night?" Briar asked, cutting to the heart of her twin's rambling.

I glanced between them.

"Maybe we'll catch up to whoever's ahead of us. It would be nice to have the train come more often. I hate how infrequently we can get to the Center, and you know you do too."

"What's the Center?" I asked.

Briar broke her gaze with Thorne and turned to me. "It's like a trade hub in our Collective. We bring our hunts there to trade for food, supplies... trouble is, it's a several days' hike on foot." She chuckled. "Not unlike this one."

"The train would get us there in a few hours, tops," Thorne said, a gleam of encouragement in his voice. And I saw it the moment it flashed in Briar eyes. Determination.

They were done just surviving the trial. Now they wanted to place.

I refused to hold them back. I was content keeping a steady, easy pace when I was sure none of us cared to win this trial. But now that they did, I wouldn't give them a reason to blame me. I stood, grabbed my pack, and tossed over my shoulder, "Well, what are we waiting for, then?"

I heard them scramble behind me, cursing as they put out the fire and stamped it out. Their jogging footsteps quickly followed as they caught up.

"Alright, Hollis. Lead us to the finish line," Briar remarked.

We pressed on through the night, with only the moon's glow lighting our way. My eyes adjusted eventually, and with the Grey siblings at my side, the shadows didn't seem as intimidating as they had when I was alone.

I really needed to thank them when we got back, or maybe before we did. Who knew what the next trial would bring, or if I'd even get the chance to see them again? The thought made my stomach clench, but I tried to push it down.

I had Ezra, and whatever was going on with the redheaded cameraman. I briefly wondered if he was the one receiving the feed attached to my chest. Was he listening in, watching over me, editing my journey into something Jax would be proud to see? For some reason, I trusted him to do that for me.

But the point was, I didn't need two more sexy strangers confusing my mind or stirring up thoughts I didn't need. And yet, they still did.

It must've been two or three a.m. when Briar's hand landed on my shoulder, freezing me in place. Her eyes scanned the darkened surroundings, her ear flicking, as if she were listening for something only she could hear. It was the familiar motion she made when she was hunting, but this time, a cold realization settled in my chest...we were the ones being hunted now.

She pressed a finger to her lips, signaling us to stay quiet, though I didn't need the reminder. The air seemed to thicken with tension, my breath catching in my throat as fear slowly crept in. Thorne's grip tightened around my hand, his fingers warm and strong, and before I could even process the comfort, he was pulling me back.

Briar didn't move, her stance unwavering, her attention fixed ahead. Thorne guided me silently, leading me away from her, away from whatever danger lurked nearby. I wanted to call out to Briar, to urge her to join us, but the fear in my gut told me that if we made any noise now, it could make things worse, but it didn't help the pull I felt the further we got from her. Thorne obviously trusted her to take care of herself in the face of whatever was out there, but worry clenched my heart.

When we reached a massive tree, Thorne pulled me behind it, his body shielding mine. He pressed me into the rough bark, the coolness of it seeping through my clothes, and then he caged me in, his chest coming flush with mine. My heart thundered in my chest, so loud I could barely hear anything else. Our faces were inches apart, our breaths mingling in the small space between us. His warm exhale brushed against my skin, sending a shiver down my spine.

We both tensed, listening, our bodies so close that I could feel the fear radiating from him. His muscles were tight. He was terrified. I could feel it in the slight shake on his body. The coil of his muscles. I lifted a hand, resting it on his chest and I could feel the quick beat of his pulse beneath my fingertips. His eyes locked on mine and I felt his fear slowly dissipate.

Thorne's hand moved to the side of my face, cupping it gently. He wasn't even aware of it, but the simple touch grounded me, slowing my racing heart. His thumb brushed softly against my cheek, and I let my eyes drift closed for a moment, finding a strange comfort in his closeness, in the heat of his body pressing against mine.

I focused on him, on the rhythm of our breaths, trying to block out the rest of the world, and the worry I felt for Briar. His eyes were dark, intent on me as we listened for his sister.

I could feel the heat of his body, his closeness starting to affect me in ways I didn't expect. My chest ached with something deeper than just anxiety, and I found myself leaning in slightly, drawn to him in a way I couldn't explain.

"Okay, I think we're clear," Briar whispered-yelled, and Thorne and I exhaled simultaneously. I expected him to step back, but he didn't. Instead, he pressed his hips forward and the evidence of how my closeness affected him was clear as it pressed against my stomach. His eyes flicked to my lips for just a brief moment, a glance so soft and fleeting that I almost missed it. Enough to send my heart into a frantic beat.

Thorne brought his hand up between the two of us, switching his camera off first, then doing the same to mine. My breath caught in my throat. Whatever he was about to say or do, he didn't want an audience for it.

I could almost taste the air between us, the anticipation heavy and thick, and I wasn't sure who moved first. But then, just as I thought he would lean in, a sudden movement tore him away from me. It was violent, sharp, and in an instant, I was left standing there, breathless and confused.

"Get the fuck off of her," a voice growled, and a sob of relief broke free from my chest.

"Ezra!" I cried out, rushing forward. But before I could reach him, he had already pinned Thorne to the forest floor. Panic gripped me. "Stop, let him go, Ezra!" I shouted. The two men were locked in a furious struggle, rolling and fighting.

"Ezra, stop, please!" I screamed again, my voice desperate, as Briar finally arrived and ripped him off of her brother.

Ezra was thrown back, but in a heartbeat, he surged forward again. I stepped in between them, raising my hand to press against his chest. His breath was ragged, his body tense with fury and anger. For a fleeting moment, a painful thought crossed my mind, that maybe he hated me for finding comfort in someone else.

The thought hit me harder than I cared to admit.

But then his eyes, those familiar, intense eyes, flicked from Thorne to me. And in them, I saw nothing but relief, admiration, and something softer, something caring. It melted the knot of panic in my chest.

"Ezra," I whispered, my voice trembling as I rushed forward. Without a word, he pulled me into his arms, lifting me off the ground as if I weighed nothing at all. He held me tightly against his chest, his body steadying mine as I felt the weight of his relief too. He inhaled deeply, like he was trying to absorb every part of me, pressing a comforting kiss to the side of my neck.

His touch was grounding, and in that moment, I finally felt like I could breathe again.

"I've been looking for you," Ezra said, pulling his head back to look at me. His voice was rough, eyes scanning me with that familiar intensity. He looked just as worn as the rest of us, tired and dirty, but there were no signs of injury. A smile tugged at my lips as I met his gaze.

"I thought he was hurting you," he added, his eyes darkening with anger as he glanced over my shoulder at Thorne and Briar.

I took a step back, shaking my head. "Not at all," I replied, trying to steady my voice, turning to face the two men. "They helped me survive, Ezra." I injected as much sincerity into my words as I could, hoping he'd understand. "They saved my life."

Thorne and Briar exchanged a glance and nodded, soft smiles gracing their lips. I turned back to Ezra, watching as his eyes shifted between them, his expression unreadable at first, then softening as he processed what I said.

"Thank you for protecting her," he whispered, his voice quieter now.

"We'd do it again," Briar answered, taking a step closer to me, her presence a comfort.

"Yeah, I was actually using my body as a human shield when you so rudely interrupted," Thorne teased, stepping forward and casually wrapping an arm around my shoulder.

I caught Ezra's eyes, searching his face for any sign of discomfort or jealousy. He was quiet for a moment, then smirked.

"Yeah, well, if I was able to rip you off, you weren't doing that good of a job," Ezra shot back, but there was an edge of playful sarcasm in his voice that helped me relax. The last thing I needed was another fight to complicate things.

I had to remind myself we were still in the middle of this damn trial.

"We should keep going," I said, stepping out from under Thorne's arm, trying to focus on the task ahead. "We can reach city limits in a few hours if we pick up the pace."

I began walking toward the direction of Praxis, trying to push all the conflicting emotions swirling inside me to the back of my mind.

Ezra was back, and the weight of the tension between Briar, Thorne, and me was thick in the air. Every touch, every look was making it harder to keep it together. I needed to focus, to get back to Praxis, before I did something I'd regret. Something reckless. Like indulging all three of them.

"Let's catch our breath for a minute," Briar suggested, brushing a sweaty strand of hair from her brow. "I could use a second to let my heart rate return to something that doesn't feel like imminent death."

"Yeah, I could go for a quick pit stop," Thorne added, stretching his arms overhead with a grunt. "Ezra here body-slammed me into the dirt hard enough to knock the hunger right back into me. I'm craving some of that leftover squirrel from this morning."

They peeled off toward a shaded patch beneath the trees and started prepping a small fire. Ezra and I lagged behind, and when our eyes met, the weight of everything finally caught up with me. I collapsed into his arms without hesitation, like I'd been waiting for permission to fall.

"You okay?" he murmured, his hands moving gently along my back, not searching for wounds, just reassurance.

I nodded against his chest. "Yeah. I promise. You have no idea how happy I am to see you."

"Yeah," he said, brushing his knuckles across my cheek. "I do."

His eyes flicked over my shoulder toward Briar and Thorne, and I saw a flash of distrust, and maybe jealousy in his gaze.

"They saved me, Ezra."

His eyes flashed back to me, softening.

"Don't let her fool you," Briar called over her shoulder as she stacked kindling with Thorne. "She's saved our asses more than once already too."

Ezra glanced down at me, and there was pride written all over his face, unguarded and warm. "I don't doubt it."

His hand rose to cup my cheek, fingers brushing lightly against my jaw. For a moment, I wished he'd close the space between us and kiss me. Which was confusing. Or awful. Or both, because not even five minutes ago, I'd been wishing the same thing about Thorne. And then there was the way Briar's humming always made me feel safe, or the look Zaffir gave me back at the cabin. I was starting to feel a lot of very confusing, very selfish things. And I needed to get myself under control before I ruined this tenuous but special alliance.

"Come have a seat," Thorne called, voice easy but eyes watchful as he sat beside Briar and gestured toward the fire.

Ezra's fingers slid naturally into mine, and I didn't resist. I didn't want to. When we sat down together, I could feel the weight of their gazes, not harsh or judging, just... noticing. Curious.

"So," Thorne said, with a glance at our joined hands, "You two an item?"

My stomach twisted, and I felt the air rush out of me. I didn't look at Ezra. I couldn't. Would he be upset if he knew how I felt when Thorne grinned at me, or when Briar brushed her fingers against mine as she cleaned the blood from my skin? Would he still care for me if he knew I'd shared something raw and personal with Zaffir that no one else had ever seen? I wasn't trying to collect hearts like trophies, I just didn't know how to stop needing the way they made me feel.

"I'll protect her," Ezra said instead. His voice was steady, grounded. "I care about her, and I want her to survive this. That's all that matters."

I turned, and the intensity in his eyes made it hard to breathe.

"How convenient," Thorne replied, not unkindly. "I feel the same way."

The two of them locked eyes, and something unspoken passed between them.

"So we're all in agreement then," Briar said brightly, breaking the tension as she turned the meat over the fire.

I looked around at the three of them, the smoke curling between us in lazy spirals.

"Why?" The word tumbled out before I could stop it, raw and unfiltered.

Their heads turned toward me, eyes sharp with attention. I immediately regretted the interruption. "I'm sorry," I said quickly. "I don't mean to sound ungrateful. I just...why me? Why are you all so focused on protecting me? What did I do to deserve that?"

It wasn't the time to question allies, not when loyalty was a rare commodity. But I couldn't help it. Their care didn't feel transactional. It felt real. And that terrified me more than it comforted me.

Briar was the first to speak, her voice soft but sure. "I can't speak for the boys," she said, shifting a little closer. Her eyes, green and steady, held mine without wavering. "But I've always been good at reading people. But you, Hollis..." She reached out and brushed a loose strand of hair behind my ear, her fingers lingering for half a second too long. "You wear your heart on your sleeve. Brave, open, and beautiful. And I.." she paused, swallowing a lump in her throat. "I really like the person I see when I look at you. I trust her."

I felt the sting behind my eyes before I could blink it away.

Ezra shifted on my other side, his leg brushing against mine. "You didn't deserve what happened to you," he said, his voice low, like it was meant only for me. "None of it was fair. But you're still standing. You're fighting for your brother. You've got this fire in you, Bex. The kind that makes people want to stand beside you."

His fingers found mine where they rested on my lap, his touch warm and steady. "You fight like hell, and I don't want you to have to fight alone."

Then Thorne, sitting across from us with the firelight

dancing in his eyes, leaned forward just slightly. "Remember what I said about the stars?" he asked.

I nodded. He had said they had a tendency to shine on the people who earned it.

"They're shining on you," he said. "And I don't mean that in some poetic bullshit way. I mean it quite literally. You've got a way of making people sit up and pay attention. It's rare. It's worth protecting." He smiled at me. "Also you're pretty hot."

The four of us broke into an incredulous chuckle, even Ezra. And it felt light, and comfortable. Then the laughter faded. There was a moment of quiet, filled only by the soft crackle of the fire and the sound of my own heart pounding against my ribs. The tears I'd tried to hold back slipped free, hot and silent.

"Thank you," I whispered, voice thick. "All of you."

I wiped my cheeks with the back of my hand, trying to steady the emotions that swelled in my chest. "I don't know why I deserve your support. But I'm not stupid enough to turn it away. Whatever happens, I've got your backs too."

Briar gave me a slow, radiant smile and laid a hand on my knee. "Good. We'll hold you to that."

Thorne's lips quirked into that charming, crooked smile of his. "I'd say we're officially a team now. Let's get matching tattoos!"

I chuckled and Briar playfully smacked his shoulder. Ezra didn't speak, he just leaned closer, his thumb drawing gentle circles on the inside of my wrist. His eyes flicked to my lips for the briefest of seconds, and the breath caught in my throat.

A team?

I think I liked the sound of that.

My map was right. A fact I was ridiculously proud of. It felt like a validation of my usefulness. I was starting to think maybe I really did stand a chance in winning for my brother and getting him what he needed.

When we finally broke through the forest, the towering, gleaming golden gates of Praxis came into view. A girlish giggle bubbled out of me, the absurdity of it all hitting me at once. We were here. We made it.

I exchanged a look with Briar, Ezra, and Thorne, and in that instant, everything seemed to shift. The excitement between us was palpable, like we were all running on the same high-frequency adrenaline. Without another word, we took off, sprinting together toward the gates.

The closer we got, the louder the roar of the crowd became. I hadn't even noticed they were there, waiting for us to arrive. I could hear them calling my name, our names, like they knew we were coming just from the cameras strapped to us.

We broke through the last few meters, and as we neared the threshold of the gates, I slowed. We came to a halt just ten feet from the line that marked the end of this trial, this chapter of our journey.

I looked over at Briar and Thorne, heart pounding in my chest. I'd gotten us here. But I couldn't be the one to cross the line first.

"Go," I urged, my voice steady despite the racing of my pulse. "You deserve it."

They exchanged a silent glance, a conversation without words. Then, Briar took a step forward and grabbed my hand, her grip firm and warm. Her eyes were soft, full of understanding.

I caught Ezra out of the corner of my eye, and his quiet

clearing of his throat didn't go unnoticed. He stood beside me, waiting, his face unreadable.

"Together," Briar whispered, squeezing my hand.

"And that leaves us, big guy," Thorne said behind us, clapping a hand on Ezra's shoulder. He sounded light, teasing. "I don't suppose you wanna hold my hand too?"

I could practically hear the eye-roll in Ezra's silence before he elbowed Thorne in the ribs. There was a brief moment of huffing, followed by the unmistakable sound of Thorne's chuckling. "Okay, no hand-holding... Got it."

The smile that tugged at my lips didn't leave. Even in this crazy, intense moment, there was warmth between us, unexpected but undeniable.

Briar led us forward, her hand still holding mine, though I could tell she was trying to let me step over the line first. But I wasn't going to let her have that. I nudged her just enough to make sure she crossed before me.

Her sneer, the kind that said *I know what you did*, was too late.

When we crossed the line, I felt the collective exhale of everything that had led up to this point. I scanned the crowd, the sea of faces cheering and clapping, but my eyes found Zaffir first.

There, at the edge of the crowd, he stood, his camera focused on us, his eyes shining with relief. He gave me a smile, and I returned it, unable to stop myself. His nod to me was reverent, thankful, proud.

The crowd erupted, their cheers deafening. And though I knew their applause was for surviving the horrors that they themselves put us through, I allowed myself to let it wash over me. I soaked in the sound, the praise, because we had earned it. It hadn't been easy. But we made it. And that was something worth celebrating.

CHAPTER
THIRTEEN

THORNE

A SHOWER HAD NEVER FELT as good as it did now. The warmth of the water poured over my head and shoulders, sluicing away the layers of dirt, blood, and grime that had clung to me like a second skin after nearly a week in the forest. I braced a hand against the tile wall, watching the water swirl dark at my feet before it disappeared down the drain carrying with it every ache, every cut, every moment of fear and adrenaline that had led me here.

For the first time in days, I felt like myself again.

Briar ended up finishing eighth and I got tenth. We probably could've pushed for a better spot if we'd actually hustled at any point before the last few miles. If we'd strategized harder, treated it like the desperate race it was meant to be. But honestly? I didn't regret a damn thing about the slow and steady approach we took. Because every night around the campfire, every lazy morning conversation, and unplanned stop in the woods gave us more time to get to know her. Brexlyn Hollis.

God, even just thinking her name now sent a pulse of something electric through me. Shivers down my spine and thoughts that had no business creeping into my mind. The way she felt pressed against me in the shadows of those trees, her breath catching, her gaze locking on mine like gravity itself had tethered us together in that moment. The way her lips parted like she was just about to...

I would have. I was going to. I could still feel the ghost of that almost-kiss. The fire of it. But then her fucking bodyguard had to show up.

Ezra. Tall, brooding, possessive. I'd half a mind to knock him clean out when he appeared, all protective glower and sharp words. But what gutted me, what made the anger coil into something uglier, was the way Bex had sunk into his arms like it was instinct. Like he was her safety and comfort wrapped in flesh and muscle.

I'd heard her a few nights when she thought we were both asleep. Those quiet, broken sobs she buried in the forest floor. And I knew she was crying for him. I wanted to reach for her, tell her it was okay. That she wasn't alone. That she had me. That she had Briar, too. That there was a whole damn world outside the orbit of Ezra that was ready to hold her up. But I didn't. Because she still needed him.

But it didn't stop me from hoping. Hoping that the longer she was around us, the more she learned the secrets to my sharp edges and smart mouth, my stubborn heart and fractured past, the more she saw me, maybe one day she'd need me too.

Not instead of him. Not in competition.

But maybe in addition.

I let my mind wander to the memory of her soft skin, the hitch in her breath as I pressed my hardening cock against her. She welcomed my touch, she was desperate for it. I let my hand drift lower and wrap around myself, hard and thick at the simple thought of her. The warm water fell over my skin, and the slick slide of soap against my palm made each touch smooth, effortless, and sinfully indulgent. I let my head fall forward against the tile, eyes slipping shut as the memory of Brexlyn Hollis spurred me forward.

Those eyes. The kind of blue that made the sky look washed out and forgettable. The way they sparkled when she was amused, the sharp, defiant glint they held when she challenged me, and the soft, vulnerable flicker she tried so hard to hide when she thought no one was looking. Her long champagne colored hair that framed her face. And her lips... thick, lush, like they were made to be kissed, bitten, ruined.

But it wasn't just her face, or the sway of her hips, or the curve of her waist that drove me out of my mind. It was her mind. That brilliant, relentless, sharp-as-fuck mind of hers. Nothing got me going like watching those gears turn, like seeing the way she absorbed everything I told her about the forest, every plant, every track, every creature. She wasn't just listening to me ramble. She learned. She remembered. And the more she did, the more I wanted to give her things to remember.

I wanted to lean in, whisper devilish, filthy things in her ear, and watch the way her breath hitched. Wanted to put my hands on her in ways no one ever had and feel her arch into me. Wanted to leave marks, memories on her skin and in her head, so no matter how far she went no matter whose arms she collapsed into, my touch and my words, would be the ones haunting her.

The fantasy of her, hair damp with sweat, lips parted,

breath ragged as she moaned my name, flashed through my mind, and a groan tore from my throat. I worked myself harder, faster, chasing the thought of making her mine, even if only in fantasy.

And when the pleasure crested sharp and hot behind my eyes, it was her name that spilled from my lips in a low, desperate growl.

I killed the water and stepped out, grabbing a towel and slinging it low around my hips. The air outside the bathroom was cooler, and goosebumps rose along my skin as I moved down the hallway. I could hear Briar's voice carrying from the main room, something lighthearted directed at Char, our ever-present camera guy. Briar was probably cracking some joke or recounting one of the million near-death experiences we'd somehow spun into an adventure this week in a ruse to get Char to lower his guard and tell us something about the Architects or the next Trial. When people feel comfortable, they let their guard down. Simple as that. And Briar was great at making people comfortable.

I didn't bother joining in on the conversation. It wasn't my scene, never had been. I kept my head down and made for my room, slipping inside and locking the door behind me with a soft click. The quiet was instant. I exhaled, leaning my back against the door for a second before pushing off and crossing the room.

Briar had always been the people person, the one who could smooth-talk a soldier out of his weapon or sweeten a tense situation with nothing but a smile and a clever story. She had this easy way about her, like every conversation was a game she already knew how to win. And people ate it up. Hell, half the time so did I. But that wasn't me, I never had the energy for that social shit.

People were exhausting. The fake smiles, the unspoken

rules, the way you had to tiptoe around words and egos like navigating a minefield. Conversations always came loaded with invisible strings and ulterior motives you had to unravel before you could get anywhere real. I wasn't built for that kind of dance. I didn't care for the performance, the half-truths, the carefully curated versions of ourselves we presented like masks at a masquerade.

Give me something solid. Concrete. Something that made sense. Math, science, those were my languages. In those worlds, you didn't *almost* find the answer. You either did, or you didn't. It was clean, unburdened by emotion or messy histories. No guessing what someone really meant, no gut instinct trying to decipher tone or meaning. Just numbers. Just facts. Just proof.

But with people? Too many variables. Too many factors you couldn't control or predict. Feelings. Trauma. Lies. The impossible-to-track chain reactions of words spoken decades ago, still rippling through their bloodstream. No matter how well you thought you knew them, you never really know anyone. Not entirely.

And that... that's what made someone like Brexlyn Hollis so goddamn dangerous. Because even with all her painful memories, I wanted to know her. To figure her out. To run the equation of her and solve for X. And something told me that girl was going to ruin me long before I ever got the chance.

Just as I finished tugging on the silk Praxis-issued pants, a soft knock sounded at my door. I didn't need to ask who it was. There were only three of us in the house, and besides I could always feel Briar coming. It was like some invisible thread stretched between us, tugging gently to let me know she was near. She was a part of me in a way no one else would ever be. Well... maybe someone else could...

I opened the door just in time for her to brush past me,

claiming a seat on the edge of my bed without waiting for an invite.

"Yeah, sure," I drawled sarcastically, closing the door behind her. "Come right in, make yourself at home."

"Figured we could watch the coverage together," she said with a shrug, already reaching for the remote like it was her room. Her easy confidence was both infuriating and comforting in its familiarity.

I hadn't turned on the coverage since we got back. Part of me didn't even want to see it. Praxis had a way of twisting everything to fit their own narrative.

"Char says your little spat with Ezra got caught in full view on my feed," Briar added casually, flicking through channels until she found the right one.

I sighed, climbing onto the bed beside her. "Of course it did. Can't wait to see what kind of villain edit Char cooked up for me. Bet he painted me as the obsessive, girl-stealing asshole." I tried to keep my tone light, but there was a sharp edge under it I couldn't quite blunt.

Briar glanced over, reading me like she always did before glancing away. "Char told me Canyon's camera guy came to him after we found Bex," she said, keeping her eyes on the screen. "Offered to cut our footage for the rest of the trial."

I frowned. "Why the hell would he do that?"

Briar shrugged, her expression unreadable. "No idea. Char was just happy to 'have some time off from the cutting room.' Could be a setup. Could be nothing. But either way, it's weird."

It was more than weird. The idea that another Collective's operator was holding the strings on our public image made my stomach twist. Brexlyn didn't need much help from clever editing to win hearts, but what about us?

"It's starting," Briar said, pointing to the screen.

We both fell silent as the feed opened with the row of us lined up, blindfolds on, backpacks strapped tight, sitting in the humming belly of the plane. It was surreal, watching it now and seeing it for the first time despite having lived it. I saw Briar lean over to whisper our plan to me, her face grim. Then we were at the door, one after another, and I felt the phantom drop in my stomach just watching us fall.

The coverage cut seamlessly between Challengers, sharp edits of screaming voices and flailing limbs, and when the footage switched to a particularly panicked individual, my breath caught. His panic was raw, his voice high and cracking as his chute tangled, snapping against him uselessly. This was Dominic. The sounds he made were horrible, terrifying. He screamed for help. Screamed for his family. My eyes stung. The only saving grace was that his camera couldn't catch his face. I knew what was coming and still, I closed my eyes before it happened. Didn't need to see it. But I heard the impact.

When I opened my eyes again, I heard my own voice call for Briar. They showed our reunion, and to my surprise, the edit was... kind. Heartfelt. The moment played genuine and unfiltered, the way it had actually felt.

Then came the part I braced for, when we found Dominic. Briar and I approached, then when we switched off our camera feeds, instead of cutting away, the footage shifted to his perspective. From his fallen body, we watched ourselves work in quiet, reverent movements, cutting his chute loose, pulling him free from the debris and wreckage, laying him out with care. Didn't make a spectacle of it. Just let it play out in silence from his 'eyes' until we lowered the chute over him, and the screen went dark.

The coverage moved on, showing other landings, other faces, but I barely registered them. I glanced sideways at Briar, catching the same stunned expression mirrored on her face.

"That was..."

"Respectful," Briar finished quietly.

I let out a breath I hadn't realized I'd been holding. "Not exactly Praxis' style," I muttered. "But... I'm glad they showed Dominic's story like that."

Briar gave a small nod, the kind of wordless agreement only we could have. No debate, no over-explaining. Just shared understanding.

The footage shifted, and the second Bex appeared on-screen, both of us stilled. There she was, dropped through thick trees and branches, the limbs clawing at her as she fell through them, the kind of landing that could've wrecked anyone else. But not Bex. She moved like her instinct was as attuned to the woods as ours, pulling herself free, finding cover, and checking her gear with practiced, shaking hands.

The audio stayed close, catching every quick, shallow breath and the soft grunts of pain and effort as she fought through it. And with every strained sound, something in my chest tightened. It wasn't pity. It was... respect. Pure and sharp, building like a quiet storm inside me.

The footage carried on, and Briar and I watched in heavy silence as the other Challengers battled their way through The Wilds. Devrin Marx from Saltspire moved like a machine, all determination and stubborn resolve. He barely stopped to sleep, never lingered to tend wounds. Just pushed forward with that dead-eyed intensity Saltspire was famous for.

Then there were the Horizon Challengers, the elected and the chosen, who managed to find each other on the second day. From then on, they moved together, a tight alliance, navigating the woods with focus. Their pace was relentless. No doubt they had intentions to win.

And then came Winnie.

The camera cut to feed from the chosen Steelheart Challenger, an elderly woman whose age alone should've disqualified her. She'd landed hard, shattering her leg. The footage lingered as she tried to crawl, dragging herself through the dirt. She called out again and again, voice cracking and wild with desperation.

Her camera tilted up to catch the open sky as she lay back, exhausted and broken. She kept trying to move, to sit up, to call out for someone, anyone. But her voice faded over the hours as the sun set and the darkness blanketed her. And when the snarls began in the distance, thick and low like some nightmare thing, she panicked.

Briar, without a word, grabbed the remote and muted it. We both turned our heads, looking away from the screen, away from the inevitable end neither of us needed to watch.

The room felt heavier for it, the air thicker.

When we finally looked back, the footage had shifted to Ezra. He was crashing through the underbrush, branches whipping at his face, calling out Bex's name. There was a desperation in his voice that settled uneasily in my stomach. Briar caught my eye, and we shared a look.

"Bex, please. Where are you," Ezra muttered to himself, his voice cracked and raw. "Please... be okay."

"Damn. They're really making him out to be this big protector. They're really gonna make me look like an asshole, aren't they?" I asked rhetorically. They were painting Ezra this man on a mission to save the girl, meanwhile, I was gonna be the cocky sonofabitch that swoops in.

I can see it now.

Hell, I'd probably do the same thing if I were trying to get ratings. Dammit.

Briar put a comforting hand on my shoulder, but didn't respond. She knew I was right.

The feed cut to Bex's point of view in full flight, sprinting through the trees, a snarl chasing after her like death itself. I leaned forward, every muscle in my body tensing as if I could leap through the screen and help her all over again. The moment in the edit was just as intense as I remembered it, the fear in her cries, the sound of her breath hitching in her throat. And then, Briar's camera caught me swinging that rock, cracking it against the creature's skull and dropping it in a heap at her feet.

But what came next surprised the hell out of both of us.

The edit didn't cut away to some Praxis-approved narrative beginning to paint me as this villain. It lingered. It moved between the three of us, Briar, me, and Ezra, all focused on Bex in our own ways. Briar's hand steadying her shoulder and cleaning her wounds, my voice murmuring that she was okay, and working to provide meals for her, Ezra's panicked search and desperate need for her safety. The footage painted a picture of people showing each other genuine care. Of people looking out for each other in a place designed to tear them apart.

And the weirdest part? It made it look like our only motive was Bex's safety. Briar, me, and Ezra, protectors rather than competitors.

The footage shifted to a quiet moment the three of us shared around one of our late night campfires. We were laughing, joking, teasing, flirting, on my part mostly. It was easy, simple, and fun.

"I told her about Felix," Briar whispered.

I turned to face her, my jaw slack.

We never talked about Felix. That was the rule, unspoken, but solid as stone. He'd tried to take us when we were kids, and Briar and I hadn't seen him for what he was. That blind spot, that failure to recognize the danger in him, was her deepest shame. She never listened when we tried to convince her that it wasn't her fault. I knew that event changed her.

And as far as I knew, she hadn't spoken his name in nearly twenty years.

But now she'd told Bex?

"What'd she say?"

"That it wasn't my fault," she replied.

"Like I've been saying for two decades," I retorted.

"Yeah, yeah," she said, waving me off.

"You must really trust her," I said carefully.

She met my eyes. "Don't you?"

I didn't hesitate. "Yeah," I said. "I do."

Briar's eyes fixed back on the screen and I knew we'd likely never speak Felix's name again. Fine by me. But a part of me was glad that someone outside of us two knew about it. Maybe now that she's shared it, it wouldn't weigh as heavy with an additional person to help carry the weight.

I glanced back at the screen just in time for the big show-down. I braced myself when I pulled her against a tree and caged her in. I waited for the fight, the anger...

But it never came.

The footage cut from Bex and I pressed together in tense silence, thinking we'd heard something in the woods, to Bex calling out for Ezra. She threw herself into his arms. Like it was a happy reunion.

I turned my head, locking eyes with Briar. Her brow was furrowed, mirroring my confusion.

The Ezra on the screen thanked us for protecting her. And on camera, we swore we'd do it again.

"I'll protect her," Ezra said on the screen. His eyes looked at Bex with a type of longing that I understood intimately. *"I care about her, and I want her to survive this. That's all that matters."*

"How convenient," I chimed in, my own eyes finding her like she was the light and I was a damn moth. I smiled at that thought. *"I feel the same way."*

Then Ezra met my eyes. It was a silent conversation, but if I read it correctly. He was telling me that the way I felt about Bex was okay. That he wasn't upset that she had more people in her corner. For a moment, it felt like he was giving me his blessing to show her I cared.

"So we're all in agreement then," Briar added. The edit flashed around the campfire, showing each of our faces. Determined and connected. A team.

Then the coverage moved on, away from us, away from her, to the Challengers who took the top seven spots.

"What the hell was that?" I muttered, still staring at the screen.

"I have no idea," Briar said, her voice low, wary.

"We looked like a team," I said slowly, the words tasting strange in my mouth. "The four of us. That edit made it look like we were a damn team."

"A team whose sole mission was to keep Brexlyn Hollis alive," Briar added, her eyes still on the now-muted footage. "We might need to send a thank you card to that Canyon Collective cameraman."

I gave a short nod, the wheels already turning in my head.

"Maybe we can be though," I started, trailing off.

"Be what?" Briar asked, her brow lifting.

"A team," I said, meeting her gaze. "Maybe we actually work with Ezra. Keep her safe. Keep each other safe. Alliances aren't the worst thing to have out here. And you said it yourself, you trust her."

Briar studied me for a long moment, narrowing her eyes. "You sure this isn't just about spending more time with her?"

I smirked. "Why can't it be both?"

She shook her head, the faintest hint of a grin tugging at her mouth. "Get some sleep, Thorne."

Briar stood from the bed, the mattress shifting under her weight as she moved to the door. Before stepping out, she glanced back.

"The trials are only just getting started."

CHAPTER
FOURTEEN

ZAFFIR

My hands trembled at my sides as I crossed the threshold into the Show Center. I didn't come here often, I didn't need to. Most of my work was done from the safety of my own quarters or sent off through encrypted channels. But today was different. Today, I'd been summoned. No explanation. No preamble. Just an insistent message that left my stomach twisting itself into knots.

The place was alive with motion. Technicians hurried between workstations, Architects barked orders over comms, and massive digital boards flickered with maps, schematics, and footage from the last trial. I could feel my heart pounding in my chest, loud enough that it felt like the sound might give me away. I wasn't supposed to be nervous, I worked for them, for Praxis, for the system. But lately, with every step I took, I felt less like an insider and more like an intruder.

As I weaved through the organized chaos, my eyes darted to the boards. Trial layouts. Projected survival rates. Trap placements. My fingers itched to grab a data slip, to memorize a camera angle, anything I could feed back to Brexlyn to give her even a sliver of an advantage. But I forced myself to look away. That was a good way to get yourself dragged into a room you didn't walk back out of.

At the front desk, a petite woman with sharp eyes and a clipped tone barely looked up. "Can I help you?"

"Zaffir Stark," I said, trying to keep my voice steady. "I was called for a meeting."

She tapped a few keys, her expression unreadable. "You're expected. Conference room's through there. She'll be with you shortly."

I managed a stiff nod and made my way toward the door, my mind already racing through every possible reason they might have dragged me in for a face-to-face. Maybe they found out I took over the Darkbranch Collective's feed during the trial. Maybe someone noticed how I cut the footage to protect the Grey siblings' interactions with Ezra, how I buried the moments that could've sparked a feud and boosted the drama. The higher-ups loved their rivalries, betrayals, bloodied faces and desperate alliances. But that would've put Brexlyn right in the center of a storm she wasn't ready for. I wasn't going to let that happen. No, it was better for her to be seen as part of a strong alliance. A team. Her and her Wildguard, as I dubbed them.

And now, maybe they knew.

I slipped into the conference room and froze for a moment, taking in the space. It was... luxurious. The kind of room no one from the outer Collectives would ever see, let alone step foot in. Thick velvet curtains muffled the sounds from the center outside. A stained glass lamp cast a warm, honeyed glow across a polished wood table that looked like it could stop a bullet. The air conditioning hummed softly, making the hair on my arms rise.

This was the kind of privilege my status bought me. And for the first time in years, I actually noticed it.

Ever since Brexlyn crashed into my life, I couldn't stop seeing the fractures in this place. The things I'd stopped questioning. The comforts I never realized others bled and died for. Every step I took here felt heavier now. Like I was carrying something with me that I hadn't been before.

I sat down and let my gaze drift to the far wall, where a row of portraits displayed some of the most decorated champions in Reclamation Run history. Their faces were etched into the collective memory of Praxis, legends born from blood and broadcast. Among them, Edgar Soonwater of Ember Collective stood out. He was a Challenger when I was still a kid, a name spoken in every household, his victories recounted like bedtime stories. My friends and I would reenact his greatest hits on the playground.

Edgar had done what no one else had. Sixteen trial wins out of twenty, placing in the top five for the rest. An impossible streak. A miracle by Run standards. After his final victory, you couldn't turn on a screen without seeing Ember. Footage of grateful families receiving resources. Smiling children holding baskets of produce, people receiving medical assistance. Edgar had saved them.

Back then, I believed it. I remember thinking how thrilling it was that he won. How good it must feel for Ember, to finally get their due. But now I see it for what it was. Even with Edgar's record-breaking performance, even with the blood, sweat, and bone he left on those trial grounds, the footage of Ember was still a pale shadow compared to Praxis. The Collective's streets were cracked, their power grids unstable, their medical supplies rationed to the ounce. And the next year, the resources all went away again, waiting for another Challenger to fight for them. Meanwhile, Praxis broadcasted from towering spires and silk-lined conference rooms, sipping from glasses no one else could afford.

The Collectives could fight, bleed, and die a thousand times, and they'd still never catch up. The game was rigged long before it ever started.

It wasn't right.

It wasn't fair.

I understand that now.

And if this meeting was the end of my career, if they pulled my feed rights, cut my access, erased my name from every server and clearance list, how was I supposed to protect Brexlyn then? How could I keep her safe from a system designed to devour people like her?

I clenched my fists in my lap, feeling my nails bite into my palms, and fixed my stare on the table's flawless, polished surface when the door opened.

I'd only seen Archon Evanora Veritas in person a handful of times each year, usually during opening ceremonies or broadcast debriefs for the Reclamation Run. But never like this. Never with just the two of us in a room, no buffer of officials or fellow producers to soften the weight of her attention.

She strode into the conference room like she owned the air itself, her sharp gaze locking onto me the second the doors opened. She wore a soft, silver pantsuit that shimmered under the stained-glass glow of the overhead lights, every movement of the fabric catching and scattering light. Her dark hair was twisted into an intricate bun atop her head, pinned with jeweled clasps and tiny diamonds that glinted like frost.

I stood as she approached the head of the conference table, lowering my head in a bow I hoped masked the pulse hammering in my throat.

"Archon Veritas," I murmured, voice steady by some miracle. "It's an honor."

It was also probably a death sentence. But I couldn't say that part out loud.

"Zaffir Stark," she said, her voice as smooth and sharp as glass. She gestured for me to reclaim my seat with a flick of her fingers, a dismissive little motion. I obeyed, sitting slowly.

"You've been in your line of work a while now, haven't you?" she asked, tapping a single polished fingertip against the tabletop, a slow, deliberate rhythm that felt more threatening than casual.

"I have, ma'am," I answered. "I've been behind a camera for as long as I can remember."

"You like telling stories, do you?"

I swallowed. "I do."

She hummed, a small, thoughtful sound. "Yes... storytelling is one of the most useful weapons a society can wield. Don't you think?"

I said nothing, just nodded, though I could feel her gaze peeling back my skin like she was searching for the softest place to cut.

"You love your work, then?" she prompted, eyes narrowing the tiniest fraction.

"I do," I replied evenly.

"You must," she said, a faint smile curling at the corners of her mouth, not kind, but knowing. "After all, I can't imagine anyone offering to take on twice the footage if they didn't love what they do."

A chill slid down my spine. My breath hitched for a heartbeat, but I masked it as best I could.

I had to play this carefully. No hesitation. No cracks.

"I didn't take on Darkbranch's feed out of love for the work," I said, adopting the cold, clinical tone Praxis expected.

"I did it out of necessity, the need to manage my Challenger's narrative."

Her eyebrow lifted, the slightest arch of interest. She wasn't convinced yet, but she was listening. "Is that so?"

I nodded once. "Canyon hasn't elected a Challenger with a viable shot at survival in years, let alone one capable of contending for top placements. The past several seasons, my work's ended early, Challengers washed out in the first few trials, leaving nothing to edit, nothing to broadcast. No story to tell."

I leaned forward slightly, threading just enough ambition into my voice to sound like one of them. The words I was saying were things I may have said in earnest a few weeks ago, but now they felt false. "This year... I saw potential. An opportunity to prolong my time in the Run and improve my standing. Their success is my success, after all."

It felt strange, and colder than I liked, to talk about Brexlyn and Ezra like that. Stripping them down to assets and survival percentages when all I wanted was to keep them breathing.

I wondered if she could see through it. If she could feel the falsehood clinging to my words like static.

But if she did, she gave no sign. The Archon simply leaned back in her chair, that unreadable smile still playing at the corners of her lips, and studied me like a piece on a game board.

"I heard there was an altercation between the Canyon elected and the Darkbranch chosen," Archon Veritas said, her voice as smooth and sharp as glass. It wasn't a question. She already knew the truth. There was no use pretending otherwise.

I should've realized Char would scrub the footage before

passing it off to me. I was lucky he'd let me handle the edit at all. Foolish to hope he wouldn't keep eyes on it.

"Yes," I admitted quietly.

Veritas didn't react, didn't blink. "Why wasn't it included?"

I took a slow breath, tried to shrug like it didn't matter, like my pulse wasn't thundering in my ears. "Because the Canyon fool forgave him before the fight even got good," I said, keeping my tone casual, irreverent. "I had a cut with the altercation in, but it was... dull. Barely a tackle, no blood, no real fists thrown. Frankly, it was boring."

"Boring," she echoed.

"Yes, Archon," I nodded. "The real story wasn't the scuffle, it was what came after. The shared interest in protecting the girl. For some reason those three put aside their goals and focused on her. So, I thought the edit should mirror the same. And based on the viewership metrics, the commentary threads, and the rising favor scores... I believe it was the right call."

I didn't dare fidget, though my heart felt like it might punch clean through my ribs. I prayed she couldn't hear it from where she sat. Or see the panic clawing at the edge of my carefully practiced expression.

Veritas hummed, leaning back slightly, one manicured finger tracing a slow circle against the table's polished surface. "Yes... I've seen the data. It appears this...Wildguard has garnered quite the following."

I inclined my head. "They have."

It was impossible not to notice. The public was ravenous for them. The bold, reckless girl fighting for a brother no one but her could save, and the three dangerous and powerful competitors who kept risking themselves to keep her safe. The footage of Briar tending to her wounds had gone viral. Thorne protecting her from the bobcat was winning him some serious points in sympathy threads. Even Ezra, green-eyed and sharp-tongued, had charmed the viewers when he whispered reassurances to her and nearly cried with relief at finding her after days of non-stop searching.

I knew I was supposed to be jealous of it. Of the way Thorne's body pressed against hers as they hid behind cover. Of Ezra's mouth brushing the vulnerable skin at her throat when they reunited. Of Briar, her hand gently pressing against her injured face, fingers ghosting along the curve of her cheek, pulling soft, breathy sounds from her lips.

But I wasn't.

I wasn't jealous at all.

If anything, I envied that I wasn't also there. I found myself wishing I could have been there in the flesh and blood reality of it, rather than trapped behind a screen, scrubbing through hours of footage. Watching moments I'd never get to feel, never get to be part of.

I'd catch myself leaning closer to the monitors when her laugh cracked through the comms, when she smiled at something one of them muttered, when she let herself soften for half a second, and I'd realize how pathetic it was to feel so desperate for a girl who already had three other people pining after her.

But I couldn't look away.

"Our little lottery pick has certainly made quite the impact," Archon Veritas murmured, her voice silk over steel. She folded her hands beneath her chin and leaned forward, those sharp, predator's eyes pinning me in place. "We haven't had a fan favorite stand out this early in the broadcast in quite some time."

I swallowed hard, forcing a polite smile. "Thank you,

Archon," I replied, though I wasn't entirely sure it was meant as a compliment.

A long, loaded silence stretched between us. Veritas let it hang there because she wanted me to feel the weight of her gaze, the careful calculation behind those pale, gleaming eyes.

Then she spoke, her tone light but razor-sharp. "You understand, of course, that your job isn't simply to tell the best story" She let the words sink in like a knife twisting slowly. "It's to tell the right story."

I felt a cold ripple down my spine. I nodded once, careful. "Of course, Archon."

"The people need heroes and villains, Mr. Stark," Archon Veritas continued. "They need cautionary tales, and they need shining examples. We give them both. We always have. The narrative shapes loyalty. It shapes compliance."

She let the pause stretch, her eyes locked on mine, cold and deliberate.

"And most importantly," she added softly, "it shapes hope, a dangerous, volatile thing when placed in the wrong hands... or stoked too high."

Her meaning was clear, but she chose to spell it out anyway.

"Go ahead and let them root for her. For the girl with the sick little brother. Let them cheer when she stands her ground, or when her allies bleed for her. We want their hearts invested." Her lips curved into something too sharp to be a smile. "But make no mistake, what we don't want, Mr. Stark... is a martyr."

My throat tightened.

"Now, of course, with favor like hers we'll do what we can on our end to keep her in the Run for as long as possible. But say she dies in a trial," she tossed out and I tried to school my expression when imagining that horrible outcome. "We want the audience to feel sad, heartbroken. But not betrayed. Her death should make good TV, not spark riots in the streets. If you build her too high, if you turn her into something untouchable... if her fall makes the wrong kind of sound...it won't be the Collectives who suffer the consequences."

She tapped a single, lacquered fingernail against the table. *Click.*

"It'll be you." The words hit harder than any shout could've. I swallowed hard and gave a stiff, measured nod. "It will be all of Praxis."

"Understood, Archon."

"Good," she murmured, glancing toward the door. She smiled then, though it didn't touch her eyes. "It would be... in your best interest to remember that. Especially with such volatile pieces on the board this year."

"And since you have such a clear vision for their story, I've relieved the editor for Darkbranch, and you'll be taking on his duties as well. I assume that's amendable?"

I nodded. "It is, thank you, Archon."

"I'm sure we won't have to have this conversation again."

I shook my head.

She tapped a slender finger against the table, a signal more than a gesture. The door behind me hissed open, and two guards appeared in the frame.

"Good. See to it that we don't. You're dismissed."

I stood, bowed my head once more, and turned to leave, not too fast, not too slow. Just the right amount of deference.

"Oh, and Mr. Stark?"

I paused in the doorway, turning back to face her.

Archon Veritas clicked a button on the remote, and the screen behind her flickered to life. Winnie Fetter's final moments, the sweet old woman from Steelheart, filled the room. The grainy footage from her camera shook as the wolves descended. Her screams pierced the air again, the wet, snarling sounds of teeth on flesh following close behind.

The first time I saw it, it made my stomach turn. But now, with Veritas watching me like she crafted the ending all on her own, it made something deep in me splinter.

"Your Brexlyn is a lovely girl," she said, voice smooth as glass. "But you'd do well to remember that you are Praxis. And she is Collective. Wolves and lambs." As if punctuating her point a wolf snarled as it ripped into Winnie.

"Yes, ma'am." I tried to school my expression. To hide the way the violence on the screen made me want to scream, or cry, or fight.

I stepped out of the room, feeling Veritas' eyes like a weight between my shoulder blades. I walked away as fast as I could but Winnie's screams chased after me.

I had a feeling they always would.

BEX

IT TOOK another three days before the last of the surviving Challengers crossed the finish lines and reentered Praxis city limits. Two innocent lives were claimed during the Transportation Trial. Dominic, the one the Grey siblings had told me about, and Winnie of Steelheart. Poor woman never had a chance. Her age put her at a disadvantage before she even hit the ground, but I still wished her end hadn't been so brutal. No one deserved to go out like that.

I didn't watch the coverage. Couldn't bring myself to. Zaffir kept me updated though, even though he'd been a little standoffish since our return, assuring me that my little makeshift adventuring party had come across surprisingly well. Apparently, people were already calling us the 'The Wildguard.' Praxis citizens rooting for the four of us, together.

I didn't hate the sound of that. Actually...it was kind of nice.

The idea of facing what was ahead as a team felt like a

bloom of hope. I found my thoughts drifting toward them more than I probably should've. The memory of Briar's careful, steady hands tending to my wound. Thorne's infuriatingly charming grin and the way he made me laugh when everything else felt like it was crumbling. Ezra's relentless search for me, the ferocity in his protection when he finally did.

And in the quietest hours of night, when the weight of it all pressed too heavy against my chest and those memories refused to leave me alone, I'd let my hand wander lower, chasing a release that was never quite enough, but dulled the ache for a little while.

Ezra and I had slipped into a quiet, unspoken rhythm. Every morning, without fail, he'd appear in the kitchen as if summoned by my presence. We didn't exchange many words, we didn't need to. The silence was comfortable, stretched soft between us. He'd move around me with that crooked, knowing smirk, his eyes lingering a little too long, and I'd pretend not to notice the way my pulse kicked up every time our shoulders brushed or our hands grazed reaching for the same pan.

There hadn't been a repeat of that night in the hallway after the party... not yet. But it hovered between us, thick and electric in the quiet moments. In the glint of his gaze when I bit my lip. In the drag of his hand along the counter when I passed too close. We were both waiting. For what, I wasn't sure. A safer moment, or maybe a more reckless one.

And maybe, selfishly, I was waiting to figure out how to tell him about my night with Zaffir when his eyes feasted on my core as I pleasured myself to his words. Or maybe about how a sinful part of me also wanted Briar and Thorne to kiss me in the heat of the trial too. About how messy and tangled my heart had become inside this chaos. I knew it wasn't fair to him. I owed him honesty before either of us reached for something more.

This morning though, when I padded into the kitchen on bare feet, the space was empty. A small, selfish sigh of relief and disappointment left me. I made my way to the cabinet, reaching up on tiptoe for my favorite mug. The silk of my nightdress whispered up my thighs as cool air brushed higher against my skin.

And then, the warmth of a body at my back.

A firm chest pressed against me, trapping me between him and the counter. A hand reached past mine to pluck the mug from the shelf, and his hips pressed flush against my barely-covered backside. I gasped, my body going rigid and then trembling, goosebumps erupting along my arms.

"Morning," Ezra's voice rasped in my ear, low and rough from sleep. It sent a shiver down my spine, and my thighs clenched involuntarily, heat blooming low in my belly.

He set the mug down in front of me, but didn't step back. I swallowed hard, feeling the question hanging unspoken in the air between us.

Maybe we weren't waiting anymore.

"Good morning," I replied, breathlessly, trying to turn in his arms, but he kept me pinned there.

"What's for breakfast?" He asked, but his tone was deep, dark, promising.

"I.. uh... haven't chosen yet." I replied, flustered and heated. My cheeks were hot with anticipation.

"Hmmm, well, you look delicious," he said, brushing his nose against the column of my throat, drawing a downright vulgar moan from my lips. "Maybe I should have a taste."

Wetness pooled in my core, and I instinctively arched my backside against him, he groaned, his hardened cock pressed against me.

With a flat hand, he applied light pressure on the space between my shoulder blades, forcing me to bend over the counter. My breasts pressed against the hard surface and the move only jutted my ass into him even more, and we both released satisfied sounds at the friction. I was folded completely across the counter, my cheek pressed against the cool marble countertop, and I felt his hands slip to my hips, gripping me like his life depended on it.

I needed to tell him about Zaffir, Briar and Thorne. Needed to tell him I wasn't sure if I could choose just one of them, but the words died in my throat as I felt him lower himself to his knees behind me. His breath dusted over my thighs and the minute his fingers hooked in my panties and pulled them down my legs, I didn't know if I'd ever be able to speak again.

I felt his breath dance across my now exposed pussy, which I knew was glistening with wetness. Then his tongue swiped through my wetness and I bucked into the counter.

Ezra groaned with appreciation as he dove his tongue in through my folds again, and the vibration was deadly. I felt my fingers try to dig into the countertop beside me, but I couldn't find a grip.

He flattened his tongue, pressing it deep inside of me and then gently flicked it, reaching desperate parts of me with even more desperate parts of him. His fingers trailed up my legs until one found my clit and pressed down in soft commanding circles as his tongue continued to slide through my center like a ravenous man.

"Fuck, you taste even better than I remembered, Bex," he whispered against my core, pressing gentle teasing kisses to the sensitive skin that surrounded my soaked folds as his finger continued its slow, sensual circles on my clit.

I pressed my hips back, searching for him again. Needing

him to bring me to the mountaintop and jump with me over the edge.

"This is mine," Ezra growled before diving back in with ferocious, feral licks, working in tandem with his fingers to bring me to an absolute blissful moment of tension.

But my mind was screaming at me through the haze of pleasure. He thinks I'm his, and I need to tell him now...

"Ezra,' I forced out, as he slid a finger into my pussy along with his tongue. The fucking bastard really knew how to do this. "Ezra..." I started again. "I need to...tell you..." I gasped out, pressing my hips back against his face, my skin tingling with pleasure.

"Tell me what, sweet girl?" he asked between devilish swipes of his tongue.

"I... oh my," I cried out as his finger hooked inside of me and pressed against that perfect spot.

"I.. fuck," I tried to focus. "I need to tell you about Zaffir." I yelled out, and to my shock, he didn't stop his pursuit of my pleasure. His tongue pressed against my core, deeper, slicker.

"You wanna tell me about how he watched you fall apart on your fingers?" he whispered, and I felt my whole body stiffen, only to immediately come unraveled under his expert touch again.

"How did you-" I began.

"How does she taste?" I heard another voice call out from behind me, and I knew it was Zaffir. His presence fell over me like a blanket, and I knew he was getting a clear shot of exactly what Ezra was doing to me. I didn't shy away. I liked feeling his eyes on us.

"Like nothing I'd ever tasted before," Ezra said, dragging his tongue up along my slit to press against my tight puckered hole. I gasped, and bucked against the counter, my hips digging into the edge.

"Is our girl needy?" Zaffir teased, and I couldn't stop the whimper that escaped my lips. "I take that as a yes," he said, and I could hear the smirk in his voice. "Brexlyn, do you like it when Ezra puts his tongue there?"

I was too lost in sensations to even contemplate being embarrassed or confused at this situation. All I felt was pure lust and desire.

"Yes," I replied.

"Hmm, I'm a little jealous," Zaffir teased. "Ezra's gotten to taste you twice now, and I haven't."

Ezra pressed his fingers in deep curling them. I moaned. My mind was a lost storm of sensations and heightened emotions. I didn't know where my pleasure began or ended, it just was. I was mindless with desire, which is probably why I said what I said next.

"Then come and have a taste," I said, low and breathy. The sultry tone felt simultaneously like nobody I've ever known and so much like the real me.

"Is that what you want, Brexlyn? My tongue in that perfect cunt of yours?"

Fuck, his mouth was dirty. I think I loved it.

"Yes," I answered.

"Do you want both of our mouths, baby?" he challenged, and my whole body clenched around Ezra's fingers which were pulsing lazily in my pussy.

"Oh, fuck," Ezra whispered. "I think our girl really liked that thought."

Our girl.

They've both said it now. And there didn't seem to be any animosity in it.

"Ezra, sit down and put your back against the cabinet," Zaffir ordered in that commanding tone I remembered so well from our night in my room. Ezra's fingers and mouth slipped from my core, and I missed the touch instantly. I felt Ezra reposition himself between my legs, his head leaning against the cabinet below me. Zaffir gripped my hips, and pulled me back, repositioning me so that my clit was pressed directly against Ezra's waiting and willing mouth.

"Oh!" I cried out as he ravaged my clit with his expert tongue.

"That's it, Brexlyn," Zaffir murmured, his voice rough, low, and threaded with a hunger he wasn't even trying to hide. "You're doing so well."

I felt him move behind me, his body brushing against mine, heat radiating off him, his breath at my ear. My pulse stuttered, then quickened, my skin alive with every place we touched.

"Are you ready for me?" he asked, and there was something almost reverent in his tone.

I nodded, the air thick and electric between us.

But he didn't move right away.

"Are you sure?" he whispered, voice tightening, as if it hurt to ask. "You know who I am. You know what this is. Praxis and Collective..."

I whimpered as Ezra continued to swipe his tongue against my clit.

"People would hate us for this... punish us for it. You'd be at risk. We both would," Zaffir whispered, somehow making the warning feel seductive.

There was a flicker of hesitation in his touch then, like some last-ditch instinct to pull away before we crossed a line neither of us could ever come back from.

But his words didn't douse the fire in me, they fed it.

I turned my head enough to meet his gaze, my voice steady even as my heart pounded.

"I'm sure," I said, meaning it more than I'd ever meant anything.

Something in his expression shifted then like a storm breaking open behind his eyes, lust and defiance crashing together.

"Good," he growled, lowering to his knees. "Because I've never been the best at following rules."

Then his tongue swept through my slit and I bucked against the two of them as they both drank my pleasure from me. Their faces must have been close, I felt them fight against each other for the honor of devouring me, their tongues trying to reach for the same spots in my core. Then I heard the most sinful sound in the world. Their tongues clashed against each other and for a moment they stopped drinking me, and drank each other.

"Oh my God," I whispered. Feeling my whole body shiver at just how much the thought of their mouths locked, and their tongues fighting against each other with my arousal on their taste buds turned me on.

"Hmmm," Zaffir hummed, and Ezra's tongue returned to my clit. "Did you like hearing me taste your cum off of Ezra's tongue, Brexlyn?"

"Yes!" I screamed out.

Zaffir's tongue danced along my opening, dipping inside gently, and reverently. It wasn't rushed or ferocious. It was delicate and searing. Then he licked upward, traveling to the puckered hole, his tongue dancing around it, soaking it with his saliva and my slick arousal that coated it.

Someone pressed a finger into my slick opening just as Ezra sucked my clit into his mouth and Zaffir pressed his tongue against the tight opening. The sensations were overwhelming, all consuming, and the orgasm slammed into me with a weight I was glad I didn't have to carry alone. Their strong hands held me in place as I fell apart.

My release wracked through my body for several long moments. I had no idea how long I was sitting there, my core dripping onto the man beneath me, but they let me sit there and ride wave after wave of delicious release. Then I stood slowly. I carefully stepped over Ezra, and then turned to face them for the first time.

They were both staring at me, their eyes dark and searching. Hungry. Ezra stood and pressed his shoulder against Zaffir.

I flicked my eyes between the two of them and saw evidence of my release glistening on their lips. I couldn't stop myself. I sprang forward, pressing my lips to Ezra's, desperate for a taste of us. His tongue danced along mine, and the burst of flavor was so sinfully us. I pulled back, and his wide eyes with blown pupils watched back. Then I turned to Zaffir and kissed him. This was a rather filthy first kiss, but I wouldn't have wanted it any other way. His hands wrapped around my waist and he kissed me like he'd been waiting years to do so.

When I pulled back, all three of us were breathing heavily, our shoulders heaving with exertion and excitement. We watched each other for a few deliciously silent moments, then Zaffir turned to look at Ezra. The same hunger in his eyes. My nipples pebbled beneath the silk and almost painfully pressed against the fabric as I waited for them to show me what I only heard before.

"You want to see what our mouths did when you couldn't see them, don't you?" Zaffir asked me, but didn't pull his eyes from Ezra who had turned to meet his gaze, his body tense, but in an anticipatory way.

"Yes," I answered. "Show me."

Zaffir grabbed Ezra's neck, and pulled him forward, latching his mouth onto his. All three of us groaned at the same time at the erotic and perfect display. Zaffir took charge of the kiss, but Ezra pressed back with fervor and eagerness. I pressed forward, unable to help myself and brought my mouth to theirs. As my eyes closed, I didn't know who's lips were whose, or who's tongue was where, but for a few blissful moments we did nothing but chase sensations.

A knock at the door had us all breaking apart, taking a few steps from the erotic hold we just had on each other.

Our eyes met in a sort of playful and reverent agreement. No words had to be spoken yet, but we knew that there was something here. Something building and it was as special as it was dangerous.

The knock sounded again, and Zaffir cleared his throat. "I know you're in a nightgown babe, but you might be in the best position of all of us to open the door," he said with a smirk, indicating the thick outlines in their pants. God, if we hadn't been interrupted, I would have loved to get a look at those up close and personal.

I forced a smile, smoothing my hair down as best I could while padding across the room toward the front door. My pulse was still thudding from Ezra's proximity, and Zaffir's dirty words, my skin prickling with leftover electricity. I took a steadying breath and reached for the handle.

When the door swung open, my jaw damn near hit the floor.

"Hey there, roomie," Thorne grinned, standing shoulder to shoulder with Briar, both of them lugging duffel bags. His eyes did a quick, unabashed sweep of me, and his grin widened. "Damn, that's one hell of a welcome outfit."

It took me a beat too long to register what he meant, until

I remembered the silk nightdress, the way it barely covered anything, and the glaring fact that I wasn't wearing a single thing beneath it.

"We were told you knew we were coming," Briar said, her voice softer, carrying a faint note of apology as her heated gaze flicked down, then respectfully back to my face. God, I probably looked like a wreck. A well-satisfied wreck, but a wreck nonetheless.

"That's my fault," Zaffir called from the kitchen, amusement in his voice. I turned just enough to see him leaning against the far end of the island beside Ezra, both of them looking entirely too pleased with themselves. "I was on my way to tell you, but," he shrugged, smirking, "got a little distracted."

I felt my face flush hot, the kind of deep, traitorous blush that climbed down my neck.

"Can we come in?" Briar asked, one brow raised, polite despite the whole situation.

"Oh, yeah, of course. Come in," I stammered, stepping aside as gracefully as one could while half-naked in front of three very attractive men and one stunningly beautiful woman.

The two of them brushed past me, carrying the scent of cool air and woodsmoke, and I quickly closed the door behind them, pressing my back to it for a moment longer than necessary.

Briar and Thorne dropped their bags by the couch, both turning to face me at once. The sight of them hit me harder than I expected, like something in my chest unspooled all at once, and I hadn't even realized how tightly wound I'd been. I hadn't seen them since we were yanked apart after crossing the finish line three days ago, and now that they were here, standing in my living room like no time had passed, it hit me just how much I'd missed them.

Without thinking, I rushed forward and threw my arms around Thorne's waist. He let out a surprised laugh, his arms wrapping around me without hesitation as I melted into his warmth.

"Hey there, love," he murmured, one hand sifting gently through my hair, smoothing it down like he'd done it a thousand times before.

I pulled back, my eyes immediately finding Briar. She was already watching me, her expression softer than I'd ever seen it. I didn't hesitate. I stepped into her, burying myself in her arms. She held me tighter than Thorne had, like she was afraid if she let go, I'd vanish.

"I missed you too, Hollis," she whispered against my hair.

When I finally stepped back, I offered them both a small, bashful smile. "Not that I'm not happy to see you, but... what are you doing here?"

"I believe I can explain that," Zaffir's voice cut in, smooth and infuriating as ever, as he stepped out from behind the kitchen island. "I may have... accidentally gotten their camera operator fired."

I blinked. "You what?"

"There's a long version," Zaffir said, a flicker of something unreadable crossing his face, "but the short of it is I'm officially their new camera op. And since it's easier for the camera team to live in-house with their Challengers for daily check-ins, interviews, b-roll..." He gestured vaguely at the room. "Well, here they are."

"You got him fired?" Briar asked, one brow arched.

"Accidentally," Zaffir corrected smoothly.

"Because you asked to edit our footage too?" Thorne

pressed, his tone somewhere between suspicion and amusement.

I whipped my head toward Zaffir, narrowing my eyes. He what?

"Yeah… something like that," Zaffir admitted quickly, offering me a crooked, unapologetic grin. "What can I say? The fans are desperate for more Wildguard content." He shot me a look that sent a fresh wave of heat rushing through my bloodstream.

I glanced around the room, acutely aware of four sets of eyes fixed on me, each carrying their own brand of heat. It was the kind of attention that made me want to both bask in it and bolt out the nearest door.

"So, Ezra, buddy," Thorne started, his grin all sharp teeth and trouble as he tossed an arm over the back of the couch. "You wanna be bunk buddies? Unless, of course," he turned to meet my eyes, "you want to open *your* room to me, love," he added, sending me a wink that made my stomach flip.

"No," Ezra bit out, his voice low and rough, eyes narrowing on Thorne like he was seconds away from lunging and finishing what they started in the woods.

Zaffir raised a brow, glancing between them like a man watching a match he didn't mind betting on. "Okay, okay," he intervened smoothly. "Ezra can crash with me. You two can take his old room."

I didn't miss the flicker of shock, followed quickly by interest, that passed across Ezra's face. My mind went straight to ten minutes ago, and I wanted a repeat performance immediately.

"So," Thorne drawled, kicking his feet up on the coffee table like he owned the place. "What's for breakfast? I'm starving."

Ezra didn't look away from me. His gaze pinned me where

I stood, heavy with everything unspoken and sinful. His lips curled into a smirk.

"We already ate," he murmured, voice dark and loaded.

I could've combusted right there.

This was going to be... *very* interesting.

EZRA

THE NEXT SEVERAL trials were simpler in concept but no less lethal.

For the textile trial, we were herded to the top floor of a crumbling ten-story building on the outskirts of city limits. Each of us was handed a pile of mismatched fabrics, sheets, tablecloths, blankets, whatever could be scavenged. Along with a single spool of thread and one needle. The task? Fashion a makeshift rope, climb down, and hope you didn't meet the ground headfirst.

I'd never sewn a damn thing in my life. By the time I pricked my finger for the twelfth time and bled all over a pale blue sheet I was trying to attach to a fraying green tablecloth, I admitted defeat. Instead, I shifted over to help Bex however I could. She was nimble with the needle, her fingers steady and sure, no doubt from patching up the hand-me-downs she and her brother had scraped by with.

Briar and Thorne teamed up too, working side by side as if

they'd done it a hundred times before. They chatted easily with Bex, laughing like old friends. I guess surviving several days alone in a forest together does that to people. Now that they were our housemates too, I couldn't help but wonder if their bond with her would only tighten, and selfishly, I hoped mine wouldn't unravel because of it. If Bex had room for all of us in that battered heart of hers, I could learn to share her affections.

Franklin Shale, the chosen from Horizon Collective, was the first to test his makeshift line. He made it to the third patch before the knot gave out, sending him plummeting. The sickening crunch of his body hitting the ground echoed up to us. Bex buried her face in the crook of my neck, trembling as I held her. Franklin didn't die right away, we heard the screams as they hauled him off, but judging by the sounds he made, I bet he wished he had.

Cayal Orin of Ember and Fenly Nots of Stormwatch were the first to reach the ground unscathed, claiming first and second. Nile Fulton and Dani Cale from Oasis and Steelheart weren't far behind, taking third and fourth.

Once Bex finished her line and Briar and Thorne completed theirs, the three of them made the smart call to twist their ropes together for extra strength.

I volunteered to stay behind, anchoring the top of the rope until they reached the bottom. It seemed fair since I didn't actually do anything to contribute to the competition. Bex protested, but thankfully her other admirers talked her down.

She landed fifth. Thorne, sixth. Briar, seventh.

I was alone then. The last of our little group, and I knew I'd have to move slower due to my weight and my lack of an anchor. Every shaky knot I checked twice. By the time I reached the ground, Devrin Marx had already made it down, claiming eighth.

Which left me with ninth.

Not great.

But considering I was still breathing... not bad either.

The fuel trial was every bit the firestorm I figured it'd be. A classic straight-shot race from one side of an open field to the other, only this field was laced with pressure plates buried under cracked, dry earth, each one wired to barrels of unstable fuel. One wrong step and you'd light up like kindling, taking out anyone dumb enough to be standing nearby.

Bex was the first to speak up when we were brought to the starting line. "Spread out," she whispered, eyes darting between us. "I don't want one of us taking the rest down with a single bad step."

None of us argued. Even though every instinct in me screamed to stay close, to keep them within arm's reach. Truth was, none of us gave a damn about winning this one. Fuel was valuable, sure, but not worth a body count.

When the horn sounded, most of us hung back, watching as the others crept forward like they were navigating a minefield. Which, technically, they were. For a race, no one moved fast.

Beron Golader, the elected from Wildfold, was the unlucky bastard who made the first mistake. His foot must've caught a trigger because one second he was there, and the next a blast of heat and flame shot up from the ground, tossing him like a ragdoll through the smoke. The heat hit us even from a distance, and instinctively we ducked, shielding our faces from the blast. He survived, barely. He'd be down a leg, and half of his face. But I knew they wouldn't let him quit. They'd patch him up and send him back out for the next trial.

We took it slow after that. Careful steps, measured moves. By the time we crossed the line, we'd placed dead last, well except for Beron who couldn't even finish. Not a single point for our Collectives. But we still had all our limbs, still had each other.

In the nights between the trials, the five of us would record our talking heads, sometimes solo, but often together per Zaffir's insistence that the world wanted to see us as a team. We'd sit around the living room, playing games, telling stories. Getting to know each other. Thorne was a cocky sonofabitch, but he had some redeeming qualities too. And I'd be lying if that super computer brain of his didn't impress the hell out of me.

Briar was magnetic in a way that sneaked up on you. She told stories about the secrets she could pull from a room just by watching those in it. That's one hell of a skill. I got it, though. I found myself telling her more than I meant to, more than I should have, just because she got me to lower my guard. But my biggest secret? I was still keeping that one locked up tight.

And then there was Zaffir. I was honestly surprised by how not-awkward things were between us. We didn't talk about it, whatever had happened between us. Not out of shame, I don't think. It just... didn't need words. We were letting it unfold on its own terms. I've always preferred the company of women, but I've never been one to shut the door on what my mind and body wanted, no matter who it came from. And while Praxis-born men were not, and never would be, my type, there was something about Zaffir during those nights, when the camera was off. He was unguarded and real. Maybe it had everything to do with the woman we were all orbiting like moths to flame. Bex had a way of pulling truth and hunger and hope from all of us, without even trying.

Bex.

Around us, she was radiant, like some star we all orbited without even realizing it. Her laugh, light and unexpected, filled up the space between us. Every time she spoke, we all leaned in, caught in some invisible pull. I don't think she knew the effect she had on the room. Maybe that made it all the more powerful.

I found myself hoping that each trial would be short and simple, just so we could retreat back to our little safe haven. The place where 'Wildguard,' as they call us, was starting to feel less like a publicity stunt... and more like something real. Something that might last.

The produce trial was a goddamn death trap. I knew it the second we stepped inside. The stench of rot hanging in the air, the tangled mess of vines and creaking platforms suspended over a pit lined with splintered wood and rusted metal. Produce dangled from ropes and baskets above us like bait. Some of it fresh, most of it questionable. The kind of thing you'd only eat if starving... or stupid.

The goal was simple. Gather as much fresh, edible produce as you could and deliver it to the top platform without falling to your death. Once you arrived at the top platform, they made you take a bite of each piece you collected. So, if you were one of the unlucky ones who couldn't see the difference between an apple and death, then you were screwed.

Lucky for us, we had Thorne. The bastard had a weirdly encyclopedic knowledge of poisonous plants and spoiled food. "That one's good," and "that one'll kill you in five minutes," he called out, pointing as we climbed. His voice sharp, confident.

I moved fast, strength was my advantage here. While other Challengers hesitated on weak boards and frayed rope, I pulled myself up with ease, yanking baskets toward us and tossing good fruit down to Bex's waiting arms below. She was quick too, careful but not timid. I could hear her nervous gasps every time one of us slipped or a board snapped nearby. Real fear, not the performative kind. It settled something tight in my chest.

Briar nearly went over the edge at one point, her boot catching on a loose vine as a basket gave out beneath her. She slipped, body pitching sideways toward the pit. Without thinking, I grabbed her wrist, the force of it jolting through my arm as I yanked her back. Her wide, startled eyes met mine for a beat and then she nodded. No words needed.

Beron fell to his death. I knew it was coming. A climbing trial right after he'd lost a leg and nearly his life? He never stood a chance. But even if we knew what his outcome would be, it was still painful hearing his scream and the horrible sound as his body fell to the pit below and was impaled on the metal stakes.

We crossed the finish line in third, fourth, fifth and sixth, one after another. A mess of sweat, dirt, and bruises. And when we ate our share of produce, we were met with delicious tart juices, not painful convulsing death. Not like the chosen from Ember. She took a bite of her pear and within seconds she collapsed onto the platform, foam falling from her mouth which was opened on a silent scream. Her body wracked with seizure-like symptoms, and all we could do was watch until her body stilled, and her lifeless eyes dulled.

I held Bex's hand while she rested her head on Briar's shoulder and Thorne placed a comforting hand on her shoulder from behind. God help me, I really trusted these people. And it was then that I was hit with an even more striking, and painful realization. If I lost any of them, I wasn't so sure I wouldn't lose myself too. I felt simultaneously thrilled that I'd found a little family, guilty that I was replacing the one I'd lost, and terrified that I'd lose this one too.

For the next trial, they marched us out to a stretch of farmland on the far outskirts of the city, close enough to The Wilds that the treeline looked like jagged teeth against the horizon. Each of us were tethered to a single animal, and handed a dagger. I got a sheep, fluffy and clueless, while the others each ended up with calves.

The rules were to keep your livestock alive until morning.

It was easy for the first few hours. Too easy. I knew there had to be a catch coming soon. And sure enough, not long after sundown, the howls started. Low, mournful, then multiplying until the night air was thick with them. A pack of wolves. Hungry ones.

We scrambled fast, corralling our animals into a tight circle, the four of us standing guard as the wolves descended. Thorne and Briar handled themselves like they were born for it, moving with practiced ease, no doubt from their years of hunting experience they'd shared with us. Bex was focused and fierce too, though I could see the panic in her eyes whenever a wolf got too close.

Me? I was all brute force and bad decisions. I had no finesse, or foresight. After fighting a few off with pure strength, a wolf managed to come at me from another angle and sink its teeth deep into my arm before I could even react. I roared, more pissed than anything, but my idiot sheep panicked, bolting straight into the waiting jaws of another wolf. By the time Thorne cut the thing down, it was too late. Stupid animal was dead.

Bex was on me in an instant, killing the wolf still latched to my arm and hastily binding the wound with a strip of her shirt, even though it left her calf momentarily exposed. I tried to protest, but she wouldn't hear it.

When dawn finally broke, only Thorne and Briar still had their animals alive. Out of everyone else, only three more had managed the same. The rest... Well, you didn't have to look too hard to see the blood on the dirt. Only five people completed the trial, and won resources for their collectives, but at least no other Challengers died.

When we got back from that trial a few hours ago, they insisted I take the first shower and deal with the mess on my arm. It hurt like hell, so I didn't bother arguing. The hot water stung like a mother, and by the time I was clean, the dull throb in my arm had turned into a sharp, relentless ache I could no longer ignore.

I slipped out of the bathroom and made my way to the room I now shared with Zaffir. As I stepped inside, Zaffir's gaze drifted to my bare chest before snapping up to meet my eyes.

"You need to get that arm checked out," he said, his voice softer than I expected.

"I'm fine," I muttered, turning my back to him as I started to dress.

"That was a nasty bite," he added, and I heard him get up, his bare feet padding across the floor until his hand settled on my shoulder.

"Nothing I can't handle," I grunted, trying to ignore the way his touch stirred something in me I hadn't let myself think too hard about. I'd tried chalking it up to Bex's involvement, but there was something about Zaffir that hooked me in ways I didn't fully understand.

"Maybe so, but you should still let us patch you up," he said, gently grabbing my arm to study the wound. I met his eyes and I wish I hadn't because there was a heat in them that I had been quietly avoiding since that morning in the kitchen.

Before I could pull away, a knock hit the door.

I yanked my arm free, earning a smirk from him, and he crossed the room to answer it. Bex stood there, hair damp, skin flushed from the heat of her own shower, and a first aid kit tucked under one arm.

"Welcome, Dr. Hollis," Zaffir teased, stepping aside to let her in. "Our patient is being quite stubborn." She shot him a faint smile before striding over to me.

"Sit," she ordered, her tone leaving no room for argument.

My eyes betrayed me, trailing the droplets of water slipping down her throat, over her collarbone, disappearing into the dip of her robe's neckline.

She caught me looking. The unimpressed arch of her brow told me she knew exactly where my head was at.

"Yes, ma'am," I muttered, sinking down onto the edge of the bed.

Zaffir dropped onto his bed, reaching for the cursed camera I'd grown to hate having in our room.

"Come on, not now," I groaned, shooting him a glare. Bex glanced over her shoulder at him, one brow raised.

"You know I have to feed them a certain amount of behind-the-scenes fluff every day," he said with a casual shrug, fiddling with the lighting until the room was bathed in that cold, artificial glow. "And who doesn't eat up the 'tough girl patches up her big, brooding boyfriend with lingering sexual tension' bit? It's a classic."

Bex didn't even blink. She'd gotten good at tuning the cameras and the man behind them out when she needed to. Zaffir, for all his charm and easy jokes, still wore the Praxis colors, even if it didn't always feel like it fit him. Every time he picked up that camera, it was a reminder of where he came from. Where he really belonged.

The red light blinked on, and I forced myself not to look at it. I was getting better at pretending it wasn't there, but it still crawled under my skin.

The plan was working, though. The people loved us. Bex

and her loyal protectors. Crowds had started showing up outside the trial arenas, shouting our names, waving signs. Zaffir told me there were entire threads and chat rooms dedicated to us, fans cutting together clips of our moments, setting them to music like we were some tragic, war-torn romance epic. It was ridiculous.

Zaffir kept saying it was good, that getting the people on our side gave us leverage. But I noticed the nerves he had when he thought nobody was watching. I knew he was thinking of something specific when he'd warned us not to let it go too far.

I just wasn't sure what *too far* looked like anymore.

Did *too far* mean I shouldn't kiss her where the cameras could see? Did *too far* mean she shouldn't show how much she cared about all of us? Did *too far* mean I wasn't allowed to fall in love with this fierce, stubborn, maddeningly beautiful woman in front of me?

A sharp sting in my arm yanked me out of my spiraling thoughts. I hissed through my teeth as Bex pressed a cloth against the deep puncture wounds. My instinct was to jerk my arm away, but her hand shot out, steady and firm.

"I have to clean it, Ezra," she warned, voice low and certain.

I gritted my teeth and held still, biting back a curse as she wiped at the gashes with something sharp-smelling. Antibiotic, I guessed. We didn't have this kind of thing back in Canyon. This little box, packed with gauze, creams, and ointments that promised to stop infection, was a luxury the people in Canyon would have to bleed for.

I stared at the stupid red kit like it had personally wronged me. So simple. So easy. And so far out of reach for the people that Bex loved. I could have cared less about if the people in Canyon suffered after the way they treated me, but Bex's love for them had softened my own anger.

"I know," Bex murmured, catching my glare and clearly reading the thought in my head. "I feel the same." She kept working, wiping away the blood with gentle, careful hands. "If Canyon had even a few of these... we wouldn't need to dig as many graves."

My eyes flicked up to Zaffir, locking onto him as the camera rolled. I hoped he caught the look I tried to send, 'don't use that'. It wasn't directly 'anti-Praxis,' but it was close enough to be interpreted as such. And the last thing I wanted was to paint a target on her back.

So I did the only thing I could. I changed the subject.

"I'm going to help you save your brother, Bex."

Her head snapped up, eyes locking on mine.

"That's my vow to you," I said, voice rough, the words dragging out of me like they'd been waiting to be spoken. "You've become..." I swallowed, feeling that familiar ache in my chest. "Important to me. More than I know how to say."

Has it really only been a few weeks? Because my heart felt like it had carried her name forever.

"Ezra..." she whispered, her voice trembling in a way that gutted me.

I cupped her cheek, running my thumb along the soft curve of her cheekbone. Her eyes fluttered closed, and she leaned into my touch like she belonged there. Like maybe *too far* was already miles behind us.

Not wanting to share this moment with the ever-watching lens, I pressed a gentle kiss to her forehead, even though every instinct in me screamed to claim her lips. I pulled back, let her finish tending to my arm, and forced myself to keep still.

Zaffir's communicator buzzed, sharp and insistent, and he quickly shut off the camera before hurrying out of the room to answer it.

The second the door clicked shut, I reached for her. One

hand on the side of her face, I guided her to me and pressed my lips to hers. Soft. Slow. Nothing demanding, nothing desperate, just warmth and quiet, and something like healing. She kissed me back, and for a moment, the world outside didn't exist.

But then, as if she remembered what she was doing, she pulled her lips back. Pushing me away gently, she sighed, a sound that wasn't relief. It was heavy, aching, and sad.

"What's wrong?" I asked, brushing my thumb along her jaw.

"I..." she hesitated, then shook her head. "Nevermind."

She started to stand, but I caught her wrist and gently tugged her back down beside me.

"Talk to me, Bex," I murmured, my voice rough with the fear of whatever she might say.

"It's stupid," she whispered, but her eyes shimmered with unshed tears.

"I doubt that," I said, pulling her against my side, holding her there like it might stop her from slipping through my fingers.

"I just... sometimes it feels like it's all a show," she admitted, her voice barely audible. "Us. Thorne and Briar too. This whole little team the people love to root for. And I get it, it's working, it's helping, but..." She swallowed hard. "I'm starting to have *real* feelings. Honest-to-God feelings for all of you. And if it's just for the cameras... I just need to know so I don't get myself hurt."

The ache in my chest was sharp and immediate. Because my heart wasn't mine anymore, it belonged to her, and I'd gladly let it break if it meant keeping hers whole.

I reached for her face, tilting her chin up until her tear-bright eyes met mine.

"Let me be clear, Bex," I said, my voice steady even though

my heart thundered in my chest. "If I haven't made it obvious enough, then that's on me. Because I love you. And believe me when I say that I'm just as surprised as you are. Hell, I never knew I'd be able to feel something like that again, but then you happened."

Her eyes widened, a soft gasp escaping her lips.

"You..."

"Love you," I finished for her.

And I watched it happen, the way those words crashed over her, breaking through the walls she'd built. Relief, fear, joy, and something that looked like hope flickered across her face in quick succession.

"I wasn't letting myself," she confessed, voice shaking. "Fall for you. Any of you. Because I couldn't tell what was real... what was just for show."

I nodded, swallowing the lump in my throat.

"I know," I said quietly. "And honestly maybe at first I wasn't all that sure either."

She looked like that had wounded her. I gripped her hands. "Bex, I won't lie and say I didn't let Zaffir spin the story he wanted. At first at least. We agreed that if people saw a connection between us, they'd want me to stick around. Then I could protect you in the trials."

She sucked in a breath.

"So, the hand holding, the limo..." her eyes widened as if the thought returned in brutal force. "The Welcome Ball?"

"No, God, no, Bex. I was never pretending with you. I just let the camera see it. From the start, I was drawn to you. You were fascinating, beautiful, and you looked at me like I was a person, not a criminal. I hadn't felt that in a long time. But I kept telling myself that's all it was."

I ran a hand through her hair. "But then I saw you dancing with Thorne. His hands on your waist, your eyes watching him, his eyes watching you, and I felt jealousy like I'd never felt before. And desire like I'd never imagined." I took a deep breath. "And then I spent three days in the woods searching for you, not sure if you were alive, dead, or out there in pain somewhere. And that's when I knew. That this," I brushed my fingers over her cheek, "this is the only thing that's felt real to me since I won that fucking election."

She smiled at me, soft and quiet, like she could see straight through the walls I'd spent years building. Past the bravado and the bitterness I wore like armor. She looked at me like she could still see the man I used to be. The one who'd been beaten and broken. Betrayed by the only people he'd ever trusted. Sold out by the only place he'd called home.

The door opened, and Zaffir slipped back in, his usual focused swagger noticeably dulled. His expression was off, too distant, too subdued for the demanding camera op we knew.

"Hey," I called, brow furrowing. "What's wrong?"

His glazed-over eyes blinked like he was just remembering the rest of us existed. "Oh, uh... nothing."

"Doesn't seem like nothing," Bex said, already moving toward him. She placed a gentle hand on his arm, and he melted into her touch. Their eyes met, an entire conversation happening in silence between them.

"I'm okay, Brexlyn. Promise." His voice was soft, tired. "I just... I've got an extra project to prep for. And your next trial kicks off tomorrow morning."

He ran a hand through his wild red hair, disheveling it further.

"What kind of project?" I asked.

"You'll find out soon enough," he replied, and there was a weight in his voice that tightened my stomach.

"What is it?" Bex pressed before I could.

Zaffir hesitated, his gaze flicking between us. The struggle on his face was clear. His Praxis loyalty warring with whatever it was he felt for her, for us.

"I think..." he sighed. "I think we did our job too well."

"What's that supposed to mean?" I asked.

He looked at me, something like regret in his eyes. "The four of you are being sent to a live interview tomorrow night after the trial. The public demand, and the support for your little team, has gotten too loud to ignore. And the producers want to cash in while the fire's hot."

Bex frowned. "And that's a bad thing, why?"

Zaffir's jaw clenched. The truth sat on his tongue but he refused to share.

"Trust goes both ways," I told him quietly, meeting his gaze.

He nodded once, then lowered his voice. "I was... warned. About turning you into a martyr."

"A martyr?" Bex echoed, alarm in her voice.

He nodded. "You've reached a level of public favor we haven't seen in a Challenger in years. If something... happened to you in the trials now, if you died on that screen..."

"The people would riot," I finished for him.

"Exactly." He glanced toward the door as if afraid someone might overhear. "Archon Veritas wants her people invested, but not obsessed to the point of acting on it."

Bex's brow furrowed. "Wait... you think your edits made people like me too much?"

Zaffir gave a small, sad smile. "I think the people saw the real you, Brexlyn. And they fell in love with you, just like we knew they would. I think the Archon's realizing that attention breeds power. Power breeds influence. And if you wanted to, you could turn those hearts and minds against Praxis."

"That's ridiculous," Bex scoffed, shaking her head. "I could never do that."

But Zaffir caught her hands in his and held them tight. "Yes," he said softly. "You could." He cupped her cheek and ran his thumb along her bottom lip "You already have." His meaning was clear. It was obvious in the way he'd produced his edits. The way he sanitized our worst sides for the public's eyes, but kept the honest and raw truth of who we were there for all to see. The way he had shared with us secrets we never should have known... He was Praxis, sure, but Bex had him seeing things differently.

And for a heartbeat, the room felt still.

"I don't want to cause problems," Bex whispered, her voice barely carrying. "I just want to win what I need for my brother... then go home."

"And I'm going to do everything I can to help you do that," Zaffir promised, no hesitation in his voice.

The thought of her in danger made my blood run hot, made my fists clench. But the idea of someone like her, someone genuine, kind, and good, rallying the people against Praxis and their sadistic Reclamation Run, against the way they hoarded resources and dangled them over our heads like scraps to starving dogs... that was a dangerous, intoxicating idea.

"Ezra?" Bex's voice pulled me out of it.

"Yeah?"

"You said something under your breath."

"Nothing important," I shrugged. "Just... wondered what life might look like if we weren't under Praxis' boot anymore."

The words hung heavy in the air. The treasonous thought seeping into our minds. None of us spoke for a long moment, but I knew we were all thinking the same thing.

"So, what should I do tomorrow? At this live show?" Bex asked quietly. "Go out there and make people hate me?"

Zaffir shook his head, a tired sigh escaping him. "No. But it wouldn't hurt to..."

"To what?" she pressed.

He hesitated, then said it. "To thank Praxis."

"Thank them?" she echoed in disbelief just as I muttered, "Fuck that."

"I know," Zaffir said quickly, holding up a hand. "I know how it sounds. But if Archon Veritas even suspects you're becoming a threat... if she senses for a second that you might turn the people against her, the favor you've built won't save you or your brother. Not anymore."

He looked between us, eyes sharp, serious.

A line drawn in the sand.

If it were just me, I'd like to think I'd use that spotlight to speak out, to light a match and burn this whole nightmare down. But it wasn't just me. I didn't have anyone waiting for me on the other side of this, but they did. Bex did.

And it was a nice dream, imagining we could do something about the selfish rule of Praxis. But that was a risky game I don't think any of us were prepared to play.

BEX

THE NEXT MORNING arrived faster than any of us wanted.

We'd slept through most of the day after the livestock challenge, our bodies wrecked from staying up all night fending off those damn wolves. Credit where it's due, the Architects of this year's trials weren't pulling their punches. Every test felt crueler than the last.

I loved my little team. My Wildguard. And if I'm honest, there was something intoxicating about knowing other people out there loved what we were building too. But Zaffir's warning clung to the edges of my mind like a shadow in my sleep. If I wanted to protect the people I loved, if I wanted to keep Jax safe, the smart move was to keep my head down, stay quiet, and survive long enough to get home.

But that's what we've all been doing since Praxis took control, falling in line, biting our tongues, keeping low to avoid the crushing weight of their rule. And where had that gotten us? Fighting to the death for scraps, living without the basic things every human deserves, while Praxis perched in their ivory towers, drowning in luxury and excess.

I didn't realize how wide the gap truly was until I got here, walking these streets, treated like one of them, even if it was all for show. Things my people had bled for, died for, and been denied generation after generation, were handed to Praxis citizens like candy tossed to children at a parade.

It was almost enough to ignite something dangerous in me. A voice that nearly begged me to take this moment and use it. A flicker of rebellion in my chest.

Almost.

But every time it started to spark, Jax's face cut through the flames, bright and all the reason I needed to hold the line. I couldn't risk everything, not for a dream I might never live to see.

I was just one girl, after all. And one girl could never change the world.

I kept to my typical morning routine, and made my way to the kitchen where I found Zaffir. He sat at the kitchen counter, his gaze fixed on something on the screen in front of him. His eyes narrowed as if whatever he was reading was clawing at his nerves. When I stepped up beside him, he flinched, just for a second, before his shoulders eased at the sight of me.

"Good morning, gorgeous," he greeted, and I liked the way the words sent a flutter to my chest.

"Good morning, Zaffir," I answered. Finding a mug and pouring myself a cup of coffee.

"How did you sleep?" he asked. I smiled and turned over my shoulder to glance at him.

"Fine," I said. "And you?"

He nodded. "Was up pretty late preparing for this evening."

His eyes darted down to the screen in front of him, his brows furrowed and his hands fidgeting.

"What's on your mind this morning?" I asked, taking my cup and leaning on the counter opposite of him.

"Oh, nothing," he replied, entirely unconvincingly. I gave him a pointed stare until he sighed. But it was shaky and disjointed. Not at all the cool collected Zaffir I'd grown accustomed to seeing.

"I'm just...nervous. About your trial. The interview," he said, not meeting my gaze.

I nodded. "Yeah, me too."

There was panic in his gaze, I felt it from across the room, painful and thick. His breath was shallow, chest rising too fast, too hard. His fingers twitched like he was fighting his own body, like he didn't know where to put his hands.

My feet were moving before I realized it. I crossed the space in a blink, stepping up beside him and pulling his head to my chest. He came apart in my arms, every rigid muscle trembling before melting into me. I held him tighter, grounding him, anchoring him. His arms circled my waist with a desperation that stole the breath from my lungs. It cracked something wide open in my chest.

I didn't say anything. Just held him. Quiet and steady, as his breathing slowed, as the storm inside him dulled to a quiet hum. His grip loosened. His jaw unclenched. The panic passed. We just breathed together.

After a long moment, he pulled back, just far enough to look up at me. There was a pause, charged and heavy. A breath where everything could tilt, shift, break wide open. His gaze flicked down to my lips, then back up to meet my eyes.

We hadn't kissed since that morning with Ezra, both of us caught in that rush of lust and adrenaline. We'd never touched like that without that heady desire buzzing through us. I told myself that's all it was. Lust. Blind passion. It couldn't be anything else. He's Praxis. I can't feel this way about him.

And yet.

He looked at me like he was asking. Not demanding, not expecting, just asking. And I couldn't think of a single reason to say no.

So I didn't.

He kissed me. Soft. Careful. Nothing like the man who'd once ordered me to touch myself for his viewing pleasure. This kiss was real. Raw. Sweet and terrifying and perfect.

His tongue traced the seam of my lips, and I opened for him, let him in. My hands tangled in his wild red hair. He gripped my waist, pulling me closer. Always closer. Still not close enough.

When we finally broke apart, his forehead rested against mine. Our breath mingled, warm and slow.

"I'm feeling much better now," Zaffir murmured, a smile in his voice.

I laughed, soft and breathless, smacking his shoulder playfully before slipping out of his hold and stepping back behind the counter, before I could change my mind and stay right there, forever.

"I mean it," he said, smiling brightly at me. "Thank you."

I nodded. And a quiet moment passed between us. There were feelings and emotions swirling within me. None of which I was prepared to address so I changed the subject.

"Got any advice for me today?" I asked, keeping my voice light, teasing.

He met my eyes, and there was a quick flash of fear. Not for himself, for me.

"I wish I did," he said, voice low. "It's... a brutal one."

I gave a small nod. I didn't want to put him at risk. Even wanting to ask felt selfish.

"Can you tell me anything?" I probed.

He nodded. "You're not gonna like it."

"Of course I'm not," I answered, trying to hide the fear in my tone.

"They intend to take advantage of the pairs of Challengers that are still in the Run," he said. And when he noticed the confusion on my face he clarified, "You and Ezra will be partnering for this trial."

Okay. That didn't seem too bad. But there were only fifteen of us left. A few Collectives had already lost Challengers.

"Some Collective's don't have two Challengers anymore," I pointed out. The color drained from his face.

"I know," he said quietly.

And in that instant, I knew this trial was going to take a particularly rough toll.

"We'll be okay," I answered. Not surprised that I meant it. Ezra and I were a good team, I trusted him and if we needed to work together to make it through this trial, I knew we could do it. I also knew Briar and Thorne had been having each other's backs since birth, so they would no doubt be able to handle anything the Architects threw at us, too.

"Yeah," he smiled softly. "You will."

He tapped something on his screen, hesitated for a moment, then stood.

"I need to hit the restroom before we leave," he announced a little too loudly, performing for whatever unseen eyes might be watching. Then he slipped away, leaving the screen open on the counter.

I frowned after him. Was that intentional?

Curiosity pulled me around the counter, and I glanced at the display. A mess of images, parts of something I didn't recognize, tubes, hoses and nozzles that meant nothing to me.

My stomach twisted. Maybe I'd imagined the moment. Maybe he wasn't trying to tell me anything at all. And now I was being nosey.

I shook my head and turned toward the door. The transport would be arriving soon. And whatever waited for us out there, it wouldn't care whether I was ready or not.

Nova arrived, with all her effervescent and bone-chilling tenacity. She handed each of us a bag with our wardrobe for the trial. Skin-tight wetsuits, a dead giveaway that water was going to be involved in whatever was coming. Then the four of us were separated into two different vehicles. Ezra and I in one, and Thorne and Briar took the other.

We pulled up to a sprawling warehouse, its massive structure stretching for what felt like miles in every direction. Endless corridors and towering walls blurred past the windows as the transport carried us to the front entrance.

Cameras were already in place, Zaffir among them, and a crowd of eager fans had gathered, their cheers rising in a wave as Ezra and I stepped from the vehicle. Their excitement felt electric, but all I could think about was what kind of hell waited for us inside.

I searched the area for the other Challengers but saw no one as we were led through the doors and into a windowless room. Zaffir trailed behind, camera in hand, recording every tense step as the door shut firmly behind us.

The room was empty, no props, no clues, nothing but the door we'd come through and another one straight ahead. A single, ominous exit. The air felt heavy with anticipation.

Another trial, another nightmare.

A crackle over a hidden speaker cut through the heavy silence of the room.

"Welcome, Challengers," came the sickly-sweet voice of Annalese Wyley, the ever-cheerful host of this nightmare. Her voice echoed from somewhere overhead, far too chipper for what we knew was coming. "Who's ready for the next trial?"

Silence. Not a single one of us gave her the satisfaction of a response.

"Today's challenge is for water filtration systems," she continued brightly. "As all members of the Collectives know, clean drinking water is vital to the survival of a functioning society."

Especially in the desert. I stole a glance at Ezra, who gave me a stiff, terse nod. We both knew how important this one was, how it could mean life or death for our people back home.

"Beneath your feet," Annalese went on, "runs miles of submerged tunnels and canals. Hidden within those flooded passages, you'll find the scattered components of a water filtration system. Your goal is to collect the correct pieces and assemble the system before your partner is submerged in water."

The blood drained from my face. My lungs tightened.

"But you must be careful," she added, voice dipped in a mock warning. "Some of the pieces are decoys. Grab too many, and you'll be weighed down. Grab the wrong ones, and... well." A pause. "You might run out of time."

I turned toward Ezra, reading the storm already brewing behind his eyes.

"Now," Annalese's voice chimed back in, "for those of you lucky enough to still have two Challengers left, it's decision time. One of you will dive. The other will be bound in the filtration chamber. Putting your life in your partner's hands. For those Collectives where only one Challenger remains, you will be diving. Make your decisions now."

I barely had time to register the words before Ezra stepped forward.

"I'll swim," he said quickly, his voice tight but steady. "I'm fast. I can carry more, even if I don't know what's what. Let me do this. I swear, Bex, I swear I'll keep you safe."

His eyes were pleading. I could see it, could feel it.

I glanced toward Zaffir in the corner, his camera trained on us. But for a fleeting second, his expression softened, and he gave me the smallest, almost imperceptible nod.

I inhaled sharply.

"No." My voice was firmer than I expected. I turned my full gaze back to Ezra. "I've seen a water filtration system before." Just this morning, actually, but I wasn't going to say that. "I know what to look for. I can do this."

He opened his mouth, ready to argue, but stopped. Maybe it was the finality in my voice. Or maybe the fact that deep down, he knew this was the smarter call.

I gave him a small, grim smile. "I can do this."

"I know you can," he said, pushing a strand of hair behind my ear and letting his hand rest on my cheek.

"You just stay alive for me, okay?" he asked.

"You too," I whispered, and to hell with the cameras. I rose up on my tiptoes and pressed a soft kiss to Ezra's lips. For a moment, the world outside of us disappeared, no trials, no fans, no cameras. Just the warmth of his hands settling around my waist and the familiar press of his forehead against mine when we parted.

He held me there for one precious, stolen moment, both of us knowing it very well could be our last.

"Please send out the Challenger who will be staying behind," Annalese's voice echoed once more, slicing through the silence like a blade.

Ezra drew in a steadying breath, his thumb brushing once against my hip. "I'll see you soon," he promised, voice low and rough with emotion, then turned and disappeared through the unexplored door at the front of the room.

I was left alone in the quiet, every second stretching unbearably long. My palms itched. My pulse hammered. I tried to stay still, to keep my nerves invisible, but my fingers betrayed me, fidgeting with the seam of my wetsuit as minutes crawled past.

Finally, the speaker crackled again. "Challengers, please enter the room."

I swallowed hard, squared my shoulders, and moved toward the door Ezra had vanished through.

The room on the other side was massive, its walls made of smooth, cold concrete. A single, enormous tank dominated the center of the chamber, easily ten feet tall, maybe more. It was a simple hulking cylinder of reinforced glass. The whole room curved around it like an arena, with walkways leading up to it and overhead rigging clinging to the high ceiling.

And inside the tank were ten figures.

Each one was chained by their wrists to thick metal poles bolted to the tank floor. My breath hitched when I found Ezra, his emerald eyes cutting through the haze to find me instantly. His expression was fierce, burning with a kind of protective anger, but also filled with something softer, something meant just for me.

I dragged my gaze around the tank, scanning the others. Thorne stood a few places down from Ezra, his lips curling into that intoxicatingly smug grin even now. It felt grotesquely out of place, but in a strange way, I was grateful for it. The fear hadn't claimed him yet. Or if it had he wouldn't let the cameras see it.

I searched for Briar next, heart pounding, but before I could spot her, a piercing scream ripped through the room.

"No!"

It was Dani Cale of Steelheart. She bolted toward the tank, her hands slapping hard against the glass. "No, please! Not my son!" Her voice cracked like a whip in the tense chamber.

My stomach lurched as my eyes snapped to the figure she was staring at. A boy. No older than thirteen, maybe younger. His face pale, eyes rimmed red and wide with terror as he clung to the chain around his wrists. His gaze never left Dani, silently begging, sobbing without sound.

A horrible understanding settled over me like a lead blanket.

Dani's Collective partner, Winnie, was dead. And in her place, Praxis had dragged someone Dani loved into this, a son who'd never been chosen, who shouldn't have even been here.

Around the room, more cries of anguish erupted.

Gasps. Curses. Shouts. Someone punched at the tank with no luck. Someone else sank to their knees.

There were five others like the boy, faces I didn't recognize, people who weren't Challengers. A middle-aged woman with salt-and-pepper hair. A young man, barely older than me, his hand gripping the chain so tightly his knuckles had gone bone white. A father. A mother. A child. A wife.

They'd plucked them from their Collectives to fill empty slots. Collateral. Leverage. A message.

This is what happens when you fail. This is what you risk.

The air thickened with grief and fury. Tears shimmered in the eyes of hardened competitors. Rage simmered beneath trembling hands. I felt it too, a storm rising in my chest, sharp and bitter.

But through the horror, a single, selfish relief clawed its way to the surface…It wasn't Jax. My brother wasn't in that tank.

I let myself have that one breath, one quiet, desperate thank you to whatever force of chance had spared him this time. I lifted my gaze, locking eyes with Ezra once more. He was still watching me, his expression unreadable through the fogged glass and swirling water, but his eyes were unwavering. I clung to that look, let it steady me.

This was too far. Too much. The tiny spark of unrest that had been growing in my chest flamed to life.

Around us, Praxis guards moved in, shoving the other Challengers back into formation with rough, unflinching hands. Boots thudded against the grated metal catwalk we stood upon, a caged floor suspended high above a rushing channel of water. The current below snarled like a living thing, violent and relentless.

Annalese's voice crackled over the loudspeakers again, unnervingly cheerful against the charged, frantic air. "You must retrieve the pieces of the water filtration system and return them here. Only then can you release your partner from the tank."

I felt my pulse surge, my fingers twitching at my sides.

"You have..." she began, but her voice was drowned out by a massive, metallic groan. A thick, rusted pipe leading to the tank lurched open, and water burst forth with a deafening roar. It gushed into the chamber, cascading in fat, cold streams as the tank began to fill. Annalese's voice barely cut through it.

"...until they drown. Go!"

Before I could move, the floor beneath my feet split open.

I barely had time to suck in a startled gasp before the ground vanished and frigid water swallowed me whole. It hit like a fist, stealing the warmth from my limbs and leaving my skin prickling and numb. I kicked hard, breaking the surface long enough to snatch a long thick breath before diving under again.

There was no time. No margin for hesitation.

Ezra was counting on me.

I propelled myself through the submerged tunnel, cold water biting at my skin, my lungs already aching from the shock of the drop. The walls of the narrow shaft scraped against my shoulders as I swam, and each twist in the passage forced me deeper into a maze of submerged corridors.

It wasn't a straight shot.

These canals were winding, disorienting, a labyrinth designed to waste time we didn't have. There were sharp turns and dead ends, narrow channels barely wide enough for me to squeeze through. And nowhere... nowhere... to breathe.

My chest burned, pressure building as my lungs begged for air. I fought against the rising panic clawing at the edges of my mind. Not yet. Not yet.

I spotted an offshoot just off to the left.

Kicking hard off the nearest wall, I headed toward it and burst into a tiny, domed chamber where a pocket of stale air waited like a blessing. I gasped, the air tasting sour and metallic, but it filled my lungs just the same. I coughed, clinging to the rough stone wall as my body trembled with adrenaline. I spied on the peak of the dome a camera, pointed down at me. I wanted to look away from it. Not make eye contact with the people watching and waiting for me to fail.

Something caught my eye at the bottom of the chamber, a glint of metal or hardened plastic.

I dove without thinking, hands outstretched, fingers closing around a cold, cylindrical object. It was heavy and slick, but I clutched it tight and surged back toward the pocket of air, breaking the surface with a sharp gasp.

I turned the object over in my hand, water streaming down my wrist. Recognition struck fast.

This was one of the tubes from Zaffir's diagram. I could see it clear as day in my mind, thanks to the picture he provided me with this morning.

I needed to thank him for that if I made it out of here alive.

No. Not if.

When.

"One down," I whispered, my voice ragged and hoarse in the confined air pocket. No time to savor the win.

I drew in another deep breath, pushing off the wall and plunging forward into the next stretch of tunnels, my mind already calculating, how long until the next air pocket? How many pieces were out there? How fast was the tank filling?

No time.

I swam harder.

By the time I reached the next pocket of air, my chest felt like it was caving in. Every muscle in my body screamed for rest, for warmth, for oxygen. I'd come across two decoy pieces and one nozzle I actually needed. Three more pieces. Three more, and then I had to somehow find my way back to the tank. Back to Ezra. The thought alone made my head swim, whether from determination or the steadily growing lack of air, I wasn't sure.

I probably lingered too long in that tiny chamber, greedily dragging in precious, ragged breaths of the stale, metallic air. My head throbbed, a pulse pounding between my temples like a drumbeat, and dark spots bloomed at the edges of my vision.

A sudden splash tore through the silence.

A figure burst up beside me, water surging with the movement, and I jerked back in alarm, my shoulders slamming against the cold, slick wall. The chamber was barely big enough for one of us, let alone two.

It was Devrin, Saltspire's elected. His wild, furious eyes met mine as he surfaced beside me, gasping like a drowning man, a low, feral growl rising from his throat. He sucked in a breath and then his gaze dropped to my hands.

To the objects I held.

I followed his gaze and felt my stomach drop. His hands were empty. No tubes. No nozzles. Nothing.

Panic bolted through me.

"No-" I managed to utter, voice ragged and cracked, but he was already moving.

Devrin surged forward, shoving through the water with vicious intent. His hands clamped down on my shoulders and drove me back against the wall, my head snapping against the cement with a sickening crack. A burst of pain exploded through the back of my skull, hot and cold at once, and the world tilted sideways.

"Stop!" I shouted, thrashing in his iron grip, but my limbs felt sluggish, disobedient.

His hands slid down, rough and possessive, searching, until they found the tube and nozzle clutched against my chest. He yanked, trying to rip them from my grasp.

Instinct took over. I shoved my foot between us and kicked, catching him square between the legs.

He let out a sharp, strangled noise of pain.

"Shit," he spat, rage twisting his face, but I didn't wait for him to recover.

I wrenched myself free, pushed off the wall, and dove, my body burning with effort as I swam through the dark, churning water. The cold bit at my skin, every stroke a war against my weakening limbs.

It wasn't until the water around me began to bloom in cloudy, crimson ribbons that I realized what had happened.

I was bleeding.

I felt it now, a warmth spilling from the wound, mingling with the cold water. My head throbbed, my vision blurred, and nausea twisted my gut. I needed air. I needed to stop the bleeding. I needed to get away from Devrin.

I swam harder.

If there was one advantage, it was that the spreading blood would cloud the water, making it harder for him to see me if he was still following. Clutching the nozzle and tube, I shoved them down the front of my wetsuit, tucking them tight against my chest. It was uncomfortable, heavy, but at least they were hidden.

As I swam, I scoured the floor of the tunnel with my blurred, stinging eyes. I snatched up the first two items my fingers brushed against, whatever they were, and pushed onward. My vision dimmed, and I fought to stay conscious.

Then I hit something.

A body.

I braced for another attack, heart hammering, but when I looked up, relief flooded through me so suddenly I nearly sobbed.

Briar.

Her face appeared through the haze, eyes wide in horror as she took in the sight of me, blood clouding the water, my trembling, unsteady limbs. Her hand reached out, catching my shoulder.

I tried to warn her, to shake my head, but Devrin's hands closed around my waist from behind, yanking me back with bruising force. Briar dove forward, trying to fight off the manic who'd attacked me.

I forced myself not to scream. To save my breath. My fingers tightened around the two decoy objects in my grip, and with what little fight I had left, I shoved them hard into Devrin's chest, forcing him to take them.

He hesitated, just for a moment, then ripped them from my grasp and kicked off, swimming away toward the tunnels we'd come from.

Briar moved after him instantly, ready to give chase, but I grabbed her arm, my weak grip barely enough to hold her.

I shook my head and her gaze snapped to mine.

She took one look at the state I was in, the blood still spilling from my head, and grabbed my wrist, pulling me with her. Good. Because my limbs were starting to give up, heavy and useless.

She dragged me through the water, fast and relentless, until we broke into a larger chamber, one with a pocket of air near the ceiling.

The moment we broke the surface, I gasped, choking on the stale, precious air as Briar hauled me into the tiny air pocket of the chamber. The cold, red tinted water lapped at my chin, and my arms felt like dead weight, but her hold was strong, steady, anchoring me in place. Her chest heaved against mine, breath ragged and fast as though she'd been the one bleeding out.

"Hollis, come here," she rasped, voice breaking on my name. "You scared the absolute shit out of me."

Her arms clutched me tighter, one hand at the back of my head, careful of the wound, the other around my waist, holding me flush against her like if she let go, I'd slip away forever. Her chin rested against my damp hair as we both fought to catch our breath.

For the first time in what felt like hours, warmth sparked somewhere inside me.

"Are you okay?"

"Alive, yes" I managed weakly, a ghost of a smile on my lips, "Okay? Debatable."

I felt her laugh, a soft, strangled sound, more relief than humor.

"What the fuck just happened?" she asked, her voice a mixture of fear and fury.

I leaned my head against her shoulder, the exhaustion catching up to me. "Devrin," I whispered. "He attacked me... tried to take the pieces I'd found."

I felt her entire body tense, the water shifting around us. Her breathing hitched and when she pulled back, I could see the storm in her eyes, the rage, the terror of almost losing me.

Without a word, Briar reached down to her wetsuit, fingers fumbling at the seam of her pant leg. She yanked at the fabric, tearing a long, jagged strip free. Her hands were shaking. She cradled my head in her palm and carefully began wrapping the makeshift bandage around the gash at the back of my head.

It stung, and I winced, but the pressure steadied the spinning world.

"This'll keep pressure on it," she murmured, eyes flicking to mine. "It's still gonna bleed, but it'll buy us time. We need to get you out of here."

I nodded, my throat thick with emotion. I opened my mouth to thank her, to crack some weak joke, to say something, but she was already moving.

Her hand cupped my cheek, fingers sliding into my hair, and before I could breathe another word, she kissed me.

It wasn't careful, wasn't sweet or hesitant. It was desperate and fierce, trembling and alive. A collision of mouths. Water, blood and terror still clinging to us both. It was the kind of kiss you gave someone when you thought you might never see them again.

And because I needed this and I needed her, I kissed her back.

My hands fisted into the front of her wetsuit, pulling her closer as life bloomed inside me again, a warmth that spread through my aching body, chasing away the numbness. The world narrowed to the heat of her lips, the sharp, uneven way she breathed against my mouth, the taste of water and copper and fear. The feel of her breasts pressed against mine.

When she finally pulled back, her forehead rested against mine, both of us panting, and for a moment, nothing else existed.

"Don't do that to me again," she whispered, voice breaking. "I swear to God, Hollis."

I smiled, small and pained but real. "Not part of the plan, I promise."

She let out a shaking breath, then brushed a damp lock of hair from my face. "We've got to move. Can you swim?"

"Yeah, but we should be fast." I answered. "Do you have any pieces?"

"These," she said, pulling them from the neckline of her wetsuit. I glanced at them. She had two pieces right, and one decoy. I took that one from her hands and let it fall.

"Damnit, I wasn't sure. I helped Pa put one together once when I was a kid, but it's been a while." She cursed under her breath.

"I know what they look like. I can help," I replied, still hiding Zaffir's secret assistance from the watching cameras.

"Let's do it. We'll find what we need and get back to our guys. Together."

"I like the sound of that," I teased.

Her smile cracked through the tension, a crooked, aching thing, and she pressed one more quick, fierce kiss to my temple before wrapping an arm securely around me and diving again.

CHAPTER
EIGHTEEN

BRIAR

I DON'T THINK I truly understood fear until I saw Brexlyn underwater, blood trailing from her head, panic in her eyes, thrashing through crimson-tinged water with a hulking figure closing in behind her.

I'd been swimming for at least an hour at this point, lungs burning, muscles screaming, chasing down the final scattered pieces we each needed to survive this trial. When I found her, when I saw what had happened to her, I could have killed Devrin with my bare hands. I still might, but surviving and getting back to Thorne and Ezra was the most important thing now. My revenge on that Saltspire bastard would have to wait.

Bex was quick. Sharp. Even with the injury. She moved with purpose, zeroing in on the right pieces with barely a glance. It was that damn brilliant mind of hers. She'd probably seen one of these contraptions once years ago and still remembered every curve, every connection. It was stamped on her brain.

But the blood loss was catching up with her. I saw it in the way her limbs lagged, the sluggishness in her strokes. We had to move faster. She had all her pieces now. When we finally surfaced in one of the narrow, half-submerged chambers, I managed a shaky grin.

"Go," I panted. "Head back. I'll be right behind you."

She shook her head, water streaming down her face. "I'm not leaving you behind."

"You need to get out of the water. And Ezra, he's waiting for you."

"The longer we argue," she insisted, "the longer it'll take for both of us to get back."

Her eyes blazed, refusing to even entertain the idea of abandoning me. God, she was stubborn. I almost argued again, but my heart fluttered. Thrilled that she didn't want to leave me. Finally I nodded, and together we dove again.

Three more descents, and I finally snagged the last piece I needed. Relief crashed through me... until I surfaced and realized I had no idea which way was back to the tank. My head spun.

The canals all looked the same. Dark, endless stretches of underwater tunnels with only the occasional pocket of air.

Thank the stars for Brexlyn. She surfaced beside me, panting, eyes dull with exhaustion but sharp with focus. She'd been mapping the paths in her head the whole time, of course she had.

I let her lead, following the faint movements of her hand in the murky water. But she was fading. Her strokes lost strength. She started to drift. I grabbed her arm and hauled her up to a pocket of air.

"I'm okay," she murmured, though her skin had gone gray, lips tinged blue.

"You're about to pass out," I choked, panic clawing at my chest.

"Three... lefts," she whispered, head tipping against my shoulder. "And... a right."

Then her eyes fluttered shut. Her body went limp in the water.

"No, no, no..." I caught her, cradling her head above the surface. "Hollis, wake up for me, baby," I pleaded, my voice cracking. Her lashes didn't even flutter.

I had to move. Now.

I timed her breathing, watching for the faintest rise and fall of her chest. Every second mattered. Then, tightening my grip around her, I dove.

Three lefts. A right.

Each turn, I prayed she'd hold on. I stopped at every air pocket I could find, forcing us both above the water. She gasped in thin, ragged breaths, unconscious but still clinging to life. Every time she took in air, a spark of hope reignited in my chest.

One last stretch.

My muscles screamed in protest. The weight of the pieces shoved into our wetsuits threatened to drag us down. I cursed God. Cursed Praxis. Cursed the Run. But I didn't stop.

And then, ahead, I saw it. The faint shimmer of light above, the outline of the cage, our way out.

With everything I had left, I kicked hard, breaking the surface with a ragged gasp, Brexlyn clutched in my arms. Water crashed around us. Relief and terror surged through me in equal measure.

I hauled Bex onto the solid ground, my chest heaving, arms

shaking from exertion and terror. Water slicked off her body as I laid her flat on her back, and for a moment, the world narrowed to the sight of her still, pale face. My heart thundered in my ears.

"Come on, Hollis," I whispered, tearing the weighted pieces of the machine from her wetsuit, flinging them aside like they meant nothing, because right now, they didn't. Not if it meant losing her.

I pressed my palms against her chest, my own hands trembling. "Come on, baby, please. Breath," I begged, voice cracking like glass under pressure. I leaned down, forcing a desperate breath into her mouth. Then another.

The water still clung to her lips, my tears mixing with it, blurring my vision as I worked. I pressed again, harder. Another breath. Another.

"Come back to me, Hollis," I pleaded, voice rough and breaking apart at the edges. "We need you. *I* need you."

There were so many things I hadn't said. So many things I wanted to ask her, to tell her. Somewhere between those endless trees in the Wilds and this hellish trial, she'd found a way into the deepest, most guarded corners of me and made herself at home there. And it had been so effortless. So natural. I wasn't ready to lose that. Not now. Not ever.

We weren't finished. Not even close. We haven't even started yet.

And then, she coughed. Violent, ragged, water spilling from her lips as her body shuddered back to life. Relief cracked through me, and I fell back on my heels, gasping for breath, the weight in my chest finally breaking.

"Hey," I croaked, brushing the wet hair from her face as she blinked up at me, dazed and weak, but alive.

Only then did I glance up and spot the camera pointed directly at us.

Zaffir stood behind it. Our Praxis-assigned cameraman.

His eyes were glassy, face stricken. I'd seen the way he looked at Bex around the house, how his walls would drop when she laughed. And right now, the raw fear and grief on his face spoke volumes. There was history there. Unspoken things. His world had almost ended in front of him.

Then my gaze snagged on the tank.

The people inside, the ones still bound to those metal poles, were rising, the water creeping higher. Panic clutched at my throat as I locked eyes with Thorne. His face was pressed against the glass top of the tank, desperately clinging to the last few inches of breathable air. Ezra wasn't far from him, straining against his restraints too.

And then Brexlyn's voice, ragged and weak, cut through the panic. "Briar..."

I scrambled to her side. "Hey, beautiful," I murmured, slipping an arm under her shoulders. "We gotta move. Now. We have to get them out of there."

She groaned, pain flickering across her face.

"I know, baby, fuck, I know." I helped her sit up. "But Ezra needs you." Her gaze sharpened when I mentioned his name. And that was all it took.

Her bloodshot eyes locked on mine for a beat. Then she nodded, jaw set despite the tremble in her limbs.

We both started fumbling with the pieces I'd dragged out of her wetsuit, hands shaking as we fit them together. It wasn't perfect. It was desperate, frantic. But Bex was still sharper than anyone else in this goddamn place even with a head wound.

"This tube," she rasped, "into this chamber." Her voice was barely a whisper, whether from exhaustion or fear of being overheard, I didn't know.

Our fingers brushed as we connected the final pieces on each of our devices. They clicked into place.

"We've got it!" I shouted, holding up the makeshift device.

A Praxis guard strode over, taking his sweet time examining our work. Every second felt like a year. I clenched my fists, biting back the scream clawing up my throat. Finally, he grunted his approval and handed us each a key.

I grabbed Bex's hand. "Come on."

Running on pure adrenaline, we climbed the slick ladder up to the top of the tank. The access hatch was barely wide enough for one of us at a time.

"Go get him," I said, cupping her cheek. Her skin was ice-cold, but she nodded, eyes gleaming with that familiar reckless fire. No hesitation.

And then we dove.

The icy water hit like a wall, but I forced myself to move, homing in on Thorne. He'd slipped under completely, face pale in the shifting light.

I reached for him, and fumbled the key into the lock on his handcuffs. It was jammed. I cursed, twisting harder. It gave. His wrists came free.

Without a word, we kicked off the side, swimming hard toward the exit. Through the murky water, I spotted Brexlyn with Ezra clutched to her, his face a mixture of fury and desperation as he dragged her upward with him.

We burst through the surface together, gasping and heaving. I climbed out first, then turned to reach for Bex.

As we climbed down from the tank, she nearly collapsed, her body giving out as she slumped into Ezra's arms.

Ezra was murmuring to her, soft words I couldn't make out, but I could feel the weight of them. Words thick with love and gratitude, whispered promises and desperate relief, his hand stroking her soaked hair as she clung to him like a lifeline.

Then Thorne stepped up in front of me, eyes bloodshot,

water still clinging to his skin. He pulled me into a rough, shaking embrace.

"Close call, sis," he muttered against my ear, his breath ragged. "I was starting to really doubt the whole 'you can trust me' speech you gave me."

"Glad you're okay," I said, gripping the back of his neck and holding him there for a beat longer than either of us might have admitted we needed.

And then a scream tore through the room. "No! No, please!"

My head snapped toward the sound just as Dani Cale stumbled forward, her hands trembling as she held up her device to the guard standing by the tank.

"You've got the wrong configuration," the guard said flatly, barely sparing her a glance. "You have the wrong tube."

"No, no, please, please... Check again. Give me the key!" Her voice cracked, raw and breaking. She rushed toward the tank, slamming her palms against the glass where her son was thrashing beneath the rising water, the chains keeping him trapped as panic overtook him.

"Baby, I'm here. Momma's here," Dani cried, her voice shattering on every word as she tried to catch his eyes through the water-streaked glass.

"Give me the key!" She screamed again.

"You have the wrong configuration," the guard repeated.

She screamed, slamming her fist against the tank.

"You can't do this!" she cried. But the guard remained still and unyielding.

She turned away from the child in the tank, took a steadying, decisive breath, and then she climbed. Her hands fumbled for the ladder, soaked and shaking, but she didn't slow. No one moved to stop her.

She didn't have a key. Wasn't even trying to bring one.

She wasn't going in there to set him free. She was going in there to drown with him.

I felt the bile rise in my throat, my stomach twisting as she slipped through the hatch and disappeared into the water.

"Let's go," Ezra said quietly, his voice rough. He was cradling Bex's head against his shoulder, shielding her from the unfolding nightmare. I saw the tremble in his jaw, the way his eyes refused to drift toward the tank.

None of us wanted to see what came next. We turned away as a new wave of water crashed into the chamber, as the tank began to overflow, the sound of it rushing in loud and relentless. And then we left. Left the room, left the tank, left those last terrible sounds behind us. We didn't look back.

I closed the door behind us, locking us into one of the small holding rooms where they'd corralled us before the trial. Ezra had Bex pressed into his side, one hand fisting the fabric of her suit like he could anchor her there. Thorne sagged against the wall, sweat and water trailing down his face. And Zaffir stood stiff and pale in the corner, his camera lowered, a look of sick, soft horror on his face like the weight of what he'd filmed was finally breaking through the detachment.

He powered down the camera with trembling fingers and moved toward Bex, his whole posture shifting as he crouched in front of her.

"Hey, beautiful," he said softly, his voice cracking a little at the edges. "Let's get that head of yours patched up, huh?"

Bex managed a weak smile, her lips ghosting the word, "Thanks."

Zaffir grabbed a first aid kit from the corner and started working, pulling the makeshift bandage I made from her head.

"Quick thinking, Briar," Zaffir commended, brushing matted hair from the area and cleaning the gash with shaking hands.

"Yeah," I replied. Ezra peeled away from Bex and let Zaffir work, coming straight for me, eyes storm-dark.

"What the fuck happened to her down there?" he hissed, his voice low but tight, vibrating with fury.

"She was attacked," I said, my own anger curling sharp beneath my skin.

"By who?" Thorne asked, straightening.

"Devrin," I spat, the name like poison in my mouth. "Asshole thought he could take the pieces she already collected."

Ezra's face contorted, his jaw clenched so hard I could hear his teeth grind. "I'm gonna kill him."

"Get in line," I muttered, clapping a hand on his shoulder.

I risked a glance at Bex. She was doing her best to follow Zaffir's instructions, but I could see it, the pallor, the tremor in her fingers, how she bit down on her bottom lip to keep from making a sound every time he touched the wound.

"She lost a lot of blood," I said grimly.

"She needs to rest," Thorne murmured, his gaze locked on her like she might slip away if he looked anywhere else. The idiot was head over heels, even if he didn't have the spine to admit it yet.

And then Zaffir's voice cut through, low and tight. "Unfortunately, all of you have an interview to prepare for."

It felt like a slap.

"You're joking," Thorne snapped, stepping forward. "She's in no condition for that."

"I know that," Zaffir bit back, his face flushing, eyes bright with unshed fury of his own. "You think Praxis gives a shit?"

And that was it. The crack in my temper split wide open.

"Aren't *you* Praxis?" I snarled, venom flooding every word. "Or is that just when you're holding the fucking camera?"

Zaffir's head snapped up. He stood, stepping toward me

so fast the chair he'd been kneeling by skidded back with a scrape.

"You think you can buddy up next to us when we're at the cabin, but then stand by and watch them put us through *that!*" I said, pointing furiously to the door we'd just arrived through. Where on the other side a mother was actively drowning with her child.

"I don't have a choice, Briar," he barked, eyes blazing, nose to nose with me now.

"You think that buys you a free pass?" I growled, shoving him back a step. "You think you get to stand behind your lens during the trials then go home and pretend that you're not part of this? That you didn't watch that kid drown tonight? That you didn't watch a mother climb in to die with him and just...keep filming?"

Zaffir's face twisted, a muscle ticking in his jaw. "I'm trying to keep you all alive."

"By what? Making us look palatable for broadcast? Making the public love us so they cry when Praxis inevitably kills us?" I shouted, shoving him again, harder this time.

Ezra was there in an instant, grabbing my arm. "Briar, enough."

But I wasn't done. "You don't get to pretend you're one of us. Because you're not."

"I'm trying to protect her!" Zaffir roared, pointing to Bex. His voice cracked on the last word. "Every fucking day. Altering your edits. Omitting things. But it's a risk I'd gladly take for her. For all of you!"

He came at me then, catching me off guard. His shoulder collided with mine, and then Thorne was pushing him back with maybe a little too much force. The room erupted in shouted voices as Ezra and I tried to pull them apart.

"Stop it!" Bex's voice cut through the chaos like a blade.

Everyone froze.

I turned to see her pushing to her feet, swaying, blood streaked down the side of her face, her eyes burning with something fierce and terrible and heartbreakingly brave.

"Please..." she whispered, and somehow the whisper was louder than any shout.

Zaffir stilled beside me, his chest heaving. I released my grip on his collar. He didn't move.

"Zaffir may wear the colors, but he's no more Praxis than any of us," she said, her voice steady though her legs trembled. "I've known that for a while now, and I think you have too."

Zaffir's gaze found hers, and his face crumpled. A soft, strangled sound escaped him, half sob, half apology.

"I'm sorry," he choked, tears slipping free now, streaking down his face. "I'm so fucking sorry."

"I know," Bex murmured, crossing the room with painful slowness and pulling him into her arms. His shoulders shook under her touch, grief and guilt breaking him apart.

"I'll be okay for the interview," she added, turning her head to look at the rest of us. "I can rest after. I'm fine."

She was lying. Every one of us knew it. But none of us called her on it.

Zaffir scrubbed a trembling hand down his face and backed away, sinking into a chair like his legs might give out.

I took advantage of the quiet moment and made my way over to her, each step came heavier and heavier like my body was only just catching up with the trauma I'd just put it through. She looked up as I approached, and her mouth curled into the gentlest smile. It hit me square in the chest.

"You scared the shit out of me in there, Hollis," I whispered as I knelt in front of her. Her hand reached for mine without hesitation, and I wrapped my fingers around hers like

I'd never let go again. Like she was the only thing tethering me to this earth.

"You saved my life," she said softly. I didn't feel worthy of the words, or of her, but I'd accept them anyway. "Again," she added, letting out the faintest chuckle, worn at the edges but still somehow light.

"We really have to stop meeting like that," I offered, trying for humor, though it came out a little strangled beneath the lingering fear still coiled inside me.

Her smile didn't fade. If anything, it deepened, a little sad now. A little too knowing. "I have a feeling it won't be the last time," she murmured. Her gaze dropped to where our hands were joined, like maybe she was grounding herself in the same way I was.

I brought her hand to my lips and pressed a soft kiss to her knuckles. She lifted her other hand, curling her fingers beneath my chin and guiding my gaze back to hers.

"Thank you for saving me," she whispered again, and this time the words settled somewhere in my bones.

"Thank you for staying alive," I breathed. "And I... I wanted to apologize. For kissing you. Earlier."

Her expression shifted slightly. Just a flicker of curiosity beneath the calm.

"Not because I didn't want to," I rushed to add, heart in my throat now. "God, I did. I've wanted to for a while. But I shouldn't have surprised you like that. You were scared, and I was just so relieved you were alive, and in that moment, it felt like...like it was the only thing I could do. But that doesn't make it fair to you."

I hesitated, drawing in a breath I didn't know what to do with. "And maybe you only kissed me back because you were thankful. Or in shock. I don't know." We've gotten close over the last few weeks, but she's never made a move to kiss me.

Even with those quiet heat-filled moments we shared in the Wilds, or the way she glances at me when she thinks I'm not looking. I can't just assume she wants the same thing I do. Or that she feels the same way. "And I need you to know... if you don't want that... if friendship is all this is for you, I'll be okay with that. I just... don't want you to feel like you owe me anything."

It was the part I hadn't said out loud until now, the fear that had been quietly gnawing at me since the moment our lips met. I would never want to mistake gratitude for affection, or make her feel like she owed me anything. I couldn't bear that.

"Briar." Her voice brought me back, soft but firm, and when I looked up, her eyes were locked on mine. Steady. Clear. "Let me be perfectly upfront about this. I want so much more than just friendship from you."

For a second, I forgot how to breathe. My heart did something unsteady in my chest, and before I could say a word, she leaned down and kissed me.

Not like before. Not rushed or desperate. This kiss was deliberate and tender. A promise tucked between parted lips and the press of her fingers against my jaw. Her mouth moved with mine slowly, like we had all the time in the world now. And although I knew we didn't– for this moment, we pretended.

Every stroke of her tongue against mine quieted the doubt. Every sigh between us wiped away the hesitation I'd carried. This was her. Wanting me. Choosing me.

When we finally broke apart, we just smiled at each other, grinning uncontrollably. All girlish and breathless, cheeks flushed and eyes shining.

God, she was beautiful when she blushed. I made a mental note to make her blush more often.

Then came a knock at the door.

The tension in the room snapped taut again. Zaffir hastily scooped up his camera, flipping it back on while Ezra moved to open the door. I stood, and put my body between Bex and the door, just in case it was Devrin and I got my chance to kick his ass.

A Praxis guard stood waiting on the other side of the corridor, his posture rigid and weapon slung across his chest. His face was unreadable.

"Trial results have been determined," he announced. "Briar Grey, first place. And Brexlyn Hollis, you've been disqualified for failure to exit the canals under your own power."

The words hit like a slap. A sick, sharp silence followed, broken only by the shallow sound of Bex's breath beside me.

"What the fuck did you just say?" Ezra snapped, stepping forward before anyone could stop him.

"She almost died in there!" Thorne added, voice sharp and shaking.

"She should have won," I cut in, the heat in my chest boiling over. "You're telling me she gets nothing because I helped her swim for the last ten minutes?"

The guard's hand drifted toward his holster. "Stand down," he said, voice firm. His fingers fully wrapped around the butt of his weapon.

I heard someone curse under their breath behind me. My heart pounded in my throat.

Then Bex stepped forward, her voice barely above a whisper, but somehow it sliced through the rising panic like a blade.

"Stop."

We all froze. She reached out and touched my arm, just lightly enough to ground me.

"It's okay," she said, looking only at me. Her lips trembled, but her eyes held steady.

"Hollis—" I started, but she shook her head.

"I'm alive," she said quietly. "That's enough."

The air seemed to shift with her words. The tension held for one more fragile beat, then began to bleed out like a slow exhale. We all stood down. Our anger, still there, but less confrontational. Less reckless.

The guard's hand slipped away from his weapon. He studied us for a moment longer before finally speaking again.

"This way."

He turned sharply and started walking. We followed in reluctant silence, still raw with the injustice of it all but too drained to push back further.

He led us through a maze of sterile, winding halls that echoed with the weight of everything we weren't saying. Eventually, we emerged at the front of the facility, where a row of black Praxis cars idled at the curb.

And then I saw him.

Devrin. Being escorted to his car. Alone. His face contorted into a mask of anger.

My feet moved before my brain could catch up. I gripped his shoulder and spun him around. My fist collided with his jaw, the crack of bone against bone sharp and satisfying. He dropped to a knee, clutching his face.

"Fuck you," I hissed, and drove my knee into his nose.

Blood sprayed as he reeled back, coughing and spitting crimson onto the pavement.

"It's a competition, you fucking psycho bitch," he snarled, wiping his mouth with the back of his hand.

I knelt, grabbing the front of his suit and yanking him in close, my face inches from his bloodied one.

"You almost killed her."

"She gave me the wrong pieces," he spat. "If anyone's a murderer, it's her. Vera is dead because she tricked me."

"No," I growled, fury thick in my throat. "You don't get to claim that. You got your partner killed because you couldn't be bothered to earn your win. You stole. You cheated. And it cost a life."

Before he could respond, he jerked his head forward, head-butting me. Pain bloomed across my cheekbone. I surged forward again, ready to tear him apart. But hands gripped my arms, pulling me back.

"Enough!" Thorne barked.

Ezra grabbed my other side, but he wore a satisfied smirk at the state I'd left Devrin in. Bex was there too, breath ragged, eyes wide. Her gaze met mine. Calm. Steady. Forgiving.

"It's okay, Briar," she promised, and just like that, the fight bled out of me.

I let them pull me back, let them lead me toward the waiting cars. One last venomous glare at Devrin, who grimaced through bloodied teeth, before I let it go.

Inside the car, Bex slid in next to me, leaning into my side like it was the most natural thing in the world. I draped my arm around her shoulders, holding her close, feeling the exhaustion in her frame.

"You know what he said isn't true, right?" I murmured into her hair. "You didn't cause that."

She looked up at me, eyes bright with unshed tears, and nodded. "I know," she whispered.

I pressed a soft kiss to her temple and traced soothing, absent patterns down her back as she drifted off against me.

CHAPTER
NINETEEN

BEX

My head throbbed, a dull, persistent ache behind my eyes as a small army of stylists descended on me the moment we arrived. I barely registered their voices as they scrubbed away the blood from my skin, bathed me in scented water that stung the cuts on my skin, and wrapped me in silks and gauze and glittering jewels. Their hands worked quickly, painting my face in soft, practiced strokes, dabbing away the evidence of exhaustion until I looked like someone who belonged here. Someone Praxis would be proud to display.

I hated it.

Worse than the ache in my head, worse than the raw throb of my temple where dried blood had been carefully wiped away, was the knot in my chest. The ache of absence. I'd been whisked away from my partners the second we arrived, led down a different hall while the others were taken to their own stylists, their own cages to be polished and prepped for the show.

My partners.

The words echoed in my head. Maybe it was selfish to think of them that way, but I did. Zaffir, with his soft heart and haunted eyes. Ezra, steady and fierce. Briar's protection, Thorne's humor. They were mine, and I was theirs. At least I felt like they were.

I startled when Zaffir appeared beside me, offering a glass filled with something thick and vaguely green. "It'll settle your stomach," he murmured, his voice rough around the edges but gentle. "And keep you on your feet."

I took it without question, downing half before I could think about the taste. Whatever it was, it worked. The spinning slowed, the edges of my vision steadied. I shot him a grateful look as Nova finished smudging black smoke around my eyes and brushing shimmer across my lips.

Then she stepped aside, letting me face the mirror.

I groaned softly. It wasn't bad, the makeup was the familiar dark palette of the Collectives, but the rest of it...felt distinctly Praxis. The dress clung to me like liquid night, black beads and tiny jewels stitched into the corset bodice. It shimmered in the light, every movement sending a ripple of reflected color across the fabric. The neckline plunged deeper than necessary, the train of it trailing behind me.

It was stunning. And it would have fed my family for a year.

"Don't look so glum, girl," Nova said, tossing a glance my way as she dabbed powder along my jawline. "You're a fan favorite. That's something to be proud of."

I met her eyes in the mirror, wishing I could find the words to explain just how hollow that title felt. How little pride I felt for the things I'd had to do just to survive.

"Yeah," I said flatly, the word sitting heavy in my mouth.

She looked at me a moment longer, her sharp gaze softening just slightly, like a crack in armor. Then she turned back to the vanity, adjusting a gold pin in her hair.

"I'm glad you didn't die in the canals," she said, her voice almost offhand—like she was commenting on the weather—but the words carried a note of hesitation. A flicker of worry she hadn't meant to reveal. It was the first real glimmer of humanity I'd seen in her.

"Thank you," I replied, and to my own surprise, I meant it.

I forced myself to stand as a girl in a pale silver pantsuit appeared at my side, headset snug against her head, a clipboard in her arms. She smiled, professional and a little too rehearsed.

"You ready?" she asked.

I didn't answer. Didn't need to. She was already steering me down a long, winding hallway.

"Good luck," Nova called after me. And I hated that I almost missed her presence as I was led away. She was a horrible woman with annoying tendencies, but at least I knew what to expect when she was around.

"You're going out first," the young girl said lightly.

"What about the others?" My voice came out rough, hoarse from disuse.

"They'll follow after," she replied with a dismissive wave.

"But–"

I didn't get to finish the thought. A roar of sound cut through the corridor, the distant thrum of the crowd filtering through the studio walls. It was dizzying. My stomach flipped, bile clawing its way up my throat.

"And what a day it's been!" Annalese's voice boomed over the speakers. "Three Challengers perished during today's trial, and three visitors as well, making this the deadliest single trial in Reclamation Run history!"

The crowd erupted in cheers. Cheers. Over death.

I gripped my stomach, the bile burning its way higher, but I swallowed it down.

"And we are all thrilled to announce," Annalese cooed, "that we have a special guest in the studio with us tonight. You've asked for it, you've begged for it, we've seen the threads, the posts, the cries for more! So please, help me welcome, from Canyon Collective, Brexlyn Hollis!"

The door to the stage slid open.

The bright lights blinded me for a moment, as they warmed my face. The crowd was packed, bodies packed shoulder to shoulder, faces alight with feverish excitement. I froze, just for a breath. My heart was pounding so hard it filled my ears, drowning out the cheers.

Then I stepped forward.

Annalese bounced toward me, practically glowing beneath the harsh studio lights. Her golden jumpsuit clung to her like a second skin. She looked like a living trophy.

Before I could brace myself, she linked her arm through mine, her manicured nails cool against my skin. The contact made me tense, but I forced my face into something resembling a smile as she led me toward a long, gleaming couch that looked more like a prop than an actual piece of furniture. I sank down onto the plush cushions, my body heavy, aching. Annalese slid gracefully into a rounded chair opposite me, crossing one glittering leg over the other.

The crowd still hadn't quieted. They screamed, chanted my name like it belonged to them now.

"Brex-lyn! Brex-lyn!"

It made my skin crawl.

I didn't belong here. I wanted to run, to disappear into the shadows.

My gaze found the cameras, unblinking, predatory things trained on me from every angle. And behind one of them stood Zaffir. He didn't smile, but he met my eyes and gave me a sharp, quick nod. A reminder. Steady yourself. Play the part. Survive.

Annalese beamed at the crowd and then turned her weaponized charm on me.

"Brexlyn," she purred, "I know I speak for most of Nexum when I say you've quickly become one of our absolute favorite Challengers in Reclamation Run history, isn't that right?" She gestured to the crowd, and they roared their approval like obedient dogs.

I managed a soft, "Thank you all," though it barely carried over the noise.

Annalese didn't miss a beat. "From the moment we first met you, saying goodbye to your best friend and little brother," she reminded them, voice syrupy sweet. The crowd responded on cue with a collective, sentimental *awww*. "And vowing to win the medical trials for him. We were all so touched."

I swallowed the knot in my throat. "I love them," I said, voice steady even as my stomach twisted. "I'd do anything for those two."

Annalese clapped her hands together like a delighted child. "And you've shown that to us, trial after brutal trial. You and your fellow Canyon Challenger have already outperformed anyone from Canyon in over a decade. Tell me, how does it feel to carry your Collective's hopes like this?"

I hesitated, turning the words over in my head before choosing the truth. "It feels like it's still not enough."

The room shifted. The crowd quieted just enough for the tension to settle. Annalese blinked, a flicker of unease beneath her perfect exterior. "How so?" she asked, the question light but laced with warning.

I dropped my voice to a whisper. "Because no matter how

well we do this year. We'll be right back at zero in twelve months."

For a split second, I saw it, the flash of irritation in her eyes. And then it was gone, replaced by a dazzling smile.

"But what a beautiful year it'll be," she crooned, "because of you!"

The crowd erupted again, and I caught Zaffir's subtle shake of his head. *Careful,* his look warned.

Annalese forged ahead, perfectly unshaken. "Now, Brexlyn, there are twelve Challengers remaining. How do you think you fare for the medical trial?"

Twelve. That meant eight people–innocent people–have already lost their lives in pursuit of Reclamation.

I straightened my shoulders, forcing resolve into my voice. "I think I have a team behind me that's going to help me save my brother's life. And that means everything."

That, apparently, was the right answer.

Annalese beamed, her expression alight like I'd finally delivered the line she'd been waiting for all along. A puppet hitting its mark. "Beautifully said," she praised, her voice smooth as glass. Then her smile sharpened, too bright. "Speaking of your brother... Praxis has a little surprise for you."

My stomach dropped, my pulse stuttering. Hope and dread twisted together, rising thick in my throat. I forced myself to keep my expression neutral, but inside I was already bracing for a blow I couldn't predict. If he was here...if they did something to him. What twisted game was Praxis going to play?

The screen behind Annalese flickered to life. At first it was just static.

And then two faces.

Faces so familiar, so achingly perfect and heartbreakingly

far away that the breath caught in my chest. My eyes burned as tears blurred my vision.

"Jax?" I whispered, my voice cracking like glass underfoot. "Ava!"

"Bex!" Jax's face lit up, his eyes going wide as he recognized me. "I can see you!"

I felt the tears spill over as I pressed my hand to my mouth, trying to trap the sob that threatened to escape. "I can see you too, sprout," I choked. "Oh God, Jax... it's really you."

He grinned, but it was a little too stiff, a little too rehearsed, and I saw it, the tightness around his mouth, the way his shoulders didn't move when he spoke.

"Hi, Bex," Ava added her soft eyes meeting mine, with something that looked like guilt.

"How are you both?" I asked quickly.

"I'm okay," Jax said, because of course he would, he was never one to admit his pain, even to me.

"We miss you," Ava added.

"I'm so sorry I'm not there with you."

"It's okay," he cut in quickly. "Ava's pretty cool."

Ava smiled, but it didn't quite reach her eyes as she playfully rubbed her knuckles on top of his head. He chuckled and swatted her hand away. My heart constricted at the ease the two of them shared. I loved them so much.

I didn't give a damn that the entire arena was watching, that my mic was live, that my face was undoubtedly plastered across every screen in the Collectives and in Praxis itself. None of it mattered.

"And you," I pressed, desperate, my voice lowering as if that could protect him. "Your legs? Are they- ?"

He shrugged, a gesture so familiar it hurt. "Eh." That tiny wince in his expression undid me. I knew what that meant. I knew he was lying through his teeth for my sake.

"I miss you, sprout," I whispered. "I miss both of you."

"We miss you too," Jax grinned, that same crooked smile he used to give me when he knew he wasn't fooling anyone. "But you're kind of kicking ass, so... that's pretty cool."

The audience laughed. I barely registered it.

"Hey, watch your language, sprout," I teased through tears.

Annalese's voice cut through, slicing the moment clean. "Your sister has been doing some truly extraordinary things out here, Jax," she purred. "How's Canyon reacting to her success?"

Jax's gaze darted up to Ava, a silent exchange. He swallowed. "People are real proud. They... they keep saying you guys might finally make a difference. Ava says you might be the one who changes everything."

The words should've filled me with pride. Should've felt like a rallying cry. But they just made my throat tighten. Because deep down, I knew. No matter what I did here, no matter how hard I fought, it wouldn't be enough. Praxis didn't play fair. Praxis didn't lose.

And Jax... Jax was going to suffer for it.

"Ava, do you have anything to say to Brexlyn?" Annalese prompted. And Ava's mouth opened before she pulled it shut again. Sighing, her eyes filled with unshed tears.

"Ava?" I asked, leaning forward as if she were really in front of me.

"It's not fair," she whispered.

"I know," I responded quietly. "But I'm trying to do what you told me to. To come back home to you guys. In one piece."

She nodded, tears slipping down her cheeks. "I really do believe you can do what no one else ever has. What Canyon, and all of Nexum has been waiting for."

I narrowed my eyes. What was she talking about?

"We'll need to end the call here shortly," Annalese announced, chipper and heartless. "Is there anything else you'd like to say to your sister, Jax?"

He didn't hesitate.

"I love you," he said softly.

I swallowed the lump in my throat, nodding. "I love you too, sprout. I'll see you both soon. I promise."

"May the stars shine on you, Brexlyn Hollis," Ava whispered through her tears, echoing her words from the vote.

Then the screen blinked to black.

And the cold hit me instantly. Like someone had doused a fire inside me, leaving only ash and empty air. The crowd roared their approval, but it felt distant.

"What a heartfelt reunion," Annalese cooed, turning toward me with a grin sharp enough to cut. "Brexlyn, tell us, how did it feel, seeing your brother again?"

I forced myself to clear my throat, dragging the sleeve of my jacket across my damp cheeks. "Too good to be true," I managed.

"And Praxis made that happen for you!" she chirped, all faux warmth.

I met her gaze then, steady and sharp.

"Now that you've seen him..." Annalese leaned in, her voice dropping like she was letting me in on a secret, though the whole world was watching. "Has your focus been renewed?"

I exhaled slowly. "Yeah. It has."

"And are you more determined than ever to win those resources for him?"

I didn't look away. "Of course I am."

She smiled, satisfied, the trap snapping shut.

"And why do you feel you have the best chance to win?"

I stepped straight into her scripted segue, my voice steady. "Because I have a team."

Her face lit up like I'd handed her the final piece of a puzzle. "And what a team it is!" she turned toward the audience with a dramatic sweep of her hand. "Shall we bring out the Wildguard?"

The crowd erupted, but all I could think of was Jax's face on that screen, and the knowledge that Praxis was watching us all.

The studio practically shook from the cheers.

My heart pounded as I turned my head toward the side of the stage. And then, there they were.

Ezra, Briar, and Thorne strode into the light, each of them stunning in their own right. Ezra wore his dark button-down with the sleeves rolled to his elbows, his forearms dusted with fresh bruises and scratches, but he carried them like medals. Briar had gone sharp and sleek, her tailored jacket hanging open over a tight black corset top, silver chains catching the light at her throat. Thorne, of course, looked like sin and defiance wrapped in leather, his jacket slung over his broad shoulders, his dark shirt clinging to lean muscle.

They looked untouchable. Like they hadn't almost drowned hours ago. Like they hadn't been one wrong move away from death.

They crossed the stage toward me, and for the first time all evening, the ice in my chest cracked a little.

Thorne moved ahead of the others, claiming the seat beside me with an easy grin. He shot the others a wink, playful, cocky, before draping an arm over my shoulders and pulling me in. The familiar warmth of his presence, the casual protectiveness of the gesture, grounded me.

"Is it hot in here, or is it just them?" Annalese teased, fanning herself dramatically and earning another wave of whoops and hollers from the audience. The room felt like it vibrated with the sound, the pulse of the crowd thrumming against my skin. "You four have been the talk of the trials," she continued, her grin wide and knowing. "I mean... have you ever seen this much chemistry outside of the science based trials?" She winked, and the audience roared with laughter.

Then she turned those sharp, glittering eyes on me. "Tell me, Brexlyn," she said, leaning in just enough to make it feel conspiratorial. "What's the story with you four?"

I glanced at my Wildguard. Ezra with his steady, unreadable gaze, his mysterious mask firmly in place. Briar offered me the faintest, reassuring smile, and Thorne, ever cocky, gave me a wink and a shoulder nudge. For half a second, my eyes flicked beyond the cameras to where Zaffir stood, arms crossed, watching me. His jaw was tight, and when our gazes locked, he gave the smallest smile. One meant for only me.

"They're my team," I said, my voice soft but steady. "They've risked their lives for me. And I'd do the same for them."

"Awww," Annalese cooed, as the audience sighed and clapped at my answer. "But, please, for the love of Nexum, put us out of our misery and tell us, is there a little romance budding here?" She leaned forward, elbows on her knees, grinning like a predator who knew she'd just cornered her prey.

I took a long, steadying breath. My stomach knotted, my pulse a relentless drum beat beneath my skin. The images they'd no doubt already seen flashed through my mind, Ezra's kiss, Briar's desperate lips on mine in the canals, the near-scandalous moment with Thorne pressed against me in the dark in the Wilds. No amount of clever editing could erase the way we looked at each other when we thought no one was watching.

"Do you want there to be?" I shot back with a crooked

smile, trying for cheeky even as my heart stuttered against my ribs. The crowd loved it, shrieking and whistling.

Annalese let out a delighted laugh, clapping her hands. "Let's run the clips!"

The lights dimmed, and all eyes turned to the massive screen behind her. A soft, swelling instrumental played as a montage unfolded, and my heart lodged somewhere high in my throat.

It started simple. Ezra holding my hand in his as we exited the train. Thorne as he spun me around at the Welcome Ball, his eyes never leaving mine. Briar kneeling beside me in the Wilds, her hands gentle as she cleaned the wound on my cheek. Then came the things I hadn't noticed, stolen glances I never felt, lingering touches I hadn't realized lingered too long. The way they studied me when I wasn't looking. They way they watched me like their world revolved around my movements.

Ezra watching me as the sun rose over Praxis, his face softening in a way he never let the world see. Thorne sitting beside me while I slept on the forest floor, his eyes only on me. Briar trailing behind me in the forests, a half-smile playing at her lips as I navigated us back to Praxis.

Then there was me.

The way my face crumpled when Ezra was bitten by that wolf. The reverence as I tended to the wound. The panicked way I scrambled to Briar when she nearly fell in the produce trial. The bright, unguarded laughter I gave to every ridiculous thing Thorne said. The way I stared at Briar as she hummed. I thought I'd been careful. I thought I'd hidden it well. But up there, laid bare for everyone to see, it was painted clear as sunrise.

Then came the kisses. Ezra pulling me in with a look that claimed me as his, and me falling into it like I'd been waiting my whole life. The crowd erupted. Then Briar, drenched and desperate, finding me in the canals. That kiss was frantic, the kind you give when you think it might be your last.

The montage ended with a shot of the four of us crammed into the back seat of the limo, Ezra's head tipped against mine, Thorne's arm slung over my shoulders, and Briar's hand resting over mine in my lap. It was quiet and intimate in a way I hadn't realized the cameras had caught. The music faded out, leaving only the sound of the crowd's sighs and scattered cheers.

And it was only then, in the echo of the music and the spotlight of a thousand watching eyes, that I realized I was crying. Silent, hot tears slipping down my cheeks. Not from embarrassment. Not from fear. But from the terrifying, aching certainty that I loved them. All of them. In ways I didn't know how to carry in a world like this.

I blinked hard, the sting of tears blurring the screen for a beat before I lifted my gaze and found Zaffir. Behind the cameras and the blinding lights, his eyes were already on me. His usual sharp, unyielding expression had cracked, just for a heartbeat. I saw it in the way his brow softened, in the flicker of something tender and aching in his gaze.

He'd made that montage. I knew it in my bones. No one else could have strung those moments together with that kind of care, with that kind of quiet, aching intimacy. It was too deliberate, too personal, too much like someone who knew the weight of every stolen glance and every touch that lingered.

I smiled at him. A thank you written on the curve of my lips. And something more. A message I hoped he'd catch that said 'the only thing missing was you'.

"I've never seen a better love story," Annalese squealed, practically bouncing in her seat. The audience hooted and hollered in agreement, their energy crackling through the studio like a live wire.

"Wildguard," she grinned, turning her attention to them, "talk to me. How did this even happen? How do four hearts even find love in the middle of the trials?"

Thorne was the first to speak, his voice easy and unguarded in that way only he could manage. "I think it's no mystery to anyone watching how damn special she is," he said, gesturing toward me with a soft, crooked smile. "Anyone who's got eyes would fall for her. We just had the privilege of being close enough to convince her to fall back." He was playing it up for the crowd, but I recognized some truth behind the performance.

The crowd let out another chorus of *awws* and cheers.

Annalese, never one to miss a chance to stir the pot, leaned forward. "And there's no jealousy? I mean, Thorne... she's kissed the other two now at this point, but not you." Her voice dripped with mock scandal, like she was setting a match to dry kindling.

"No jealousy at all, Annalese," he replied playfully.

"You're not desperate for a kiss?" she teased. "Because I think we all are, aren't we?" she said, riling up the audience again into a loud roar.

"Kiss her! Kiss Her! Kiss Her!" They cheered.

"You're right," Thorne replied smoothly, the crowd rushing to hear his every word. His gaze cut to mine, electric and impossibly tender. He stood, slow and deliberate, like every movement was choreographed for maximum effect.

Then he looked at the screen behind us, now dark, and smirked. "And according to that little highlight reel, it looks like I've got a hell of a lot of catching up to do."

The crowd roared. My heart hammered.

Before I could process it, he reached for me, his hand

sliding into mine, warm and steady as he pulled me to my feet. His other hand settled on my waist, sending a jolt of heat through me, and my palms found his chest, feeling the steady thrum of his heart beneath his shirt.

"What d'you say, love?" he asked, his voice loud enough to be carried to the crowd. "Wanna help me even the score?"

Then, softer, lips brushing the shell of my ear, "Let them have their spectacle, love. But later, I'll show you what a real first kiss feels like."

I nodded, completely dazed, drowning in the storm of it, the blinding lights, the electric pulse of the room, the hunger in his touch.

Thorne grinned, wicked and breathtaking, then dipped me without warning. I gasped, my fingers fisting in his shirt as his mouth found mine. The world dropped away, the lights, the cheers, the cameras, until there was only the press of his lips, the brush of his tongue against mine, the intoxicating taste of him.

I didn't care who was watching. I kissed him like I meant it.

When he finally pulled away and set me upright, my chest was heaving, my lips tingling. I barely registered the sound of the crowd's wild cheering or the smug grin on Annalese's face.

"What a kiss," she purred, clapping as the audience lost their minds.

I darted a glance toward Ezra and Briar, both of them watching, not with jealousy, not with anger, but with a kind of resigned joy. Like they were proud of Thorne for claiming his moment. Like they were proud of me for letting him. It made my heart twist, made my pulse pound in my throat as I sank back onto the couch beside them.

But Annalese wasn't finished.

"So, Brexlyn," she purred, leaning in like a cat that had

cornered a mouse. "No reservations? None at all?" Her voice dripped with sugar, but the sharpness beneath it was unmistakable.

I met her stare, forcing a steady breath past the knot in my chest. "None," I said. And it wasn't a lie.

"So, you know these people," she pressed, her gaze flicking to each of them before returning to me. "You know what they're capable of? You're not just swept up in the adrenaline of it all?"

I swallowed hard, the air suddenly thick. I felt Thorne's pinky brush against mine.

"I know everything I need to know," I replied evenly, even though something in the pit of my stomach turned cold.

Annalese's smile stretched wider, and I knew then she'd been leading me to this moment the entire interview. "Well," she said, sitting back like a queen about to watch the walls crumble, "that's good. Because if I were going to fall for a murderer... I'd want to be sure too."

The room seemed to freeze. A collective, sharp inhale from the crowd. My heart stopped dead.

I didn't move. Didn't flinch.

And then, slowly, inevitably, I turned my head to look at Ezra.

His eyes were already on me. Wide. Haunted. A thousand things in them, fear, apology, hope, love. No excuses. No denial. Just a desperate look that said please, please don't look away.

The silence stretched.

I felt Briar shift beside me, Thorne tensed like a coiled wire.

"He's got a body count. How can you trust him?" Annalese pressed.

The question sliced through the air, through me. Every eye

in the room snapped to Ezra, his expression unreadable, save for the flicker of fear that passed through his gaze before he schooled it away. The audience held its collective breath, waiting for me to crack, to recoil, to deliver the betrayal they hungered for.

I stared into Ezra's eyes. The world narrowed until it was just us. Every memory between us flashed like lightning.

A choice.

A line in the sand.

I knew who he was, or at least the part the world wanted me to fear. But I also knew who he'd been to me. And whatever darkness lived in his past, I'd seen worse.

I turned slowly to Annalese, my voice steady as stone. "I'd argue Praxis has a higher body count than anyone," I said, letting the words hang heavy in the room, "and yet here we all are... trusting them."

The silence that followed was suffocating.

Thorne stiffened beside me, his jaw clenched so tight I thought it might shatter. Briar's fingers curled into fists against her thighs. Ezra went impossibly still, his face pale, eyes locked on me like he wasn't sure whether to thank me or mourn me.

And Zaffir looked like he was about to be sick.

I'd done it. There was no taking it back.

"Well," Annalese forced a brittle laugh. "That's a bold statement."

"My story isn't a happy one," Ezra said, his voice low but steady, slicing through the tension like a drawn blade. The cameras shifted, the crowd leaned in, and for the first time in this entire farce of a show, no one was looking at me.

They were looking at him.

"There's death in my history," he went on, his gaze fixed on the floor, the weight of his words dragging the air heavier with each syllable. "But not by my hands. Not the way you seem to be alluding to, at least."

I opened my mouth, "You don't have to-"

He stopped me with a sad smile. "I do."

He took a breath and leaned forward, elbows on his knees, every inch of him stripped bare in a way I don't think anyone had ever seen before.

"I had a best friend," he began quietly. "His name was Kade. We grew up together, same small corner of Canyon, same trouble, same scraped knees and empty pockets. When the resources dried up and people started choosing themselves to look out for, we chose each other. Moved in together when we were old enough. Shared everything. He was my family when I didn't have one left."

The room hung on his words, the mysterious, silent man finally speaking more than a sentence. Even Annalese stayed quiet.

"When times got bad, we took whatever jobs we could find. Last winter, the only work left was in the mines outside the southern barricades. Dangerous work. Shoddy equipment, collapsing shafts. Everyone knew it was a death trap, but if you wanted to eat, you didn't get to be picky." I knew the mines he spoke of. I'd almost considered working there myself when Jax was growing up and needing to eat more than I could scavenge or afford.

He swallowed hard, his jaw working like he was fighting a war behind his teeth. "I was supposed to be on shift that day. Me. Kade wasn't even on the schedule. But I'd gotten sick, some fever that had me seeing double. I was trying to tell the foreman I couldn't go down, and he'd threatened to fire me if I left him short staffed, but Kade... he just grabbed his gear and said, 'I got you, Ez. You'd do it for me.' And then he went."

I felt my throat tighten. Ezra's voice cracked just a little, but he kept going.

"There was a collapse. Shaft Nine. They buried him alive down there with seven other men." He stared out at the crowd now, his expression sharp, eyes glassy but unyielding. "When we finally got down there and dug them out... Kade was...."

Someone in the audience let out a quiet, broken sound.

"But it wasn't an accident," Ezra continued, his voice colder now. Sharper. "The supports were rotten. The emergency systems failed. The reports said they knew it was unstable, they recommended serious repairs before it was fit for work again, but it was cheaper to send men in anyway."

A ripple of horror moved through the room.

"I found proof," Ezra said. "Receipts, reports they tried to bury. Testimonies. I went to the authorities, to the press. I thought... I thought if I showed them, if I screamed loud enough, someone would do something."

He let out a bitter laugh. "They did something alright." The tension in the room drew tighter.

"They planted evidence," Ezra spat. "Made it look like I sabotaged the shaft. That I'd rigged explosives to cause the collapse. Said I had a grudge against the company, against Kade. That I'd killed him."

I felt a chill run through me as his eyes locked on mine.

"They charged me with murder in a sham of a trial. Blamed me for the death of the only person I ever trusted."

A stunned, strangled kind of silence settled over the room. No one dared breathe.

"I might be the reason he's dead," Ezra breathed, voice quiet now, almost a whisper meant for me alone. "But I didn't kill him."

I reached for him, gripping his hand in mine. Ezra clung to me like I was the only thing tethering him to solid ground.

The crowd sniffled, a few people openly sobbing. Someone from the back shouted, *"We still love you, Ezra!"* and just like that, the tide turned. He bared his soul to them, for me, to cover the wreckage I caused with my reckless mouth. And I hated myself for it.

He brought my hand to his lips, pressing a kiss to my knuckles. I squeezed his fingers tighter.

"I'm so sorry," I whispered, my throat tight.

"It's okay," he murmured back, though we both knew it wasn't.

Another wave of *"awws"* rolled over us, the crowd so easily swayed, so quick to forgive what moments ago they would've killed for. How fickle they were. How blind.

"Thank you for sharing that piece of you, Ezra," Annalese said, her hand clutching her chest like some self-appointed martyr. As if she wasn't the one who'd nearly gutted him in front of everyone.

"Unfortunately," she continued with a bright, brittle smile, "that's all the time we have for tonight, folks! Thank you, Wildguard, for joining us. We'll be cheering you on, won't we?"

The crowd erupted in cheers and applause, but the sound rang hollow in my ears. Because I could already feel Jax's medicine slipping further out of reach. Briar and Thorne, marked by association. Zaffir, who hadn't even said a word, painted a traitor by proximity. And Ezra... Ezra, who'd just salvaged us all with his own bloodied history, would carry the heaviest weight.

I'd signed my death warrant tonight. Maybe all of ours.

The noose was tightening. And it was my fault.

EZRA

I THOUGHT TELLING Kade's story, *my story*, would destroy me. The idea of digging up those pieces of my past, of laying bare the darkest, bloodiest corners of my life for the world to gawk at, had felt unbearable. I'd spent a long time convincing myself I'd break if I ever let them see it. If I let anyone see it.

But then I saw the way the color drained from Bex's face on that stage. The way her reckless, beautiful defiance on my behalf painted a target on her back. And at that moment, it wasn't a hard decision. It was the easiest one I'd ever made. I knew Kade would've thought so too.

While pulling the attention off of her, I somehow set myself free from the weight of that secret.

When we made it back to the house, the truth of it all finally hit me. I muttered something about being tired, excused myself to my room, not to hide, not out of regret, but to finally breathe. For the first time since I got that damn message that my best friend, my brother in every way but blood, had been buried beneath the rubble.

I laid on the bed, arms splayed out, staring up at the cracked ceiling, and for once it felt like I could move without the world pressing in on my chest. It didn't matter if no one truly believed me, if the stain of the accusations never washed clean. At least tonight, they'd let me speak. They'd listened. Unlike those bastards who closed my trial before I'd even opened my mouth, who condemned me without a word of my defense.

"They know the truth now, Kade," I whispered to the empty room. I let myself believe he could hear me.

A soft knock broke the silence.

The door creaked open, and there she was. Bex. Still dressed in her interview outfit, all sharp lines and dark Collective colors. Her hair was a little messy but damn, she was beautiful.

"Can I come in?" she asked softly from the threshold.

"Please," I said, scooting over and patting the empty space beside me.

She crossed the room in a heartbeat, kicked off her shoes, and climbed in, curling against me like we'd done this a thousand times. Her head settled against my chest, and I felt the tightness in my body ease, my hand instinctively finding her hair and combing through it carefully.

"How's your head feeling?" I asked, my voice low.

"Better," she murmured. "A doctor stopped by and gave me something for the pain."

There was a beat. A pause. Then she added, quieter, "He said I was lucky."

The way she said it, like the word tasted rotten in her mouth, cut through me.

Lucky.

Lucky to survive an attack. Lucky to be paraded like a pawn in a game. Lucky to be given a resource she would never have received in Canyon.

None of us were lucky.

We were fighters. Survivors. Every breath we took now was the product of a war we had to fight.

"It's not luck. It's courage."

She didn't reply, just nestled a little closer, her fingers curling into the fabric of my shirt.

For a while, neither of us spoke. The quiet wasn't heavy though, it felt... earned, like a breath neither of us realized we'd been holding finally let out. But then, her voice broke the silence, soft and laced with guilt.

"I'm sorry you had to do that, Ezra. That I forced you into it."

I shook my head and shifted, angling my body so she could see the truth in my face. "No, Bex. Don't you dare think for a second that any of what happened out there was your fault."

"But you were covering for my mistake," she argued, her voice breaking on the words. "I was stupid and reckless. I never should have said any of that."

"You didn't say a damn thing that wasn't true," I told her, my voice low and steady. "If anything... It's my fault. I should've told you why I was on the ballot before it came to that. I should've never let them catch you off guard."

She shook her head, stubborn to the end. "I told you I didn't need to know."

"And I should've told you anyway," I said, my thumb tracing the curve of her cheek as I cupped her face. "You deserve to know every part of me, Bex. The good, the bad... the parts I still hate when I look in the mirror. I want you to know me. The real me."

Her hand came up to cover mine, holding it against her

skin. "I already knew who you were, Ezra," she whispered. "I've known since that night at the train bar. You can lie to a thousand cameras, but you never could lie to me."

Something in my chest cracked open at that, something raw and aching and so goddamn grateful it hurt.

I couldn't stop myself and I didn't want to. I leaned down, pressing my lips to hers. She let out a soft, desperate sound against my mouth, and I felt her fingers tangle in my shirt, pulling me closer like she could crawl inside my skin.

My hand slid to the back of her neck, holding her in place as my mouth claimed hers, tasting the hint of fire and sorrow and stubborn hope. The kiss deepened, hunger blooming between us like something feral. It was messy, aching, a tether between two people who knew the world was coming for them and wanted to steal whatever pieces they could before it did.

Her leg slid over my hip, her weight settling against me as she moved to straddle my lap. My body responded before my mind caught up, heat flaring under my skin as her hands cupped my face, her lips never leaving mine.

My cock was achingly hard beneath her warm core. She moved her hips, gliding her covered center over mine, and the friction was sinful and all too tempting.

I broke the kiss, barely. Logic winning out over lust. "Your head.." I whispered. "You should rest."

She bent down, pressing a promising kiss to my throat before whispering in my ear. "I'll rest when I'm dead." Her hips swirled again, pressing her core against my hardened length. I gripped her hips with selfish and desperate fingers and guided her back and forth, relishing in the soft sounds the movement elicited from her throat.

I reached behind her, and without a care in the world, ripped the back of the stupid dress wide open. She gasped, but then sought my lips again with more fervor. I tore the dress from her body, pulling the remaining fabric over her head until it revealed her bare breasts, and panty clad core. Sitting up, I claimed one of her nipples with my mouth. My tongue darted across the hardened peak as she arched into my hold.

"Ezra," she exhaled, clawing at my button down until she pushed it off my shoulders and down my arms.

I needed her more than I'd ever needed air to breathe. Which is saying something considering I was moments from drowning just this morning.

I quickly slid my pants off my body as she rushed to remove her panties. Finally, we were both bare before each other, our chests heaved, our breath mingled, our eyes were locked. I pulled her hips down, until her wet core pressed against my cock. We both groaned, then she rocked her hips, slowly teasingly sliding her slickness along the length of me. My head fell back at the pure sensation of it.

"I need you," she whimpered, and I forced my eyes open so that I could watch her as she lifted, wrapped a delicate hand around the base of my cock and lined me up with her slick entrance. The tip of my cock was notched at her opening, and I could already feel her stretching for me. Her teeth caught her bottom lip as she met my gaze, then nodded.

With my hands on her hips, I pulled her down onto me at a tantalizing slow pace. I wanted her to feel every single inch of me. I wanted to stretch her. To alter her body to fit mine. She was made for me.

For us.

And I wanted her body to know it.

When I was finally seated fully inside of her, we both exhaled a long satisfied sigh. She felt perfect.

"How do you feel?" I asked, knowing that even if it took every ounce of energy I had, I'd pull her off of me if she needed me to. I scanned her face looking for any sign of pain. But all I saw was undiluted lust.

"I feel like I need you to make me come now," she said before lifting and slamming back down onto my length.

"Fuck," I cursed as the sensation sent a shockwave of ecstasy through me. My girl wanted to be fucked, so she would be fucked. I tightened my hold on her body and lifted her just enough so I could piston my hips up into her. She gasped with each powerful thrust. Her hands clawed at my shoulders.

I'd never seen something more beautiful than my girl, hair messy, makeup smudged, skin perfectly pink. Her breasts bounced as she slammed down onto me, so perfectly tempting, so I took a nipple into my mouth again. Grazing my teeth along them, I bit down slightly, which earned me a low growl of approval from the temptress who was riding me like she owned me. Which she did. Heart, body and soul.

"More," she begged. And I wasn't one to leave my girl wanting for anything. So I slipped my hand between us and pressed my thumb against her throbbing clit. She bucked against my hand, her eyes falling closed as her head tilted back. I slammed into her, working her clit in tandem with each thrust. Her hold on my shoulders tightened and I knew she was close to her release.

I released my last hold on her hips and let her take over guiding her body down onto me at the pace she needed as she chased her orgasm, and brought my free hand to her neck, pulling her lips to mine again.

This kiss was all tongue, teeth and desperation. Her moans grew heavy and loud as she bounced on my cock faster and faster. My balls drew up tight to my body as I felt my own wave crest. Finally, her slick channel clamped onto me as her release found her. The pressure of her body claiming mine ripped my own release from me as well. I rested my head on her chest and held her tightly as we both rode out the waves of passion rushing through our bodies. My cock throbbed, and her muscles tightened around me. I'd never felt something so goddamn perfect.

When our breathing slowed and our hearts stopped racing like we were still running from the world, I felt her body tremble, a soft, breathless laugh slipping from her lips. I opened my eyes to find her looking down at me, her hair tousled, her cheeks flushed, and that wickedly beautiful smile curving her mouth. She looked like chaos and salvation wrapped in one. Like something I'd never stop chasing as long as I lived.

I reached up and claimed her mouth again, because how could I not?

"I am desperately in love with you, Brexlyn Hollis," I whispered against her lips, the words tasting like a promise I didn't know I was brave enough to make until right then.

She sucked in a sharp, startled breath and then smiled, eyes gleaming.

"And I am in love with you, Ezra Wynstone," she whispered back, her voice rough and sure like a vow.

I kissed her again, because no words in any language could come close to what she made me feel. But she knew. God, she knew. I loved her with every broken, bruised, and stubborn piece of me, and with every part I hadn't figured out yet. I'd give her anything. Be anything she needed. Hell, I'd share her heart with the others if that's what made her happiest. Because I wanted her to know I loved her.

And I intended to show her just how much... at least a few more times tonight.

CHAPTER
TWENTY-ONE

BEX

I SLIPPED CAREFULLY from Ezra's arms, not wanting to wake him. His face was soft in sleep, the faintest crease still etched between his brows like even his dreams carried too much weight. I glanced over at the other side of the room, at Zaffir's empty bed. He hadn't come back with us after the interview, and it didn't look like he ever made it home. Guilt prickled under my skin. I should've brought Ezra to my room. The one the boys insisted I have to myself. I hoped I hadn't made him feel like he couldn't sleep here.

Tugging on Ezra's discarded button-down, the only piece of clothing left intact after last night's chaos, I let a ghost of a smile tug at my lips.

My poor dress was beyond repair. I glanced at it. Lying there on the floor. Torn to shreds. And as my eyes scanned the ripped fabric, I found myself picturing what it might be like to truly shed the labels and the station that Praxis forced on us. It was a small ember that had been building to a flame. I wasn't naive enough to believe I had the power to change anything single handedly...but recent events had me thinking dangerous thoughts. Like...what if I could?

Buttoning the shirt, I shook my head. It was too early to have such rebellious thoughts. I padded through the house and made my way to the kitchen, where the house was still draped in early morning quiet.

I set about brewing coffee, one small, familiar ritual in a world that had spun so violently off its axis.

We had today off to prep for the coming gauntlet of trials. Nova had stopped by after the interview last night, all sugary smiles and empty congratulations. None of us had it in us to pretend it felt like a victory. Dani's screams still clawed at my mind. Nova, as always, either didn't notice or didn't care.

She rattled off the schedule, oblivious to our hollow expressions. Two trials a day for the next several days, then a brief break, followed by a longer, grueling event meant to stretch two to four days. My stomach twisted at the thought.

The coffee finished brewing, and I poured a cup, savoring the bitter warmth as it slid down my throat. Luxuries like this wouldn't come with us when we returned to Canyon, if we returned at all. Thirteen trials still loomed ahead, and though some of them shifted to more mental contests this week, I knew better than to relax. Nova claimed that the medical trials had been shuffled to the end of the Run, likely to maximize the drama now that the audience was fully invested in our team and my goal.

They were planning to make my desperation to help my brother their wicked season finale.

Nova, to my surprise, hadn't said a word about my little rebellion on live TV. Instead, she'd gleefully reported that our appearance had already blown up across the networks. My kiss with Thorne was everywhere. Ezra's confession had the public in an uproar. There were even rumblings online about ousting Canyon's leadership.

I couldn't say I'd mourn their downfall... though I'd be lying if I said I wasn't terrified of who might take their place.

I savored the rare hush of the morning, leaning my elbows on the counter and cradling my mug between my palms and languidly taking sips. The bitter warmth soothed my throat as my mind replayed the montage they'd shown last night. Beautiful, intimate moments stitched together in the soft glow of early light. Zaffir had given me such a beautiful gift. And I haven't even been able to thank him for it yet. I found that I missed him.

I closed my eyes, letting their faces drift through my head like ghosts that, for once, weren't trying to haunt me.

"Well, well, well... what's got you all smiley this morning?"

I jolted, nearly sloshing coffee down my borrowed shirt. My eyes snapped open to find Thorne leaning casually against the doorway, his signature smug grin firmly in place as he reached for a mug.

"Ezra was *that* good, huh?" he teased, pouring himself a cup and giving me a side glance that was all too pleased with itself.

I felt my face heat instantly. "I don't know what you're talking about," I lied, taking a long sip in a feeble attempt to hide behind my cup.

Thorne let out a soft, knowing chuckle and sidled up beside me, close enough that his arm brushed mine as he lifted his mug and blew over the hot liquid. My gaze, traitorous thing that it was, dropped to his lips, the memory of them against mine last night flashing like a warning sign. Or maybe a challenge.

"You kissed me on TV," I blurted, the words tumbling out before my brain caught up.

He tilted his head, one brow arched in mock offense. "Did I?"

"Yes, you did," I shot back, narrowing my eyes.

Thorne made a show of considering it, tapping a finger to his chin. "Hmm. I feel like I'd remember our first kiss, love."

I smacked his arm with the back of my hand, earning an exaggerated wince as he clutched his chest. "Glad to see I was so memorable."

I laughed in spite of myself, and before I could protest, he set his cup down and tugged me toward him by my waist, turning me to face him. His eyes softened, though the glint of mischief still lingered.

"See," he murmured, brushing a strand of hair from my cheek, "if I were gonna give you a first kiss, it wouldn't be in front of cameras. Wouldn't be for show. Wouldn't be because we needed to make the crowd swoon."

He pressed a kiss to my cheek. Then the other.

"I wouldn't do it to even some score, or because Zaffir told us to play nice for the narrative."

A kiss to my temple. To the tip of my chin.

"If I were gonna kiss you, love..." His voice dropped, a smoky promise, "I'd get you alone. I'd tease you until you couldn't stand it. Make you crave my mouth. Have you begging for it."

His lips ghosted along my throat, and my breath hitched, my body arching just slightly toward him.

"If I were gonna kiss you," he whispered, his mouth grazing my ear, "it'd be just for us. No audience. No cameras. No scripts."

When he pulled back, his eyes met mine, and the heat there was scorching. My chest rose and fell, a thousand words I couldn't say jammed up in my throat. Because damn it, I was burning for him.

And he knew it.

Then, with a patient, smoldering fire, he kissed me.

His hands cradled my face, thumbs brushing tenderly over my cheeks as if I were something fragile, something sacred. His touch was both a promise and a possession, and I melted beneath it, sinking into him like the world beyond those walls didn't exist. The kiss was intimate, incendiary, but unhurried, like he had all the time in the world to unravel me piece by piece.

His lips molded to mine with a kind of reverence that made my pulse pound, his tongue flicking along the seam of my lips, asking...no, begging...for entrance. I opened for him without hesitation, and when our tongues met, it wasn't frantic. It was deliberate. A slow, sensual dance meant to savor, to memorize, to mark.

Every pass, every stroke, every tilt of his mouth against mine poured with aching, consuming heat. My hands wove into his hair, tugging him closer, refusing to let an inch of space remain between us. Our bodies fit together in perfect, unyielding heat, fire meeting gasoline.

When he finally broke the kiss, it was only enough to let us breathe, our foreheads pressed together as we panted, breaths mingling, hearts racing in sync. His hands still cradled my face like I was the most precious thing he'd ever held.

"Now that is the only first kiss that matters to me," he whispered, voice rough with desire.

Before I could catch my breath, he stole another kiss, soft, lingering, full of promise and unspoken things, leaving me wrecked, ruined, and already aching for more when the front door flew open.

I startled, instinctively trying to step back but Thorne's arms stayed firmly around me. A protective cage I wasn't getting out of so easily. He turned us both toward the entrance, and that's when Zaffir walked in.

He looked... horrible.

Still wearing the same clothes as yesterday, his shirt rumpled, collar stained with sweat and something darker. His copper hair was a tangled, damp mess, clinging to his forehead. But it was his face that made my stomach twist. Hollow. Gaunt. Bruised. His eyes were empty, a glassy, distant stare. His shoulders sagged with exhaustion, every step dragging like his body might give out at any second. His lip busted and bleeding.

His gaze flicked up, found us tangled in the kitchen, and he gave the smallest, almost imperceptible nod.

"Sorry," he mumbled, voice hoarse and cracking around the edges like it hadn't been used in hours. Or maybe it'd been overused. The thought twisted my stomach. "I was hoping I wouldn't wake anybody."

He turned to cut across the living room, aiming straight for the hallway like he could disappear before anyone stopped him. But I was already moving, stepping out of Thorne's arms. He didn't try to stop me, he knew I needed to get to Zaffir.

I met him halfway, planting myself in front of him so fast he nearly stumbled trying not to crash into me. He looked down at me, and for a heartbeat, his expression crumpled. Pain or shame, maybe even something worse.

"Zaffir," I breathed, scanning his injuries. There were bruises, fresh ones at his jaw and the edge of his throat. His lip was split and dried blood caked his skin. A raw, chafed mark circled his wrist like a shackle had been there. Fury boiled in my veins.

"What happened?" I demanded, my voice softer than I felt.

He shook his head, eyes darting past me like he could slip away unnoticed. "You don't have to worry about me," he said tightly, trying to sidestep.

But I matched him, cutting him off again. "Too late," I challenged, lifting a hand to touch his arm. The second my fingers brushed him, he flinched, a sharp, involuntary jerk like a wounded, cornered animal. It broke something in me.

"Zaffir..." I whispered again, voice cracking.

"I'm fine," he insisted. A lie so thin it barely held shape in the air between us.

"What happened to you, Zaf?" I choked, tears blurring my vision as I looked at him. Because no one came back from wherever they took him looking like that unless something terrible happened. And from the way his hands trembled and his body flinched at my touch, whatever it was, it was worse than I could imagine.

"Who did this to you?" I asked, my voice low but sharp, trembling with the fury burning hot in my chest. It coiled inside me, heavy and molten, ready to consume the world for him.

Zaffir's hollow gaze met mine, and for a moment, the ghost of the boy I knew flickered behind those empty eyes. "Nobody you can do anything about," he murmured, his voice rough like gravel, but steady.

But I already knew.

Praxis.

Archon Veritas.

The names struck like cold steel against my heart.

"This was... this was because of what I said, wasn't it?" I whispered, the guilt crashing over me like a tidal wave. My stomach twisted, and it felt like my ribs cracked under the weight of it. Tears blurred my vision, spilling hot and fast down my cheeks. "I did this to you. I ran my mouth, I was reckless, and I...I didn't even think what it could mean for you. You told me to thank them, and instead I go and antagonize them. Call them murderers. God, I was so stupid, and childish..."

"Stop." His voice was gentle, frayed around the edges, but unshakable. His face softened, like it physically hurt him to watch me fall apart. "No, sweetheart. No, this wasn't your fault."

"I'm sorry," I sobbed, my throat tight and aching. "I'm so, so sorry, Zaffir. I was stupid. I didn't know...I didn't think..."

Thorne's hands settled on my shoulders from behind, steady and grounding. Zaffir reached for my hands, his fingers trembling but warm, curling around mine with surprising strength despite his condition.

"It wasn't what you said, Brexlyn," he whispered, and my name in his voice felt like both a blessing and a curse. "Veritas already had a reason."

I blinked up at him, confused, my breath hitching. "What do you mean?"

"She warned me once. That Praxis and the Collectives were like wolves and lambs. And you... you were off limits." He shook his head, his red hair falling in front of his eyes. "She had footage," he said, his eyes flickering with old pain. "From the trial. When Briar pulled you out of the water and you weren't breathing." His voice cracked. "She saw my face. She saw how I reacted... how it broke me. She saw how you meant to me. She saw that the lamb had all the power over the wolf."

I sucked in a sharp, shaking breath, horror twisting inside me. "She tortured you because you care about me?"

He shook his head once, slowly, like this was the one thing he wouldn't let me misunderstand. "No," he said, voice rough but clear, his thumb brushing away a tear on my cheek. "Because I love you."

My heart cracked wide open, the jagged edges splintering and bleeding in my chest. I couldn't breathe through the storm of sobs wracking my body. My throat burned, my vision blurred, and I clung to the frayed edges of myself.

"I'm so sorry, Zaffir," I choked out, my voice a broken, desperate thing. "I never meant for this... I never wanted-"

He caught my face in his calloused, trembling hands and pressed a soft, gentle kiss to my lips, silencing my panic in one breath-stealing, heart-shattering moment.

"Don't," he whispered, his forehead resting against mine as his thumbs caught the tears sliding down my cheeks. His voice was raw, cracked open and unafraid. "You opened my eyes, Brexlyn. You made me see this place for what it is. I've been living in this... poisonous privilege, so used to the blood under my feet I stopped noticing the bodies it came from. Watching Praxis take and take. Lives, freedom, futures, and give only what keeps us docile. And I told myself it didn't matter. That it wasn't my problem."

His eyes locked on mine, blazing with a clarity I'd never seen in him before. "Until you. You woke me up from the bullshit I was sleepwalking through. You gave me something to fight for. Someone to love." His voice broke, and he swallowed hard.

"I am so sorry Zaffir," I cried, pressing my fingers to his bruised flesh, feeling like each of his injuries were my own.

He shook his head, cupping my face. "No, no, hey, listen. I'd take a million nights like last night if it meant protecting you. Loving you. I'd burn this whole goddamned regime to ash if it meant you'd be safe. We might just need to be a little more careful for a while."

I let out a sound that was half sob, half laugh, because somehow, even broken and battered, he was still the reckless idiot I'd fallen for. Tears fell from both of us now, blurring the world into something unbearable and beautiful.

"They'll hurt you again," I whispered, my voice trembling, my hands clinging to his. "We shouldn't... I can't let them keep hurting you because of me."

And then, from behind us, a voice broke the fragile, bleeding silence.

"Then why don't we take them down?" Thorne whispered.

It wasn't loud. It wasn't shouted.

It didn't need to be.

Because in those four words was a crack of lightning splitting a storm-black sky.

Zaffir and I both turned to face Thorne, stunned.

Thorne stood there like a tempest barely restrained, his jaw tight, eyes fierce and unflinching. The weight of centuries of Praxis control, of blood-soaked loyalties and inherited chains, cracked and crumbled in that moment beneath the quiet, devastating force of his defiance.

"You're saying..." My voice was a rasp, the words caught between disbelief and fragile, desperate hope.

Thorne met his gaze, unshaken. "I'm saying maybe it's time we stopped fighting *for* Praxis" His hand flexed at his side, a storm gathering behind his eyes. "And started fighting against them."

ACKNOWLEDGMENTS

First, to my husband — the true MVP of most of my novels. Thank you for reading every chapter (even the messy half finished ones) and for hyping me up like I was about to publish the next great literary masterpiece.

To my mother — thank you for always supporting my dream of becoming an author, even if what I write about is "corruption in the government and smut."

And finally, to my long-standing, undying obsession with *The Hunger Games*. You're the reason this story hijacked my brain and refused to leave, even when I begged for a break. Without you, this book might never have been written.